D1524074

AUNT BESSIE VOLUNTEERS

AN ISLE OF MAN COZY MYSTERY

DIANA XARISSA

For my Facebook fans who keep me entertained on my Facebook page.

AUTHOR'S NOTE

We're twenty-two books into the series and I'm still enjoying spending time with Bessie and her friends. I hope you are, as well. I believe the series is best read in order. The last words in the titles run alphabetically to make it easy to know the order in which to read them. Each story is complete if you prefer not to read them all, however.

Bessie first appeared in my romance novel *Island Inheritance*. Because she'd recently passed away in that story, I set the first in the cozy mystery series about fifteen years before the romance. The first Bessie story took place in April, 1998, therefore, and the stories have continued at a pace of about one a month since then. This book is set in January, 2000. We're getting close to the end of the alphabet now. I have plans for Bessie beyond Z, however. More details will be forthcoming in future books.

This is a work of fiction and all of the characters have been created by the author. Any resemblance that they may bear to real people, either living or dead, is entirely coincidental. Of course the setting, the Isle of Man, is a real place. The historical sites mentioned in this book are also real, although the events that take place within those sites in the story are all fictional. The businesses within the story are entirely fictional and have been located where convenient for the story. They are not necessarily located where any real businesses exist on the island. Any resemblance that they may bear to any real businesses is also coincidental.

The Isle of Man is a United Kingdom crown dependency and I use British English (and Manx) for spellings and terms throughout the book. There is a short glossary at the back for anyone who is unfamiliar with any of the words or terms. As I've lived in the US for many years now, I'm sure many Americanisms are now sneaking into my writing. I try to correct them if they are pointed out to me.

I love hearing from readers. Please feel free to get in touch. All of my contact information is available at the back of the book.

CHAPTER 1

"*I* really appreciate this," Mark Blake said as he pointed his car west.

"It's not a problem," Elizabeth Cubbon assured him.

"You'd say that even if you'd had to cancel something important to help me. That's just how you are, Bessie," Mark replied.

"Maybe, but I didn't have to cancel anything. I didn't have any plans for today." Known as Bessie to nearly everyone, she knew she had a reputation for always being willing and able to help out when needed. She'd done more than her fair share of volunteer work over the years, especially with Manx National Heritage, the governmental body charged with promoting and protecting the island's history.

Mark chuckled. "Whatever, I'm still enormously grateful. After all the work you did for Christmas at the Castle, I wouldn't have blamed you one bit if you refused to help me with any more projects."

"This one sounds fascinating, though," Bessie countered. "I've always wondered what's inside the various structures around Peel Castle."

"We aren't expecting to find much of anything, but I know we'll find boxes of old promotional materials in some of them. That's why I asked for your help, you know. I'm hoping you'll be able to remember when some of the various promotions were run."

"I'll do my best. I remember one summer, maybe in the late sixties, when every visitor received a commemorative pin. Is that the sort of thing you mean?"

"Exactly that. Some of the items will be dated, I hope, but over the years we've given away cups, coffee mugs, pins, toys, and goodness knows what else. Someone was meant to be keeping records of what was given out, but no one seems to know where those records are now. I want to try some new things, but I'm hoping to get inspiration from what was done in the past."

"I'm surprised things have been kept for so long."

"None of the spaces around the castle are actually usable for much of anything, so people have fallen into the habit of just shoving boxes into every spare corner. That's the other reason why I'm doing this, actually. The whole of Manx National Heritage is trying to clear out as much rubbish as possible. I know for a fact that we have six boxes of guidebooks from the nineteen-eighties at the castle. There's no way we'd ever use them again. Today, they all get sent for recycling."

"It sounds as if a good clear-out is well overdue."

"It is, yes. Some of our staff have been reluctant to discuss the matter, but there have been a few changes made lately. I believe things might begin moving in new directions within MNH."

"I hope that's good news."

"I do, too. I believe we're going to see some modernisation, anyway. We'll see."

The drive across the island didn't seem to take very long. Bessie glanced at Tynwald Hill as they drove past it. "July seems a long way off," she remarked.

"It will be here before we know it. We want to try some different things with the Tynwald Day festivities, too, actually, although that may have to wait another year or two."

"What are you thinking of changing?" Bessie asked nervously. The annual Manx National Day was one of her favourite celebrations.

Nearly everyone on the island met in St. John's to celebrate the island's heritage. Tynwald, the nation's parliament, met in the open air in front of the assembly. All laws passed in the previous twelve months were read out in both English and Manx and anyone with a grievance could come forward and present it to the government. Besides the official activities, there was food, entertainment, and fireworks.

"Nothing major," Mark assured her. "One thing we've been talking about is trying to do different things each year that will leave a lasting legacy."

"I'm intrigued. What sorts of things?"

"Maybe an art piece to which everyone could contribute. We've been talking about doing something in conjunction with the arboretum, as well, maybe planting additional trees each year to mark the day."

"As long as the basics remain the same, I'll look forward to seeing what other things you can add."

"We've no intention of interfering with the basics. The day is already very special. We just want to enhance that."

Mark slowed down as he negotiated his way through the narrow streets of Peel. The castle loomed over them as they drove along the causeway to the car park. Mark pulled into a space next to a large van.

"It looks as if the others are already here," he told Bessie.

"Others?"

"I requested three or four of our youngest and strongest staff members to help carry heavy boxes around the site. I imagine we'll end up loading the van with boxes at least twice, maybe three times. When we're done, I want every space out here to be empty, if at all possible."

Bessie nodded. "I'm not sure how much help I'll be, but I'll do what I can."

"I might not have had to bother you if Henry had been available."

"How is he?" Bessie asked. Henry had been working for MNH since he'd left school. Now in his fifties, the man knew just about every inch of every historical site on the island. He and Bessie were friends, and she'd been very worried when she'd heard that he'd been rushed to Noble's, the island's main hospital, just a few days after Christmas. He'd been suffering from a very bad case of flu, and he'd ended up in hospital for almost a week.

"He's going to be fine. The doctors want him resting for another week or two, though, and then he's going to be confined to light office work for several more weeks. He isn't up to stomping all over Peel Castle right now."

"I visited him at Noble's, but I haven't seen him since he's been home. Maybe I'll ring him later this week and see if he feels up to company."

"I'm sure he won't say no. I understand he's quite bored at home."

Bessie nodded. "He's never been one for taking much time off, has he? Work is all that he knows, really."

"I took him a stack of books and he's been reading his way through them. He's never been a fan of television, although he did tell me that he's watching quite a lot these days."

"I'll take him some more books when I go. Maybe he could do some research. Marjorie should take him something that might interest him."

Marjorie Stevens was the Manx Museum librarian and archivist. She kept Bessie busy with a steady supply of old documents to study. For years, Bessie had focussed on old wills, but in the past year or so she'd begun to look at other things. At the moment she was working her way through many years of letters between a woman called Onnee and her mother. Onnee had grown up on the island but married an American and moved away. She wrote back monthly, all about her new life in America. Her handwriting was difficult to decipher and Bessie had taken a few weeks off from the work over Christmas. It was probably time she got back to Onnee, however.

"I suggested that, but Henry said he can't do anything in that area because he doesn't have any qualifications."

"Nonsense," Bessie said tartly. "I don't have any qualifications, but that doesn't stop me. I shall have words with Henry when I see him."

Mark chuckled. "I feel as if I should ring him and warn him that you're coming. He might have other company, though. I understand he's been getting some visits from a woman called Jasmina."

Bessie grinned. "She's lovely." Jasmina ran a small café in Laxey and Bessie thought she and Henry were well suited for one another.

She and Mark got out of the car and walked up the stairs to the entrance to the castle grounds. A large sign on the door told visitors that the castle was closed for the winter. Mark pulled out a key and unlocked the heavy door.

"I can't imagine having a key to Peel Castle," Bessie said. "I think I'd visit every day, just because I could."

"You can visit any time you want. Just ring me and I'll arrange it for you."

"Thank you, but that isn't quite the same as having my own key."

"I'll get you a key if you really want one," Mark offered. "I can't imagine anyone in MNH would object. You've been helping us for more years than I've been alive."

"We were starting to think we were here on the wrong day," a young man shouted across the site as Bessie and Mark passed the ticket booth.

"Sorry, traffic was bad through Douglas," Mark replied. He quickly introduced Bessie to the group of young men and women who'd come to help. There were four of them, two men and two women, and Bessie forgot their names as soon as she'd heard them.

"Where are we going to start?" one of the men asked.

"Let's start in the storage room," Mark suggested. "That's probably where most of the work will need to be done. The other spaces are a lot smaller and won't have much in them, I don't think."

The storage room was packed with boxes and dust. It felt rather crowded with Bessie, Mark, and the four young people inside it. A single bulb did little to illuminate the space.

"I hope you all brought torches," Mark said as he pulled one out of the bag he was carrying.

Several other torches appeared and were switched on as Bessie shook her head. "I didn't," she told Mark.

"You're fine. We're going to find you a place to sit that's out of the way, anyway," Mark replied.

Two of the men set up a long table in the centre of the room. There were several folding chairs against one wall. One of the women brushed dust and cobwebs off two of them and then set them behind the table.

"Bessie, you sit there. We'll bring you things when we have questions," Mark told her.

Bessie sank down onto the hard wooden chair. A cold breeze was blowing through the open door and Bessie shivered as she pulled her winter coat more tightly around herself.

"Everyone grab a box and look inside," Mark ordered. "Let's see what we find."

One of the women grabbed the box in front of her and set it on the table. "Isn't this fax machine paper?" she asked as she held up a large roll.

"It's what used to be fax machine paper," Mark laughed. "MNH hasn't had any fax machines that use that sort of paper in years. I don't know if it will recycle, but we definitely don't need to keep it."

"That's all that's in this box," the woman reported a moment later.

"It can go out to the van to be disposed of," Mark told her.

"I'll do trips to the van," one of the men offered. "I don't mind the cold and I'm trying to get more exercise."

"Brochures," someone announced. "They look old."

Bessie leaned over and took one of the brochures. "It's advertising the dance and music festival that they used to have at the castle every July," she said. "I think they stopped doing them in the early eighties."

"A dance and music festival sounds wonderful," one of the women said.

"We have a dance and music festival," Mark said. "Just not at Peel Castle any longer. I believe there were issues with the staging and the uneven ground, which is why things were moved elsewhere."

"I think you're right," Bessie replied.

"I'll keep one copy for historical purposes. The rest can be recycled," Mark announced.

"I'll take it," the other man offered. "My box is full of boxes of pens. We probably should keep them."

Mark took the box and set it on the table in front of Bessie. "I wonder how long these have been in here."

Bessie pulled out a pen and chuckled. "I remember these pens. They're quite unusual, really. I believe they were purchased all at once in the mid-seventies. The director of MNH at the time was very fond of this particular type of pen, so he ordered hundreds of them for every site around the island. A few months later he moved to Wales, leaving MNH with what was probably a ten-or fifteen-year supply of pens that no one else actually wanted."

"What's special about them?" Mark asked.

"Try writing with one," Bessie suggested.

Mark uncapped a pen and scrawled his signature across one of the unwanted brochures. The pen didn't write.

"The ink may have dried up," Bessie suggested.

Mark scribbled with it for several seconds and then sighed. "It's uncomfortable to hold, anyway. I suggest we simply throw the whole box out."

"I believe they're more comfortable if you're left-handed," Bessie told him.

"Ah, and the man who ordered far too many of them was left-handed, was he?"

"Indeed."

"To the van with the lot," Mark announced. "Put them on the discard pile. I don't believe you can recycle dried-out pens."

"Perhaps they aren't all dried out," Bessie said. "I can test them while I sit here, if you want me to."

Mark raised an eyebrow. "I don't think that's necessary."

"I'd hate to see them wasted, if some of them do work."

"If you really want to go through them all, or even some of them, I won't stop you."

Bessie took a handful of brochures and began to scribble with the next pen in the box. Around her, the men and women were unearthing box after box of old brochures, site maps with out-of-date references, and broken office supplies.

"Why would anyone keep a box full of broken tape dispensers?" Mark asked Bessie.

"I'd rather know how so many tape dispensers managed to get so badly broken," she replied.

Mark picked up one that had been snapped nearly in half. "That's a good question, actually."

For half an hour boxes were carried out of the storage room to the van at a good pace. Bessie tried several pens from each box and didn't find a single one that worked.

"I give up," she admitted eventually. "I haven't tried them all, but I believe I've tested a representative sample. They're all dried up and useless."

Mark sent the box out to the van and then set another box in front of Bessie. "What do you make of this?" he asked.

Bessie pulled out a small cardboard box and opened it. Inside she found a coffee mug with a picture of Peel Castle printed on it. "They gave these out to special guests at Tynwald Day one year," she told him. "Probably in the late seventies, but I could be wrong about that."

Mark took the mug and studied it. "It's nice. We could use these for something else now."

"They probably won't be microwave safe," Bessie cautioned him. "Things weren't in those days."

"Or dishwasher safe," someone added.

"No, probably not," Mark agreed. He counted the mugs in the box and then repacked them. "I'm not sure what to do with them, really. They're too nice to throw away."

"I'm sure there are lots of people who would love to have them," Bessie said. "Maybe you could even sell them. Maybe MNH should have a car boot sale."

"That isn't a bad idea," Mark replied. "I have some other things at the museum that we need to get rid of as well: mugs, plates, cuddly toys, that sort of thing. A car boot sale would help clear it all out and raise a bit of money for us at the same time."

"Or you could always give things away at Christmas at the Castle next year," Bessie suggested.

"That's also a good idea," Mark said. "We could give out raffle tickets for attending and give away all of the junk that's cluttering up our buildings. It would be nice to raise a bit of money with it all, but car boot sales are hard work, too. I'll have to talk to my supervisor and see which idea he prefers."

"He may have his own ideas as well," Bessie said.

Mark nodded. "For now, we'll start a new pile of things we want to keep. This is the first box for that pile. It can stay here for today, although we'll need to move it into Douglas eventually."

Hours later, they were finished with the room. There were about ten boxes of things that Mark wanted to keep, and the van was full to bursting with rubbish and recycling.

"I'm going to take the van into Douglas and empty it," one of the men said. "It's full."

"We'll break for lunch, then," Mark told him. "Stop and get yourself something while you're out."

The rest of them went to a nearby pub for soup and sandwiches. Bessie told them all about Onnee while they ate. The MNH staff were kind enough to pretend to be interested in her story, anyway.

"So she's pregnant, but her husband may be having an affair with his former girlfriend," one of the women summarised. "I wouldn't put up with that sort of behaviour. I'd be on the first boat back to the Isle of Man, I would."

"She's eighteen, with no job and no money," the other woman argued. "She doesn't know anyone in the US except her husband and his family."

"And the family isn't any help, as they are still letting her husband's ex live with them," the first woman snapped.

"I keep hoping things will work out for her," Bessie admitted. "I know she's going to stay in America, because Marjorie said there are fifty years' worth of letters. I really hope she's wrong about her husband and his former girlfriend."

After lunch they went back to the castle. Now that the storage room was done, it was time to tackle some of the other, smaller spaces. There were a few boxes stacked up in the back of the tiny ticket booth.

"Current maps," Mark announced after he opened the first box. "And current tickets. They can stay."

"This one has tickets for that Shakespeare festival from a while back," someone said as he opened a box. "There are loads of them. I'm guessing we printed a lot more tickets than we ended up needing."

"There were very small crowds at some shows," Bessie said with a shiver, remembering how many hours she'd spent at the castle the night a man near her had been murdered during a performance.

"They can go," Mark said. "If we do anything similar again, we'll need new tickets printed anyway."

The air was cold and the wind was blowing as they moved to one of the smaller structures on the site.

"I didn't know you stored things in there," Bessie said as Mark unlocked the padlock that secured the door.

"We shouldn't, but you know how it is. Someone has a box of something and doesn't know what to do with it, so it gets shoved into any empty space."

The small space was dark and everything inside it was covered in cobwebs and dust. Mark and the other men hauled three boxes out into the cold sunshine.

"Is that all that was in there?" Bessie asked.

"That and about a dozen broken chairs," Mark sighed. "The guys are going to drag them to the van while we check what's in the boxes."

The first box was full of papers that were water damaged and unreadable. The second was labeled "broken audio guides."

Mark shook his head. "Why would anyone keep broken audio guides?" he asked as he handed the box to one of the men.

The third box had been at the bottom of the pile. Mark opened it, brushing away a spider as he did so. "More paperwork," he sighed. "Water damaged and useless."

As the men carried away all three boxes to the van, Bessie and the other women followed Mark to the next small structure. There they found even more rubbish, along with a box of plates that commemorated Castle Rushen.

"Why are those here?" Bessie asked.

Mark shrugged. "Maybe we'll find a box of Peel Castle plates at Castle Rushen when we do the same thing there."

Bessie wondered if she could find an excuse to miss that experience. Although, Castle Rushen had walls and a roof, so maybe it wouldn't be as bad, she thought as the wind blew around her. "I believe they're from the early eighties," she told Mark. "I think there was an entire set, one for each historical site that MNH was managing at that point. You were meant to try to collect them all by visiting each site over the summer, I believe."

Mark made a note on the top of the box and then carried it back to the storage room. "Break time," he told Bessie as she sank back into one of the chairs. "I think we all need a cuppa. It's cold out there."

The kettle was in the ticket booth. Mark managed to find a packet of biscuits there as well. Bessie held her mug of tea tightly, letting the warmth soak into her fingers before she drank the tea.

"That's better," she sighed as the tea began to warm her from the inside.

"Maybe we should stop for today," one of the women suggested. "We've done a lot already."

"But we only have a bit more to do," Mark countered. "I think there are only two or three more places to check and I believe at least one of them is already empty."

"That's good news," Bessie laughed.

After their tea break, they all headed back outside. At the next space, Bessie was able to help identify some cuddly toys as part of a promotion from the seventies. Sadly, all of the toys had suffered from the damp and were covered in spots of mould. The next small storage area was full of nothing but broken chairs and tables.

"Last one," Mark said cheerfully as they stopped in front of a small tower that was built into a section of the castle walls. The door was hanging at an odd angle, bending the bar into which the padlock was locked. Mark dug out his keys and inserted one into the lock.

"Not working?" one of the men asked after a minute, as Mark struggled.

"It's the wrong key, I think, but it's the only key I have for all the padlocks on site."

"That one is different from all of the others," Bessie pointed out.

Mark frowned at the lock. "You're right. I wasn't paying any attention. It looks older, actually, but I thought all of the locks were replaced at the same time."

"I suppose we'll have to stop for today," one of the women said happily. "You'll have to work out where that key is, won't you?"

Mark shook his head. "I've been given all of the keys for the site. It must be on this ring somewhere."

As everyone shivered in the cold, Mark tried every key he had. None of them opened the old padlock.

"Let's go back to the storage room and warm up," he said eventually. "I'll ring the office and see what anyone can suggest."

While Mark was on the phone, Bessie made another pot of tea. When Mark rejoined them, he happily took a cup before he spoke.

"It's getting late. You lot should head back to Douglas and unload the van. I think nearly everything in there is rubbish."

"What are you going to do?" one of the women asked.

"I'm going to cut that lock off the door and see what's inside that space," Mark told her. "We'll leave clearing it out for another day, if there's anything in there. I was told that one has been empty for years, though. I just want to be certain. I have an extra padlock that I can replace it with, once I've removed the one that's there."

"Now I'm curious and I want to see what's in there," the woman said. "Maybe we should stay."

Mark shrugged. "It's entirely up to you guys. You can go if you'd rather."

After a quick chat, everyone decided to stay. Mark went into the ticket booth to get the necessary tools and then they all trooped behind him back across the site.

It took Mark and one of the other men several minutes to cut through the rusty old lock. When it finally broke, everyone cheered.

Mark grinned. "I hope we find something exciting after all of that," he said as he switched on his torch. Several others crowded behind him as he pushed open the door. A moment later, he turned back around, his face pale.

"What's wrong?" Bessie demanded.

One of the other men looked into the space and then backed away quickly. "It's a body," he stammered.

Bessie looked at Mark, who nodded slowly. Although she didn't want to look, Bessie wanted to be certain of what they'd found. It was possible they'd simply rediscovered an old mannequin similar to the ones used at Castle Rushen. "Let me borrow your torch," she told Mark.

He handed it to her without comment. The others were silent as Bessie crossed to the door and stuck her head inside. When she emerged, she pulled her mobile phone out of her bag.

"I'm going to ring 999," she said. "You all need to stay here until the police arrive. They'll have questions for everyone."

"With all due respect, Bessie, they can't suspect that any of us had anything to do with that person's death," Mark protested. "There's nothing more than a skeleton in there."

"They'll still want statements from everyone," Bessie replied. "They have a procedure they have to follow."

Everyone at the site was well aware that Bessie knew what she was talking about. In the past few years, she'd found more than her fair share of dead bodies. The group remained silent as she used her phone.

"It's Elizabeth Cubbon. I'm at Peel Castle with Mark Blake and some of the staff from Manx National Heritage. We've just opened up a storage area in one of the old towers in the outer wall and found a dead body."

"Are you quite certain?" was the reply.

"It appears to be a skeleton. I suppose, when the crime scene team arrives, they may find that it was from a school's biology department or that it's not real, but I didn't want to trample over any evidence while trying to determine that for myself."

"Very good." The woman on the other end sounded bored. "I'm sending the nearest constable. He should be there soon."

"I'd better go and wait by the castle door," Mark said when Bessie repeated the conversation. "We've been keeping it locked between trips to the van."

"Maybe the rest of us should wait in the storage room," someone suggested. "It'll be warmer and out of the wind."

A few people began to walk away, but Bessie shook her head. "I don't want to leave whoever is in there alone," she said, feeling slightly foolish.

"Bessie is right," one of the women said. "We shouldn't leave him or her alone."

"Whoever it is has been in there, all alone, for decades," one of the men argued.

Bessie shrugged and then sat down on the nearby bench. A short while later, Mark was back with a uniformed constable. The constable took his torch and looked into the small space.

"Could be a real skeleton, I suppose," he said when he emerged. "I'd better ring for backup, just in case it is."

Experience meant that Bessie knew it wouldn't be long before the castle grounds would be almost overrun by the hard-working members of a crime scene team. What she didn't know was which inspector would be put in charge of the investigation. The head of the CID in Peel had retired recently and Bessie hadn't heard who had replaced him. She was still wondering when she spotted a familiar figure walking across the castle grounds.

Of all the men and women employed by the island's constabulary, Inspector Anna Lambert was Bessie's least favourite by a considerable margin. The fifty-something woman had worked for a time at the Laxey station, where she'd been hired to assist John Rockwell with the station's administrative tasks. Eventually, she'd decided that she preferred investigative work over paperwork and had transferred to

Castletown. Bessie hadn't heard that she'd moved to Peel. The inspector stopped and had a word with the constable before walking over to where Bessie and the others were gathered.

"Miss Cubbon, I should have expected to find you right at the centre of everything, shouldn't I?" Inspector Lambert snapped.

CHAPTER 2

*B*essie took a deep breath and then began to count slowly to ten. The last thing she needed to do was say something rude to the disagreeable inspector. She was only on nine when Mark spoke.

"I'm afraid that's entirely my fault," he said. "I asked Bessie to come and help us today."

"And you are?" Inspector Lambert asked.

"I'm Mark Blake, head of special projects for Manx National Heritage." Mark quickly introduced the rest of the MNH employees to the inspector, who was taking notes as he spoke.

"Why are you here?" was her next question.

"We were cleaning house, really," Mark replied. "We've been clearing everything from the various storage areas around the site all day."

"And this was a storage area?"

"It wasn't meant to be, but neither were several of the other spaces that were being used for storage. We were just checking to make certain that it was empty."

"But it isn't."

"No, it isn't. There's a skeleton in the back corner."

Inspector Lambert nodded. "I'll take a look in a moment. In the meantime, is there somewhere a bit more sheltered where you all can wait?"

"There's a small storage room nearby," Mark replied. "We set up a table and chairs in there earlier. We even have a kettle."

"Excellent. You and your coworkers go and have tea and relax. Someone will be in to take statements from each of you shortly," she said.

As Bessie got to her feet, the inspector gave her a cold smile. "Miss Cubbon, I'd prefer if you'd remain here, please. I'm sure I'm going to have a number of questions for you."

"It's awfully cold out here for Bessie," Mark protested.

"It's fine," Bessie said firmly. While she agreed with Mark, she'd never admit such a thing to Inspector Lambert.

The inspector waited until Mark and the other MNH staff had walked away before she switched on her torch and headed for the tower door. She was only inside for a minute, maybe less.

"Get the crime scene team," she told the constable with a sigh. "I'll need a pair of trained constables to get statements from the witnesses, as well."

The constable nodded and then pulled out his mobile. As he was pushing buttons, the inspector crossed to Bessie and sat down on the bench. "Please sit," she invited.

Bessie sat back down and swallowed a sigh. The inspector stared at her for what seemed to be a very long time. Finally she spoke.

"I know we haven't always seen eye to eye on things," Inspector Lambert said. "I know you didn't approve of my techniques during some of the investigations I conducted in which you were involved. This one seems less likely to be contentious. The man or woman in there has been dead for a very long time."

"Perhaps so long that it doesn't even warrant an investigation," Bessie suggested.

"Everyone gets an investigation," the other woman countered. "I suppose if the bones were Viking era, we might not investigate, but otherwise, I intend to do my best to work out whom we've found and how he or she ended up in that tower. I was hoping you might be able to help with that."

"Me?"

The inspector looked amused. "You can't be surprised that I'm asking for your help. If the body has been in there for ten, twenty, or thirty years, then you may know whom we've discovered. I know you helped Hugh with a similar case in Laxey not long ago."

"I was able to make him a list of men who'd disappeared from the island around the same time as the body was found," Bessie replied. "I could do something similar for you if you can narrow down a date when this person died."

"Obviously, we'll do our best. I don't think it's going to be easy, though. Do you have any initial ideas on who it might be?"

Bessie shook her head. "None at all, not without some idea of a date. Men and women leave the island all the time. Most of them stay in touch with friends or family members, but not all of them choose to do so. Staying in touch is easier now, with mobile phones and e-mail, of course. Years ago, it took more effort."

"Start making a list of anyone and everyone who may be missing. We'll narrow the list down once we have a date for the body."

"I wouldn't even know where to start," Bessie replied. "Give me a gender and an approximate date and I'll do what I can to help, but that's the best I can do."

The two women frowned at each other. Eventually, the inspector spoke again. "Of course, Laxey is your home. If the dead person was from Peel, you probably didn't know him or her anyway."

Bessie nodded. "If he or she had any ties to Laxey, I may be able to help, but otherwise, you're probably right."

"That's unfortunate. I was hoping you'd be able to identify my body for me sooner rather than later."

"Mark may be able to help you with dating things. He had to cut the lock off the door. All of the other padlocks on the site use the same key, but this one was different. He reckoned it might have been older than the other locks, too."

"Interesting." Inspector Lambert sounded anything but interested.

"I'll check his statement once he's given it. I'll need yours as well, of course. I'd prefer to take that myself, once the crime scene team arrives."

It was pointless to argue with the inspector, so Bessie simply nodded and then sat back on the bench. Hopefully, Mark wouldn't leave without her. Otherwise she'd have to ring for a taxi to get home. Bessie had never learned to drive, relying on buses and taxis to get around her island home. She was fortunate to have many friends who often took her where she wanted to go, but she always had the number for her favourite taxi company ready to use when needed.

Inspector Lambert got up and spoke briefly to the first arrivals from the crime scene team. As they went to work, she gave some instructions to the pair of uniformed constables who arrived next. Then she sat back down next to Bessie. The pair were silent as they watched the investigators work. After several minutes, as Bessie began to shiver in the cold, the inspector sighed deeply.

"Let's go find this storage area, then," she said begrudgingly. "You can warm up with some tea while I take your statement."

Bessie got to her feet and followed the other woman across the grass. When they walked into the room, Mark was sitting with a uniformed constable.

"We're just about done here," the constable told the inspector as he jumped to his feet.

"I hope you've been thorough," she replied.

"Yes, I have, I mean, I hope I have," he said.

She shrugged. "Mr. Blake, you can leave. We'll have people on site for at least the next twelve to fourteen hours. MNH will need to send someone to lock up the site tomorrow morning."

"I need to stay and take Bessie home," he replied.

"I'll make certain that Bessie gets home safely," the inspector countered. "Off you go."

Mark raised an eyebrow and then looked questioningly at Bessie. She shrugged. There was no way she was going to challenge Anna Lambert's words.

"Thank you for all of your help today," Mark said to Bessie as he headed for the door.

"I was happy to help, right up until the end," Bessie replied.

"You can go," the inspector told the constable as the door shut behind Mark. He nodded and followed Mark out of the room.

"Sit," the inspector told Bessie.

Bessie dropped back into the same hard chair she'd used earlier. It wasn't any more comfortable now than it had been before. The inspector took a seat on the opposite side of the table and made a face.

"These chairs are horrible," she complained.

"Yes, they are."

"I don't suppose it would do any good to complain. They probably don't have any other chairs out here."

"There's one in the ticket booth that's marginally more comfortable," Bessie told her.

"It doesn't matter. Tell me why you're here. What brought you to Peel Castle today?"

"Mark brought me. He rang me last week and asked me if I'd be willing to come and help out for the day."

"When did he ring?"

"I'm not sure, maybe Wednesday or Thursday. I can try to recall more exactly if you really need to know."

"I may, but let's not worry about it for now. What did Mark want you to do?"

"He wanted someone familiar with MNH to be here to help him identify the things he knew he was going to find in the various boxes. There were a lot of old plates and cups and things from old promotions and nothing was dated."

"Why does it matter?"

"I believe he wanted help determining what was worth keeping and what could safely be discarded. It's always helpful to have another pair of eyes looking over everything."

"He had four other people here with him, besides you."

"Yes, but they're all young and fairly new to MNH. He asked me to help because I know more of the history."

"And no one who works for MNH knows its history?" The inspector sounded incredulous.

"Henry Costain probably knows it best, but he's at home recovering from flu. There are others who could have helped, but some have retired and moved across and others were probably busy when Mark rang."

"You believe you weren't his first choice, then?"

"You'd have to ask him that. I've no idea who else he might have spoken with about helping. We just worked together for over a month on Christmas at the Castle. I may have been the first person he thought of when he decided to start on this project."

"Take me through your day."

Bessie did her best, starting with breakfast and working forward. She didn't bother to mention everything that was discovered in every box, but she tried to identify the highlights. She was just about to talk about the last tower when the inspector held up a hand.

"Wait. Tell me again what you found in the various boxes. I want as complete an inventory as you can give me."

Sighing, Bessie did her best to remember everything. The inspector seemed to be making a list of each item as Bessie spoke.

"Right, so that takes us up to the last tower, correct?"

"That's right," Bessie agreed. "We were all pretty cold and tired by that time, and Mark told the others that they could leave if they wanted to get back to Douglas."

"Why didn't they go? Who was behind the idea of staying?"

"I don't remember who said what about staying. I believe it was just a general feeling that they'd come so far, they should stay and finish the job."

"Tell me what happened next, then."

Bessie told her about the stubborn padlock and Mark's solution before explaining what had happened when he'd found the body.

"You deliberately took a look inside the space, even though you knew what you'd find?"

"I thought maybe the two men were mistaken about what they'd seen. I've had a bit more experience in that area."

"Yes, well, I can't argue with that," Inspector Lambert replied dryly. She had Bessie start at the beginning again, from when they'd found the padlock that Mark couldn't open. After Bessie had told the story for a third time, the inspector finally shut her notebook.

"Right, now you've had some time to think. Whom have we found?"

"I wish I could tell you, but I've no idea. As I said, I need some idea of a date with which to work if I'm to have any chance of helping."

"I'll have to talk to the crime scene team and the coroner. I'll be in touch, once they've done all that they can. After everything that I've seen since I've been on the island, I'm pretty sure you're going to be the key to solving this case."

"As you said earlier, if the person was from Peel, I may be no help at all."

"It's a small island. Whoever put the body in there is probably getting quite nervous about now. I'm assuming, of course, that the island's gossip chain is hard at work, spreading the news that a body has been found at Peel Castle. Once you get home, you should ring a few people and start stirring things up, don't you think?"

"I'm not certain I want to stir things up, not yet. There are a lot of people out there who have been looking for their missing loved one for years. I'd rather not raise false hopes for anyone as to whom we may have found."

"Surely you'd be doing the opposite of raising their hopes, if you tell them that you've found a dead person."

"I believe the not knowing is harder than dealing with the loss," Bessie countered.

Inspector Lambert shrugged. "Suit yourself, but I'll be coming to see you soon. I'm expecting great things from you, especially after all you did for Hugh."

"A certain element of luck played into that case."

"I could do with some luck right about now. I need to solve a case, the more difficult the better."

Bessie wondered what the inspector meant by that, but she didn't want to ask for clarification. "Are we finished, then?" was the question she did ask.

"Yes, I suppose so, for now. As I said, I'll be in touch."

Nodding, Bessie got to her feet. The inspector had promised Mark that she'd make sure Bessie got home safely, but as Bessie headed for the door, she assumed that Inspector Lambert had forgotten.

"Hugh should be here by now to collect you," the inspector said as Bessie pulled the door open.

"Hugh?"

"I thought you'd prefer to see a friendly face after your long day. I believe he's always happy to work a bit of overtime, as well, with a new baby at home."

"Yes, I believe you're right," Bessie replied, feeling surprised. She walked to the front of the castle grounds and found Hugh chatting with one of the uniformed constables at the entrance.

Hugh Watterson was a young man in his twenties, although to Bessie he still looked closer to fifteen. Bessie had known him his entire life. As she'd never had children of her own, she'd acted as something of an honorary aunt to the boys and girls of Laxey. Hugh had spent many nights during his teen years in Bessie's spare bedroom after arguments with his parents about his future. He'd wanted to join the police from the time he'd been a very young boy, but his parents hadn't approved. Over time, as Hugh had worked hard at his chosen career, they'd come to respect his decision, and now that Hugh was married and had made them grandparents, the three had become much closer.

Hugh greeted Bessie with a hug. "I couldn't believe it when Inspector Lambert rang me and said you'd found another body."

"I couldn't believe it either," Bessie said dryly. "This one has been there for a good long time, though. I'll be surprised if it's anyone I knew."

"No doubt the inspector has already asked you to start thinking about anyone who might have gone missing in the past."

"She has, but that job will be a good deal easier once I have some idea of a date and also of gender."

"Ready to go home, then?" Hugh asked.

Bessie nodded. "More than." It had been a very long day and she was exhausted. She knew she'd been quite spoiled in her younger years, as she'd never needed a paying job, but she'd done quite a lot of volunteer work. It had been some time since she'd worked for as many hours as today had turned out to require, though. As she settled into the passenger seat of Hugh's car, she sighed deeply. Her feet hurt, her back ached, and she was starving.

"Want to tell me about it?" Hugh asked as he started the car's engine.

"There isn't much I can tell you, really. We were clearing out the various little spaces that are all over the site, and in the very last one we found a skeleton."

"So whoever it was, he or she has been there for a while."

"Unless it's a prop from an old display or something. I imagine that's the first thing Inspector Lambert will have to determine."

"I believe she's fairly certain that it's a genuine skeleton. She's treating it as a crime scene, anyway."

"If there was a crime, it happened a long time ago."

"Someone hid the body in there. That's a crime, even if the victim died of natural causes."

"Is it? Maybe it's an ancient burial that we've just discovered."

"I'm not sure there would be any bones left from that long ago."

Bessie sighed. "I hope it's an ancient burial. If it's Viking era, there won't have to be an investigation."

"Was it still partially buried or resting on top of the ground?"

"It was mostly on top of the ground. I only took a very quick look, mind you, but I could see a lot of it."

"I don't understand how it could have been undiscovered for all these years, then. I wonder if someone moved the body there more recently."

"Mark couldn't open the padlock. He didn't have the right key. He said all of the locks were changed years ago so that they all use the same key. Clearly, that one was missed for some reason."

"Doesn't MNH take regular stock of everything on the site?"

"Judging by what we found in some of the boxes we went through today, I don't think they do. There were boxes of old papers from twenty or more years ago that were waterlogged and ruined. No one would have suggested keeping them if they'd been aware that they were there."

"So the body could have been in that tower for twenty years or more."

"It's a bit of a stretch, calling it a tower. It's more just a little space in a corner of the outer walls of the site, but yes, I suppose he or she could have been there for that long, or maybe even longer."

"Let's hope Inspector Lambert can successfully date the remains, otherwise I can't imagine how we're going to discover who you found."

"Mark found the remains. I just happened to be there."

"That happens to you rather a lot."

Bessie sighed. "How's Grace?" she changed the subject.

Hugh beamed. "She's doing really well. I can't believe how well she's coping with everything on her own."

Grace was a pretty blonde primary schoolteacher. She and Hugh had been married for almost a year and had recently welcomed their first child together. Bessie knew that Grace's mother had been staying with the couple for the first weeks after the baby's birth. Presumably she'd gone home now.

"Grace's mum is back in Douglas?" Bessie checked.

"Yes, and we're all happier for it," Hugh said. He flushed. "Don't get me wrong. We loved having her stay with us and she was a huge help with the baby for those first few difficult weeks, but having another person in the house was awkward. Grace was always uptight, too, worried that her mother thought she was doing things the wrong way. Now she's more relaxed, which means Aalish is more relaxed, too."

"That's good to hear. Aalish is doing well, then?"

"She's amazing," Hugh said happily. "She's starting to take a real interest in the world now. She seems to listen intently when Grace talks to her. Grace has started singing the alphabet to her and counting her fingers and toes when she dresses her. I'm sure Aalish is going to be very clever."

"No doubt, considering who her parents are."

Hugh blushed. "Grace is clever, anyway."

"You're very clever when you apply yourself."

"Yes, I suppose so. Before I met Grace I was, well, lazy I suppose is the word. Now that I have her and Aalish to support, though, I'm doing everything I can to advance my career." He glanced over at Bessie and shrugged. "I'm going to start taking some classes at the college at night. I want to get a degree eventually."

"Good for you."

"I need one if I'm going to move up to inspector one day, and that's my goal. I'm working all the extra hours I can now so that Grace can stay home for as long as possible."

"I'm sure Aalish appreciates that."

Hugh laughed. "I'm sure she does, but Grace might not. She told me the other day that she might want to go back to work sooner than we'd planned. She misses the children, ones that can walk and talk and learn things, and she misses being useful to the world, too."

"Raising a child is incredibly useful."

"But maybe not as useful as teaching an entire class of children. That isn't me talking, by the way, that's Grace. In an ideal world, I'd rather she stayed home until Aalish is in school, but if Grace will be happier working, then we'll find a way to make that happen instead."

"Maybe you could take a year off and stay home with the baby."

Hugh grinned. "I would love that, but it would hurt my career prospects. John does everything he can to help all of the constables get lots of experience in every type of policing. If I took time off, there's no guarantee that I'd get a job at Laxey when I came back. I can't imagine working for anyone other than John."

Bessie nodded. John Rockwell took an almost paternal interest in the young men and women he supervised at the Laxey station. Everything she'd heard about him suggested that he was firm but kind to the constables, pushing them to produce the very best possible results, and anxious to help them correct mistakes or find solutions for problems both on and off the job. Although Bessie had never worked, she imagined that John would have been the perfect person to have had as a supervisor.

"Anyway, Grace isn't going back to teaching in a hurry. We're planning on her being home until at least September. If she decides she really hates being home, she can apply for a new position that starts in the autumn or go back to supply teaching."

"I'm sure some days she'll want to work and other days she'll be unable to imagine leaving Aalish with anyone else."

"Yes, that's part of the problem. She went out to lunch with her mother the other day when I was home. They were back in twenty-five minutes because she missed Aalish too much to stay away any longer."

Bessie laughed. "Poor Grace. I can't imagine how she feels."

"I can't, either. I mean, I do miss Aalish when I'm at work and I think about her a lot, but I'm out for eight or nine hours every day, plus overtime sometimes. We'd be in trouble if I couldn't stand to be away from Aalish for more than twenty minutes."

"I'm sure mums are meant to feel that way in the first few months of the baby's life. It's part of what keeps the baby alive."

"No doubt. I've never been more happy to have been born male."

They were nearly back to Laxey, so Bessie changed the subject again, asking the question that had been on her mind for hours. "When did Inspector Lambert move to Peel?"

Hugh glanced over at her and then looked away. "Maybe a month ago," he said hesitantly. "I was so busy with the baby and everything that I didn't really pay that much attention to all of that."

"All of what?"

"The transfer, that's all. As it didn't really concern me, I didn't pay much attention."

"What aren't you telling me?"

"Nothing."

"Exactly, you aren't telling me anything. Did something happen in Castletown that led to her being transferred?"

Hugh sighed. "Officially, she was moved to Peel to better redistribute the island's inspectors. One of the men in Peel moved to Kirk Michael and the inspector from there moved to Foxdale. Lastly, the inspector in Foxdale took Inspector Lambert's place in Castletown."

"How does all of that redistribute anything? It sounds as if people just moved around."

"Aye, that's right."

"And Inspector Lambert was the impetus for all of the moves?"

"That's what I heard. I was told she wasn't a very good fit for Castletown."

"Why?"

"I shouldn't tell you any of this. I could probably get into trouble if anyone finds out that I told you anything."

"I don't want you to get into any trouble. Don't tell me anything." Bessie sat back in her seat. She had other sources. She'd have the whole story by the end of the day anyway.

"You'll find out anyway," Hugh said after a moment. He pulled his car into the parking area next to Bessie's cottage. "Just don't tell anyone who told you."

"You know I won't."

"Allegedly, Inspector Lambert became too friendly with one of the other inspectors in Castletown."

"Too friendly?"

"Too friendly, as in the male inspector in question was stringing her along just for his own amusement. I was told it was limited to flirting and innuendo, but whatever it was, it was out of line. Again, this is all hearsay, but I was told that when Inspector Lambert discovered that he had no intention of actually getting involved with her, she had something akin to a breakdown. She took a short medical leave and then requested a transfer."

"The poor woman," Bessie said. "I don't care for her, but I do feel sorry for her."

"You know I don't care for her after, well, after everything that happened when she was in Laxey, but I feel sorry for her, too. I know the inspector involved and I like him even less than I like her."

"It's all quite unpleasant."

"It is, yes. At least the chief constable was able to find her another position. I suspect she'll be keeping her head down and working incredibly hard to prove to him that he was right to give her another chance after her medical leave."

"So she'll be determined to work out whom we found today and what happened to him or her."

"No doubt. If I were you, I'd expect Anna Lambert on your doorstep pretty regularly until the case is solved."

With that unpleasant thought running through her head, Bessie climbed out of the car. Hugh followed her to her door.

"I'll just take a quick walk through the cottage and make sure everything is okay," he told Bessie.

"Everything will be fine. You get home to Grace and Aalish."

"They'll wait another minute. It won't take more than that."

Bessie didn't want to waste any more time arguing, so she opened the door and let Hugh into the cottage. While she hated it when people fussed over her, she knew that Hugh did it because he cared. He'd been with her the day she'd come home to find that someone had broken into her cottage, as well. Mostly, the intruder had simply made a huge mess, but the incident had left Bessie more willing to allow her friends to check her cottage when they brought her home.

"Everything's fine," Hugh announced as he walked back into the kitchen.

"I knew it would be," Bessie said as she handed him a bag that she'd filled with homemade biscuits while he'd been stomping around above her.

"Ah, thanks, Aunt Bessie," he told her, pulling her into a hug. "And now I'd better get home to my girls."

He looked so pleased at the idea that Bessie couldn't help but smile. She followed him to the door and then locked it behind him. It was late and she hadn't even had dinner yet. After putting a portion of cottage pie from her freezer into the oven to reheat, Bessie paced back and forth across the kitchen.

Walking on the beach was generally her preferred way of dealing with everything that life threw at her, but having spent a large portion of the day outdoors and on her feet, she found that she was too tired for a walk tonight. Her mind was racing too quickly in too many directions for her to settle with a book or Onnee's letters, so she finally bundled herself up in her warmest coat and went outside. Not wanting to walk far, she sat for a while on the large rock on the beach behind her cottage. The sea air worked its usual magic, calming her mind and clearing her head. When she went back inside to eat her dinner, she felt much better.

CHAPTER 3

The cottage pie was exactly the sort of comfort food that Bessie had needed. Once she'd eaten it and a few biscuits, she was ready to curl up with a good book. She loved cozy mysteries and had been gifted with several new titles for Christmas. Three chapters into one of them, the phone rang.

"Hello?"

"It's Doona. Are you okay?"

"I'm fine," Bessie assured her closest friend.

Doona Moore was forty-something, and people were often surprised by the friendship that she shared with the much older Bessie. They'd met years ago at a Manx language class and they'd bonded as they'd struggled with the difficult language. Bessie had helped Doona through some of her darkest days during the break-up of her second marriage, before Doona found herself helping Bessie cope through a series of murder investigations. When Doona's second husband had been murdered before the divorce had been finalised, it was Bessie's turn to support her friend again as Doona appeared to be the chief suspect. Now Bessie thought that she should have rung Doona hours ago to assure her that she was okay.

"John said the body had been there for many years," Doona said.

"It wasn't so much a body as a skeleton. I'm sure it must have been there for a very long time."

"It still must have been unsettling for you. Do you want some company?"

"Not really. I was reading a good book, but I'll probably take myself off to bed soon."

"It can't be that good of a book, then," Doona laughed.

Bessie chuckled. She and Doona shared their love of reading. "It is good, but not gripping. It won't keep me from getting to bed at a reasonable hour, although I will look forward to finishing it tomorrow."

"I'm home tonight, if you need me," Doona told her.

"What does that mean?" Bessie asked.

Doona had been spending most nights in the spare room at John Rockwell's house. His former wife, Sue, had gone to Africa on a honeymoon with her new husband, leaving her and John's two children, Thomas and Amy, with John. The newlyweds had been expected to return in August, but they'd kept pushing back their return date, causing difficulties regarding schooling for the children. In late December, Sue's husband, Harvey, had rung to inform John and the children that Sue was ill. He'd suggested that she was beyond treatment and for several days John and the children waited to hear that she'd passed away.

Several weeks later, Sue was still hanging on, talking to the children most days via an unreliable telephone connection. Doona was doing her best to support the children and John through the ordeal. She and John were more than friends, but John had been married when they'd met. As his marriage had been falling apart, Doona's husband had been murdered. Once life had begun to settle, Sue had announced her intentions of remarrying and leaving the children with John for the summer. Bessie knew that Doona cared deeply for John's children and that she was in love with John, but Sue's illness was complicating an already complex situation.

"It's just difficult right now," Doona sighed. "I want to be there for John and the children, but the tension in the house is almost unbearable. The children didn't want to go back to school after their break for the holidays and I don't blame them. Sue and Harvey are ringing at all hours of the day and night, interrupting everyone's sleep and upsetting the children even more."

"Poor John, although I feel terribly sorry for Thomas and Amy, too."

"It's going to sound terrible, but if Sue is going to die, I hope she hurries up and does it. I don't know how much more of this John and the children can take."

"How are they doing?"

"Thomas is trying to be brave and act as if he doesn't much care. He's sixteen and he keeps saying he doesn't really need mothering any longer anyway."

"Oh, dear."

"Exactly. And Amy, at fourteen, well, she definitely needs a mother. She won't talk to me about how she's feeling, and she won't talk to John, either. Mostly, when she's home, she locks herself in her bedroom with her phone. We just have to hope that her friends are being supportive, because she won't let us help."

"And John?"

"Still has complicated feelings for Sue. He loved her very deeply, you know. That she'd never stopped loving Harvey, even after marrying him and having his children, was difficult for him to accept."

"I still don't see why she married John if she was in love with Harvey."

"Harvey didn't want children. At least that was the excuse she gave John. I've never met Harvey, and from everything I've heard about him, I don't want to meet him, either."

"He's said to be a brilliant oncologist."

"That doesn't make him a good human being."

"No, I suppose not. Is Sue recovering, then?"

"Harvey just keeps saying that he's cautiously optimistic. He did hint the other day that even if she has some sort of recovery, she'll never get back to her old self again. John hasn't told the children that."

"I don't blame him. What a horrible thought."

"Apparently, she's suffered from a number of very high fevers and possibly even seizures as a result. She's definitely confused when she talks to the children. She seems to know who they are, but she doesn't always seem to know where she is or how old the children are, things like that."

"How very sad. That must be upsetting for Thomas and Amy."

"It's horrible. John was considering telling Harvey not to ring again until Sue's well enough to have a proper conversation, but he didn't because he was worried that she might never recover. He doesn't want to keep her from talking to the children if every conversation could be their last."

"What a mess."

"There's more to it than that, as well," Doona added. "You know the police have been investigating Sue's illness very discreetly at John's request. They aren't telling him anything, but the investigation is still ongoing, which suggests that they've found something suspicious somewhere."

"Oh, dear."

"The kids don't know about that, either."

"Should I ask why you're at home tonight?"

"John thought it would be best to try to get things back to normal, or at least as close to normal as we can under the circumstances. He'll ring me if he hears anything from Harvey or Sue, but he's hoping the children might relax more if I'm not there."

"Are you okay?"

"Oh, I'm fine. I want to do what's best for John and Thomas and Amy. If he thinks that they'll be happier if I'm not there, then that's what's best."

Bessie could hear repressed tears in Doona's voice. "I'm sure he didn't mean it quite that way."

"I'm not sure what he meant. We haven't been able to have a proper talk in ages because the children are almost always there. Even when they aren't around, Sue's ghost looms large, although she isn't a ghost yet. Whatever she is, she's keeping me and John apart, even from thousands of miles away."

"I am sorry."

"In a way, it may be for the best," Doona surprised her by saying. "Relationships go through difficult times. If we can get through this and still be friends, let alone anything more, then we'll be a lot stronger for it."

"That's very true."

"I just wish I could help the children more. I can't begin to imagine what they're going through."

"It all makes my problems seem quite insignificant."

"What's wrong?"

Bessie grinned "Nothing, really, aside from being tangled up in another police investigation."

"Oh, that. I have to ask, how is Inspector Lambert?" Doona was a part-time receptionist at the Laxey station and had worked with Inspector Lambert when she'd been stationed in Laxey. Doona hadn't liked the older woman, and the feeling had been mutual.

"Not much different to when she was in Laxey," Bessie replied. "I hadn't realised she'd moved on from Castletown."

"Yes, there were issues there," Doona replied. She cleared her throat and then spoke in a low voice. "I'm not meant to repeat any of this, but she was very badly treated by one of the other inspectors there. He played with her feelings, flirting and even taking her out a few times. Of course, it wasn't long before Inspector Lambert found out that he was just playing with her, but it was long enough that she'd fallen quite hard for him, or so I'm told."

"My goodness."

"Inspector Lambert ended up having to take medical leave. She went across for a few weeks to recover. When she came back, the chief constable moved her to Peel. I'm sure she'll be anxious to solve this case. It's her first big assignment since she's been back."

"She's definitely eager to solve the case. She wants me to start making lists of whom we might have found."

"That's going to be difficult without knowing how long the body has been there, isn't it?"

"More like impossible, but I didn't want to tell the inspector that, not in so many words."

"As much as I don't care for Inspector Lambert, I hope you can help her. She didn't deserve to be treated so badly."

"And the other inspector got to keep his job?"

"Yes, but he's been warned about his behaviour. I believe he still thinks it was all just a bit of fun. I don't think he had any idea that Inspector Lambert took him seriously. If she'd asked me about him, I'd have warned her. He has quite the reputation, really."

"Another sad mess."

"Yes, it is, rather. Anyway, Inspector Lambert is doing everything she can to put the whole thing behind her and make a good impression in Peel. This case she's been given looks almost impossible, though."

"I can't imagine it will be easy, working out who was found and how he or she died."

"Can you think of anyone off the top of your head that you might have found?"

"I've been trying to do just that, but no, I can't. So many people have left the island over the years, and I don't know where many of them have gone. Surely, if this person was murdered, he or she must have been missed over the years. Perhaps Inspector Lambert will find a missing person report for him or her."

"When you were helping Hugh with the same sort of case last year, there weren't any missing person reports for any of the most likely candidates," Doona reminded her.

"No, not even the victim, because the family covered up the murder. I hope this isn't another case like that one. That was very sad."

"If the body has been in there for twenty or more years, I'm pretty certain whatever happened to him or her is going to be a sad story."

"I suppose you're right. Maybe it was just a very old person who wandered into the tower one day and died of natural causes. Maybe the door had been left unlocked accidentally and when someone found it open, they shut it and locked it without noticing the body inside."

"I hope whoever it was died before he or she was locked in."

Bessie shivered. "What a horrible thought, being locked inside the damp and dark tower all alone."

"It would be enough to give someone a heart attack, I reckon."

"We need to stop," Bessie said firmly. "I don't want to think about such awful things."

"You're right. Maybe the whole case will be solved by morning. Maybe there was a suicide note or maybe someone from MNH will remember that someone who loved the castle asked to be buried in there, or something similar."

"We can but hope."

"Are you certain you're okay?"

"I'll be fine. I'm going to read a few more chapters of my book and then get some sleep."

"I'm working all day tomorrow, but I'm free in the evening if you want to do something."

"Let's have dinner somewhere nice. I haven't seen you in ages. You've been rather busy."

Doona agreed to collect Bessie at six the following evening before they ended the conversation. As Bessie put the phone down, she sighed. The conversation with Doona had put all sorts of grim ideas into her head. Her book held little appeal, but she forced herself to read another chapter before giving up and taking herself up to her bedroom.

Tonight the bright pink walls made her frown. She'd loved the colour when she'd seen it in the shop, but it had been a good deal brighter than she'd expected once she'd actually painted the room. Occasionally she considered repainting, but that seemed to be far too much effort. Just about every spare surface in the room was covered in cuddly toys. For decades small children had gifted them to their "Aunt Bessie" for Christmas or her birthday. Now she picked up a large brown teddy bear and gave him a hug.

"Sometimes the world is an unpleasant place," she told the bear. He smiled back at her. She set him on the bed and went to brush her teeth, shaking her head at her foolishness. "Talking to cuddly toys is probably a bad sign," she told her reflection.

"And now you're talking to yourself," her mirror image said back.

Knowing that the world would look brighter in the morning, Bessie pulled the covers around herself and tried to sleep. It took her several minutes to drift off, and when she woke up she was vaguely aware that she'd had multiple nightmares about being locked in small, dark spaces.

A hot shower helped to clear her head. After, as she patted on the rose-scented dusting powder that reminded her of her first love, Matthew Saunders, she began to feel more like herself. After a light breakfast, she headed out for a brisk walk on the beach. She'd walked along Laxey Beach every morning that she could since she'd bought her cottage at eighteen. The fresh sea air and exercise were given much of the credit for her long life, in her mind, anyway. As she walked, she thought about Matthew.

They'd met and fallen in love in Cleveland, Ohio. Her family had moved to the US when she'd been only two years old. She'd grown up in Ohio with her sister, who was two years older than Bessie. When Bessie was seventeen, her parents had decided to return to the Isle of Man. Bessie's sister was already engaged to be married, so she was permitted to marry and remain in the US. Bessie, however, had been told that she had to return to the island. Her parents barely knew Matthew, and they didn't trust him with their seventeen-year-old daughter.

Bessie wondered now what might have happened if she'd remained in the US with her sister. Katherine had been willing to let Bessie stay with her and her new husband, but their parents refused to even consider the idea. That Katherine had eventually had ten children made Bessie think that perhaps her parents had been right in their decision. She hadn't felt that way at the time, though. All those years ago, she'd been furious. They'd practically had to drag her onto the boat for the sailing across the Atlantic and she'd cried for the entire journey. She'd barely spoken to either of them, even though they'd shared a house, until she'd received a letter from Matthew. He'd decided that he couldn't live without her and he was coming to the island to get her. As she would have been eighteen by the time he was expected to arrive, she could have done what she pleased, whatever her parents thought.

The memory of how happy she'd been when the letter had arrived was still strong, even after all these years. Bessie wiped away a tear as she thought about the days that had followed. When her parents had told her that Matthew hadn't survived the ocean journey, she hadn't believed them. When she finally understood that it was true, she'd turned her upset into anger, blaming her parents for Matthew's death. A short while later, she'd discovered that Matthew had left all of his worldly goods to her in a will that he'd prepared just before his sailing. Bessie had sold nearly everything and used that money to buy her cottage on the beach. It had already been given a name by the previous owners and Bessie had been convinced that Treoghe Bwaane, or Widow's Cottage, was the perfect place for her to recover from her loss.

When she'd first purchased the cottage, she'd thought she might one day meet someone else. Marriage and children might still be a part of her future, she'd told herself. Years later, when she did meet another man that she might have loved, she'd discovered that she cherished her freedom too much to give it up for anyone. He'd returned to Australia and eventually married someone else while Bessie had remained happily on her own in her little cottage by the sea.

Thanks to clever investments by her advocate, Bessie had never needed to find a job. Instead, she'd lived frugally on her own as the years flew past. Now all those years of cautious living meant that she had more money than she'd ever imagined. She'd extended the cottage twice in her years of ownership and had no desire to do anything further with it. Her only real indulgence was books, and in the past few years she'd fallen into the habit of buying far more than her bookshelves could accommodate. As she walked back towards home, Bessie began to wonder if she might squeeze another bookshelf into the cottage somewhere.

"Hello, Bessie," a loud voice called across the sand.

Bessie turned and greeted Maggie Shimmin with a small smile. Maggie and her husband Thomas owned the row of holiday cottages that ran along the beach from Bessie's cottage to Thie yn Traie, a huge clifftop mansion. They'd bought the land and had the cottages built, and Bessie knew that they worked hard to run their business successfully. She truly liked both Thomas and Maggie, but Maggie had a tendency to complain about everything and gossip about everyone. Some days she simply wasn't in the mood to talk to Maggie. Today was one of those days.

"How are you?" Maggie asked as she reached Bessie.

"I'm fine. How are you?"

"Oh, you know. I mustn't complain. Thomas is doing slightly better. The doctors seem to think he'll be well again by summer, which is just as well, as I can't be expected to run the business all by myself, can I? I mean, when he wanted to build the cottages, I wasn't certain it was a good idea, but he was so tired of working all those hours every week at the bank that I agreed we could try. It's turned out to be a lot more work for me than it was meant to be, though. I mean, I don't mind doing the shopping for the cottages, or even baking pies and cakes for our guests to purchase, but Thomas was meant to deal with the cleaning and upkeep. I believe I'm going to have to paint the interiors this winter, which is a huge undertaking."

"You could hire someone to do it," Bessie suggested.

"We thought about that, but painters seem to be charging a lot more than they used to for their services. It's all those comeovers that are moving here to work in the banks. They get paid a small fortune to relocate to the island. House prices have gone crazy lately because of them and now it's starting to drive up the prices on everything else. We needed a plumber the other day. Don't even ask me what he charged for an hour of work."

"I'm glad Thomas is feeling better."

Maggie nodded. "He charged us over five hundred pounds, and I don't think he even spent a full hour at the house."

"My goodness. Was that just for his labour?"

"Well, no, he had to install a new pipe and some new taps and things, as well, but still. It was outrageous."

"I shall have to hope I don't need any plumbing doing in a hurry."

"Thomas could have done the job himself if he were feeling better, but he'd have needed my help, too. My back has been playing up again and my one foot aches something awful when I walk too much. We didn't have a choice but to get someone in to deal with the problem."

Bessie nodded. "At least you can do the painting yourself."

"I don't know," Maggie sighed. "With my back the way it is, we may have to find someone to do that as well. But I mustn't complain, really. At least this time, when you found a body, it wasn't in one of my cottages."

"I didn't find the body," Bessie countered automatically.

"You always say that, but you were there, anyway, which is just the same. I heard, though, that all you really found was a few bones. Someone told me that all that could be seen from the doorway was a skeletal hand reaching out from the ground."

"Someone has an overactive imagination. It wasn't anything like that."

"So you could see the whole body?"

"I've no idea. Mark discovered it and I glanced inside so that I could tell the police exactly what we'd found. Once I saw that it was a skeleton, I rang 999. How much was actually visible didn't even register with me, but it was certainly more than just a hand."

"Interesting," Maggie said.

Bessie imagined that Maggie would be spending the next several hours ringing around the island to share that bit of news with all and sundry.

"But who is it?" Maggie asked.

"I've no idea."

"You must have some suspicions. When Hugh dragged up that old cold case, you were able to give him a list of possibilities, one of which turned out to be correct."

"Because we knew the gender of the body and when he had died. This body could have been lying there, undiscovered, for decades.

Until someone can give me an approximate date of death and work out the skeleton's gender, I couldn't even begin to guess who it was."

"I'll bet the police are going through all the old missing person reports right now."

"They may be. It's always possible that the person we found wasn't from the island, though. Maybe he or she was just visiting."

"Maybe the person sailed over on a boat in the middle of the night. The boat might have been wrecked on the rocks behind the castle. I can see a poor shipwrecked sailor dragging himself out of the sea and climbing up to the castle, looking for shelter from the storm. He crawled into the first tower he came to and then, sadly, succumbed to his injuries."

"That's one possibility," Bessie said, mentally rolling her eyes.

"Was the body in the tower nearest the castle entrance?"

"No, not at all. It was in one of the back corners."

Maggie sighed. "Maybe our brave little sailor climbed the castle wall and then collapsed on the ground beneath it, eventually managing to crawl into the tower."

Bessie shrugged. "It's far too soon to be speculating about such things. Let's see what the police and the coroner can determine before we spend too much time and effort on the matter. I'm still hoping that the body will turn out to be hundreds of years old and not a police matter."

"The bones wouldn't still be around if it was that old. I read a book about decomposition."

"Really? Why?"

Maggie shrugged. "It was fascinating, in a really macabre way. I found it at the library when I was looking for travel guides to Greece. Someone had put it in the wrong place, obviously."

"Are you going to Greece?"

"We're thinking about it for next winter. If we have another good summer season, I think we'll deserve a holiday. Warmer weather should be good for Thomas, as well. We don't want him catching pneumonia again."

"Let's hope you have another good summer, then."

"We're almost totally booked already, actually, even with another price increase to make up for losing the last cottage and for the cost of tearing it down. People seem incredibly keen to stay on Laxey Beach for some reason."

"I'm happy for you," Bessie said, even though she was less happy for herself. The summer visitors were generally polite and stayed away from Bessie's cottage, but they did get in the way when she wanted to walk on the beach. Their constant presence from April through October made the beach feel different, as well. Still, Bessie never complained.

"Thanks. Let's hope once that last cottage is gone we won't have any more murders down here. They aren't good for business."

"I keep hoping we won't have any more murders because they're simply awful," Bessie countered.

Maggie flushed. "Of course they're awful. I didn't mean to suggest that I didn't mind murders that happened elsewhere on the island, by any means."

"No, I'm sure you didn't."

"But I haven't time to chat with you all day, unfortunately. I must go and check the last cottage one more time. I'm certain we've cleared it out, but I had a dream last night that we'd left some plates and bowls in the cupboards. They'll be coming any day now to tear it down, you see."

Bessie nodded and then turned and made her way home. The message on her answering machine made her frown even more than the encounter with Maggie had.

"Bessie, my dear, it's Dan Ross. Please ring me back. Surely you won't mind talking about a decades-old skeleton from Peel Castle? Ring me."

The reporter from the *Isle of Man Times* was nothing if not persistent, Bessie thought as she deleted the message. Why he thought that she'd want to speak to him about anything at all was a mystery to her. She was relieved that he hadn't tried to guilt her into talking to him, really. A month ago, when she'd suggested that he investigate something, he'd nearly been killed for his efforts. He hadn't blamed Bessie for the experience, which was the only thing Bessie appreciated about him.

She spent some time tidying her cottage before lunch and then headed up to her office to work on Onnee's letters for a while. Onnee had grown up on the island before impulsively marrying a visiting American man named Clarence. He'd taken her back across the Atlantic to his family home in Wisconsin. There, Onnee had been shocked to meet Clarence's fiancée, Faith, who had been staying with his parents while he'd been travelling. They'd been equally surprised to meet Onnee, as Clarence's letters to home had been delayed.

A year later, Onnee was pregnant but worried that Faith was also expecting Clarence's child. Faith was still living with Clarence's parents, while Onnee and Clarence were living elsewhere.

Onnee's handwriting was difficult to decipher, but Bessie was determined to get through several months of letters today. She worked until her eyes were so tired that the words began to blur on the page. It's almost easier to read when I can't focus, Bessie thought to herself as she pushed the letter she was transcribing to one side. While transcribing, she worked from word to word, barely noticing the contents of the letters. Now she sat back with her own neatly written copies and read through what she'd found.

Mostly, the letters had detailed Onnee's daily life in Wisconsin. She read books and did her household chores, all while dealing with morning sickness and other pregnancy issues. She did tell her mother that it appeared that Faith wasn't pregnant after all. Instead, Faith seemed to have fallen ill. Clarence was spending more and more time with his former fiancée, telling Onnee not to complain as Faith needed him. The last letter that Bessie had transcribed was mostly about how uncomfortable Onnee was feeling in the last weeks of her pregnancy. The final words of the letter brought tears to Bessie's eyes.

"I want more than anything to have you here," Onnee had written to her mother. "I'm going to become a mother soon, and I need your guidance and support. I'm terrified of what is coming, and Clarence is too busy with Faith to bother with me. I worry that he won't be especially interested in the baby, either. If I had any money at all, I would book myself on the next boat back to the island. I know leaving my husband would be wrong, but I long for home and for you far more than I care for him."

As Bessie shut her notebook, she wondered if she would have come to feel the same way about Matthew if she'd been permitted to stay in the US with him. There was no way to know, of course, but Bessie once again felt that she'd ended up exactly where she was meant to be, alone in her little cottage by the sea.

The local paper that afternoon had the body at Peel Castle as its headline article. Bessie frowned as she read what Dan Ross had written. "Mystery Skelton at Peel Castle," was a less lurid headline than she'd been expecting, but he'd listed her as having found the body, "accompanied by some staff from Manx National Heritage." That was just wrong, but Bessie knew better than to ring to complain. Instead, she enjoyed her dinner with Doona and then spent her evening finishing the book she'd started the previous day and trying to forget all about what she'd seen in Peel.

The next few days passed quietly. Bessie found herself feeling oddly reluctant to go back to Onnee's letters, expecting that the next one would announce the baby's arrival. Instead, she read books, walked on the beach, and spent some time shopping and visiting friends. Doona rang daily to let her know that nothing had changed with Sue. On Thursday afternoon, Bessie decided that it was time to get back to Onnee. She was heading for the stairs when someone knocked on her door.

"Inspector Lambert, hello," Bessie said, forcing herself to smile at the frowning woman on her doorstep.

CHAPTER 4

"I think you should call me Anna," the woman replied.

"Oh, yes, thank you," Bessie said, feeling flustered. "Do come in," she added as she took a step backwards.

"I will, thank you."

Bessie shut the door behind her guest. "Have a seat. Would you like a cuppa?"

"I'd love one, if it isn't too much bother," Anna replied as she slid into a chair at the kitchen table.

"It's no trouble at all," Bessie assured her. She put fresh water in the kettle and switched it on before filling a plate with biscuits. When the kettle boiled, she made tea for both of them, handing Anna her cup before sitting down opposite her with her own.

"How are you?" Anna asked.

"I'm fine, thank you. How are you?"

"Me?" Anna laughed. "No one ever asks police inspectors how they are, but I'm fine, thank you, or at least that's the required response, isn't it?"

"It's the expected response, but it certainly isn't required."

"No? Would you prefer it if I tell you how I really am?"

"I would, actually."

Anna tilted her head and studied Bessie for a moment. "I may, one day," she said eventually. "Not today, though. Today we have more important things to discuss."

"You know where to find me when one day comes around," Bessie said. She was surprised to see Anna blinking back tears.

"Thank you," she said softly. She shook her head and cleared her throat. "Tomorrow's local paper is going to have an article about the body you found. I wanted to talk to you first, though, before everyone on the island is talking about it."

"I didn't find the body," Bessie sighed.

Anna chuckled. "Sorry, you're right, of course, and I should be precise. You were there, but Mark Blake actually discovered the body. Let me tell you what we now know about his discovery. The body, or rather the skeleton, was of an adult female. The coroner estimates that the woman was in her mid-twenties when she died. Based on his findings and some of the other things that were found with the skeleton, we believe she died in the late sixties. The coroner was unable to determine if she'd been moved after her death, but that seems likely. Having said that, he doesn't believe that she was moved recently."

Bessie sat back in her chair and tried to think. When that didn't help, she leaned forward and took a sip of tea. "She may have been in there for more than thirty years, then. I can't believe no one found her before Monday," was the first thing that popped into her head.

"Neither can I. The chief constable has been talking to the head of Manx National Heritage about that, actually. Of course, he wasn't even living on the island in the late sixties, so he can't explain why no one has been in that space in all those years."

"What does Henry say?"

"Henry? Do you mean Henry Costain?"

"Yes, he's been working for MNH for more than thirty years. He may have some idea about that tower."

"He simply said that he'd never needed to go in there. He remembered a time, several years ago, when they went through the whole site, clearing out old boxes and things, but no one had the key for the padlock on that tower, so they simply skipped over it."

47

"And they didn't bother to change it when they changed all the other padlocks?"

"Henry said they were one padlock short of being able to do every lock on the site, so they missed that one out. When they bought more locks at a later date, no one remembered to change that one. I didn't get a feeling from Henry as if anyone were deliberately trying to keep people away from that tower, although that has to be considered."

"She was murdered?"

"The coroner can't determine the cause of death," was the disappointing reply. "Because of the location of the body, we're assuming that it was murder. If it wasn't murder, someone locked the body in the tower after her death."

"Could she have been locked in before she was dead? Could someone have left her there to starve, for instance?"

"A possibility, and a very unpleasant one, at that."

Bessie nodded. "I don't suppose she could have just wandered into the tower and been locked inside accidentally?"

"Again, it's a possibility to consider, but unless she'd gone in and taken a nap or suddenly fallen ill, surely she would have shouted when the door was shut behind her."

Bessie shivered as she imagined waking from a nap to find herself locked inside the dark tower. "Horrible," she murmured.

"And unlikely. What seems most likely is that she was murdered or died somewhere else on the island and then the body was hidden in that tower. Whoever hid the body has been very fortunate for the past thirty-odd years, but his or her luck just ran out."

"Assuming that person is still alive."

"Thirty years isn't that long. The victim was in her mid-twenties, so her contemporaries will be close to sixty now."

"She may not have been from the island, of course."

"I think she was," Anna said firmly. "I think she was from the island, that she was murdered, and that her body was hidden at Peel Castle. I also think that, with your help, I'll be able to solve the case."

"I'll do what I can."

"Who was she?" Anna asked. "There can't have been many women that age who disappeared from the island at the right time. Young women were more sheltered in those days. Make me a list of anyone you can think of who would have been about the right age and who left the island and never returned."

Bessie nodded. "I'll ring a few friends, as well. Among us we should be able to come up with a few names."

"Don't ring anyone until the local paper is out. I'm not meant to be sharing any of this information yet."

"I'll start my list as soon as you leave and then add to it when I've spoken to my friends."

"I appreciate this. It may turn out to be a wild goose chase, but I have to try."

Bessie nodded. "More tea?" she asked as she got up to top up her own cup.

"Yes, please," Anna replied. Bessie was surprised. She'd thought that the inspector was getting ready to leave, but now Anna sipped her drink and helped herself to a biscuit.

"It isn't easy, being a woman in a male-dominated workplace," Anna said after a moment. "I've always felt as if I've had to be tougher, harder, more demanding than my male counterparts. I'm good at my job, but I felt as if I had to be better, work longer hours, take the shifts no one wanted, all the same things that all women complain about, I suppose."

"I can't imagine."

Anna shrugged. "You chose to live on your own at a time when women were expected to marry and have children. I'm sure you dealt with a great deal of negativity about how you lived your life."

"Some, certainly, but I didn't let it bother me."

"You're stronger than I am, then. I've moved five times in my career. Three of those times were to get away from gossip and rumours. I know you don't care for me, so maybe you're the perfect person to hear my miserable life story."

"If you feel the need to talk, I'm always happy to listen."

Anna shrugged. "I never talk about myself. That may be part of my problem, of course. The chief constable wants me to talk to a therapist. I tried that recently, but it felt contrived and awkward. This does, as well, but at least you're giving me tea and biscuits."

Bessie laughed. "I have cake, if you'd prefer."

"Cake?"

"I made a Victoria sponge yesterday. Would you like a slice?"

"I'd rather have the whole thing and a fork, but a slice will do," Anna told her.

Bessie tried not to look as surprised as she felt. Anna Lambert didn't seem the type to indulge her sweet tooth to that degree.

"I'm always incredibly careful about what I eat, of course. Staying fit is important in my job, especially as a woman. I don't need to give anyone any extra ammunition against me."

"Why do you do it?" Bessie asked as she cut them both generous slices of cake. "Why don't you find another job? I'm sure there are plenty of other things you could do with your life."

"My father was a police inspector." She stopped as Bessie put the cake in front of her. "This looks wonderful," she sighed. "I really shouldn't, but I'm going to eat every bite."

"Sometimes we all need a little treat," Bessie replied. "So your father encouraged you to join the police?" she asked, bringing the conversation back on topic.

"No, not at all. It was the opposite, in fact. He encouraged my brother to join the police. I was meant to be a schoolteacher or maybe a nurse. Policing wasn't for women, as far as my father was concerned. That just made me more determined to pursue it, of course. My brother, who's two years older, joined the police right out of school. I did the same. My father was proud of my brother and annoyed with me."

"Oh, dear."

"When I got my first assignment, all I heard from everyone was that I was only there because my father had pulled strings to get me there. It was as far from the truth as it could be, but no one believed me. I ended up moving away from home, joining another constabulary on the other side of the country, just to prove that I could advance on my own merit."

"How did your father feel about that?"

"Oh, he didn't really care. He was too busy bragging about my brother's accomplishments to notice what I was doing."

Bessie frowned. She'd never had children, but she'd always thought that if she had, she'd love and support them all equally, no matter what.

"I was young and foolish, though," Anna continued. "I was all alone in a strange city and I made the mistake of falling in love with another constable. Dean was handsome and smart and I was certain we were perfect for one another."

"More tea?" Bessie asked, beginning to feel as if something stronger might be more appropriate.

"Yes, please."

Anna waited until Bessie had refilled both cups before she continued. "There was only one problem with my happily-ever-after fantasies about Dean. He was already married. He never talked about his wife, didn't have pictures of her on his desk or anything. I convinced myself that they'd fallen out of love and that Dean and I were soulmates. Dean said all the right things about how his wife didn't appreciate how difficult the job was and how they barely spoke to one another when he was at home. We had an affair. There, I've said it. It was passionate and crazy and I thought it was love. I found out later that Dean had a reputation for sleeping with every new female constable, but no one bothered to mention that until I was already madly in love."

"I'm sorry."

"It happens. I know I'm not unique and I know I was wrong for getting involved with a married man. At the time I was sure that true love was the most important thing, but I was wrong, obviously. Once I discovered the truth, that Dean was never going to leave his wife and that I was nothing but a conquest to him, I moved again. I was embarrassed about the entire incident. This is the first time I've talked about it in twenty-five years."

"Sometimes talking about something painful can be healing."

"You may be right. Thank you for not giving me a lecture about married men and affairs."

"It isn't my place to lecture you. We've all made poor choices in the past. All we can do is learn from them and move on."

"I thought I had, learned, I mean. I moved again and I promised myself that I wouldn't get involved with any future work colleagues. I might not have been able to stick to that, except not long after I moved, I met an amazing man. He'd been burgled and I took his statement. After I was done, he asked me to have dinner with him. I was already falling hard by the end of that meal."

Bessie could see tears in Anna's eyes again. This part of the story wasn't going to have a happy ending either, of course.

"He proposed after a week. I laughed and told him it was too soon. Then I said yes. We waited almost a year to get married, though. My parents were there. My father congratulated me and then asked me when I was quitting work to start a family."

"What did your mother think?"

"I've no idea. We've never been close. She was devoted to my father. After they married, she quit work and dedicated the rest of her life to making his life as wonderful as possible. It never mattered how late he got home from work. She made him a feast every night. My brother and I were fed at five and usually sent to bed before my father got home. Eventually my brother began to be included in our parents' evening meals, but I never was."

"My goodness."

Anna shrugged. "My mother felt that being a good wife was her calling. Being a mother came second, or maybe even third, after the volunteer work that she did. My brother, even though he was clearly the favourite child, didn't feel any more loved than I did, really."

"Are you and your brother close?"

"I wouldn't say close, but we do talk. I haven't spoken to my father in years. It wasn't a conscious decision. We simply drifted apart and neither of us care enough to reach out to the other now."

"And your mother?"

"She passed away about six years ago. That was the last time I saw my father. He was devastated and my brother and I worried that he might struggle to cope on his own, but according to Alan, he's doing just fine."

"Alan is your brother?"

"Oh, yes, sorry. I ring him about once a month or so. If I forget, he rings me. I suspect his wife reminds him. She's close to her family and I think she worries about me."

"Do they have children?"

Anna nodded and smiled. "They have a boy and a girl and I love them both very much. I actually speak to them a good deal more frequently than I do their father. They're both in their early twenties and doing really well."

"And is Alan still with the police?"

"Oh, no. He moved into private security after a few years. It paid better and had better hours. Our father wasn't especially happy about it, but Alan was still the golden child, so he was quickly forgiven."

"But you were telling me about getting married."

"Yes, I was. Doug and I got married and settled down together. It was going to be perfect. We were both going to work until we'd saved up enough for a house and then we were going to start a family."

Bessie took a sip of her tea. She could tell that the next part of the story was going to be difficult for Anna to tell. "You don't have to tell me anything else," she said softly.

"I may as well tell you the whole story. This part is the worst. Doug and I were incredibly happy. He was working in a large department store, managing the men's clothing department. We were both doing well with our careers. We were really happy."

Anna stopped and then angrily swiped at her eyes, brushing away tears that were clearly unwelcome. Bessie got up and found a box of tissues. She put them in front of Anna and then sat back down.

The other woman wiped her eyes and then took a sip of her tea. Sighing deeply, she looked at Bessie. "This should be easier. It was a long time ago."

"Let's talk about something else," Bessie suggested. "I've one idea of whom we may have found at Peel Castle."

"Really? I thought you needed to think about it."

"One name popped into my head immediately. I believe she'd have been around the right age, and I'm certain she disappeared in the late sixties."

"Go on, then," Anna said. She pulled out her notebook and nodded at Bessie.

"Her name was, or I should say is, Emma Gibson. She was a schoolteacher in Ramsey. Her mother was from Laxey, but she married a man from Jurby. They lived in Douglas when Emma was small. Emma's grandmother still lived in Laxey, though, so her mother used to bring her to play on Laxey Beach. That's how I know the family."

"And she disappeared one day?"

"I'm not sure about that. I was told that she'd left the island, but I never heard that she'd come back, not even for a visit."

"Would you have heard if she'd visited?"

"If she'd come to see her grandmother in Laxey, I may well have heard. The woman used to live on the road that leads down to the beach and I used to see her when I walked up to the shop at the top of the hill."

"Used to? What happened to her?"

"She passed away about fifteen years ago. I believe her daughter still lives in Douglas. She should be able to tell you what happened to Emma. She'll be somewhere around eighty now, Emma's mum, I mean."

"It seems likely that Emma simply moved away."

"She probably did. I'm only mentioning her because I don't know for certain where she went or why. The island was smaller in those days, or it felt smaller, anyway. When people left, we all talked about them for weeks on end. I don't remember anyone talking about Emma leaving."

"Surely, if that's the case, then people talked about her disappearance?"

Bessie shrugged. "I have a vague recollection of her going on holiday and not coming back. I wish I could remember more than that, but I'm afraid I can't."

Anna made a note and then shut her notebook. "I would imagine that her mother would have reported her missing if she'd never come back from her holiday, but I'll definitely check it out."

"I'm sorry. I know it seems unlikely, but, as I said, hers was the first name that popped into my head."

"And you never know what little bit of information might break a case wide open. Perhaps your Emma is alive and well but will remember a friend who also left the island at the same time, never to be heard from again."

"I'm sure I'll be able to suggest some other, more likely candidates in a day or two."

"I'd appreciate that. Now I'd better finish my sad life story and then leave you in peace. Doug and I were happily settling into a tiny flat when I found out I was pregnant. We hadn't planned for a baby yet, but I was thrilled. Doug was less excited, but I knew he'd come around once he got used to the idea."

She stopped and wiped her eyes again. Bessie sipped her drink, not wanting to interrupt.

"We had a little girl. She was gorgeous. She looked a lot like her father. We were both over the moon. I stayed home with her for six weeks, but taking more time off would have hurt my future prospects. After a long talk, we decided that Doug would stay home with the baby for a year while I worked. It seemed the perfect solution."

"I understand more and more families are doing such things now."

"Yes, well, it was a good deal more unusual in those days, but it was what we both wanted. Three months later, Doug rang me at work. He'd put the baby down for her nap and when he'd gone back in an hour later, she'd stopped breathing. He'd rung for an ambulance, but they...they couldn't...there was nothing..." she trailed off, tears streaming down her face.

Bessie patted her arm awkwardly for a moment and then got up and prepared more tea. Anna had stopped crying by the time Bessie had refilled her cup.

"Thank you. I'm sorry. I don't like losing control."

"Considering the circumstances, it's understandable. I'm terribly sorry for your loss."

Anna nodded. "It isn't any easier, even after all these years, talking about her, remembering her. She was the best thing that had ever happened to me, and I lost her. I blamed myself, of course. The doctors said it was cot death, that nothing could have prevented it, that the same thing would have happened no matter who had been there, but I didn't believe them. I was certain that if I'd been looking after her, as I should have been, that she would have been okay. I failed her."

"You didn't fail her. You were out doing your job, trying to secure her future. You left her with her father, who was as devoted to her as you were. There was nothing you could have done to prevent what happened."

"In my head, I know you're right, but in my heart I still feel a tremendous amount of guilt. Doug blamed himself, and I'm afraid I wanted to blame him, too. Her death was the beginning of the end for us, although we struggled along for six months or so before we finally separated. I left Doug and the area after those six months. I couldn't stand the sympathetic looks from everyone and I needed to get away from the memories that seemed to be everywhere around me. I ended up in London. That's a good place to hide from everyone and everything."

"I can't imagine living in London."

"It was a good career move, if nothing else. I was there for ten years before I moved again, but this time I moved because I was offered a much better job in Birmingham. My next move after Birmingham was to the island. I thought that coming over here, taking the position at the Laxey station, would be a smart move at my age. The job was meant to be mostly administrative, and I thought I'd prefer that now that I'm getting older. I was wrong. Fortunately, a position opened up in Castletown. I didn't want to think about moving back across."

"Do you like the island that much?" Bessie asked in surprise.

"I've come to love the island, actually. The way of life, the pace of life, the people, the scenery, it's all very special. I wish I'd moved here years ago. I was offered a job here back in the seventies, but I turned it down."

"Did you like Castletown?"

Anna gave her a wry smile. "You must have heard by now what happened in Castletown. The island is too small for me to believe that you haven't."

"I've heard a few things, but I'd rather hear the truth from you."

"It was simply history repeating itself. I should have known better, really, but I was foolish. I met a man, a handsome, smart, funny man, and I fell in love almost immediately. After Doug, I'd deliberately kept men at arm's length. I'd focussed on my career, becoming harder and more shut off from my emotions. That was how I coped with my loss. When I met Jacob, for the first time in nearly thirty years I let my guard down. That was stupid."

"Sometimes we have to take chances in life. If he'd been a better person, you might have been very happy together."

"If is the right word. I thought I knew what I was doing. I told him about my past, not in this much detail, but that I'd been badly hurt multiple times. He was sympathetic and made all manner of promises. I was dumb enough to think he meant what he said."

"I'll never understand men."

Anna laughed. "I'm not sure I want to understand men. I'm not sure I want to understand how a man could lie about his feelings and deliberately mislead someone just to get her into bed. Whatever, once he'd accomplished his goal, he lost interest very quickly. I was heartbroken."

"I'm sorry."

"The chief constable was kind, anyway. He sent me to a place across for an extended holiday. There were people there that I could have talked to, trained counsellors and that sort of thing, but it wasn't required. We were right on the sea, and I took long walks and long naps and just let myself relax. When it was time to leave, I decided that I wanted to come back to the island, even though I knew that people would be talking about me."

"They aren't, really, at least not much," Bessie told her. "I hadn't heard a single word about any of this before I saw you at Peel Castle. Then I rang a few sources and asked for the skeet. I promise you that I won't repeat a word you said today, either."

"I appreciate that. I'm hoping that I can do some good work in Peel. I have no intention of letting another man into my life. Men have always been at the root of my troubles."

Starting with your father, Bessie thought but didn't say. "I hope everything works out for you," Bessie said sincerely, feeling as if she understood Anna Lambert a good deal better now. Whether she could come to like her was another matter, but she had a new level of respect for her after learning about her difficult past.

"I'm just keeping my head down and doing my job. I'll ring you or come over in a few days to get some more names to investigate. I appreciate your help."

"You're more than welcome. I'm always happy to help the police, especially when there's a dead body involved."

"I keep hoping that she wasn't murdered," Anna admitted. "Although that seems preferable to her being accidentally locked inside the tower while still alive."

Bessie shivered. "I don't much like either of those ideas."

"Let's just hope we can find a solution. I'd hate to have an unsolved case as the first thing next to my name at my new posting." Anna got to her feet. "I've taken up your entire afternoon. I do apologise. Perhaps I should have taken advantage of the counsellors when I was away. It seems I did need someone to talk to, after all."

"You know where to find me if you want to talk again," Bessie told her.

"I've told you my entire life story. I can't imagine what else we could talk about. I know your story, as well. You've had your share of tragedy, haven't you?"

"I never lost a child," Bessie countered.

"But you never got to carry one inside of you, either. I don't regret having my daughter, even though she was only with me for a short while. She was still the best thing that I've ever done." Anna wiped her eyes as she headed for the door. "No one knows about the baby," she said when she reached it. "I'd rather you didn't mention it to anyone."

"As I said, I won't repeat anything you've said here."

"Thank you," Anna replied. She opened the door and then took a deep breath and squared her shoulders before marching out.

Bessie watched as Anna climbed into her car and drove away. After shutting and locking the door, she gathered up plates and cups and began to do the washing-up automatically, her mind racing. Clearly, Anna had had a difficult life. That inspector in Castletown should be ashamed of himself for treating her so badly. As she dried the dishes and put them away, she wondered what had happened to Doug, Anna's former husband. For a moment she was tempted to try to find him. Perhaps, if he and Anna were reunited, they would fall in love again. After spinning the fantasy for a minute, Bessie stopped herself. Doug had probably remarried; he might even have passed away, or moved to Canada, or any one of a number of possibilities. Tracking him down might simply cause even more heartache for Anna.

Feeling too restless to do anything productive, Bessie took a long walk on the beach, not getting home until well past her normal dinner hour. After tea, biscuits, and cake with Anna, she wasn't particularly hungry anyway. She heated a tin of soup and ate that with a slice of toast. Still feeling emotionally drained by the conversation with Anna, Bessie didn't feel up to working with Onnee's letters again. Instead, she curled up with a few magazines that she'd purchased months earlier and never read. They were filled with celebrity gossip that was now well out of date, but as Bessie didn't recognise any of the so-called celebrities in the articles, it didn't really matter. She forced herself to read until she couldn't keep her eyes open any longer before taking herself to bed.

She woke up the next morning with a sense of purpose. Determined to do everything she could to help Anna, she started by digging out her diaries for the relevant years. With a cup of tea at her elbow, she opened the first book and began to read.

CHAPTER 5

*A*n hour later, Bessie shut her last diary from the early seventies and dropped it back into the box where she'd found it. "What was I thinking?" she demanded loudly. One of these days, she'd have to have a big bonfire and burn all of the books, she decided. Her heirs would wonder about her sanity if they read some of the things she'd written.

After a cup of tea, once she'd recovered from the disappointment of not finding anything that might help Anna, she was able to laugh at her former self. What she'd found in her diaries was a mixed bag of both too much information and not nearly enough. On one page she could find an almost hour-by-hour account of a single day when nothing much had happened. She'd recorded what she'd eaten, what book she'd been reading, how far she'd gone on each of the three walks she'd taken, and a dozen other bits of minutiae that wouldn't have been interesting at the time and certainly weren't thirty-odd years later.

Then there were pages and pages with only the minimum of notes, some of which were intriguing and frustrating in equal measure. "Man missing from ferry," one note read. Try as she might, Bessie couldn't remember anything else about the incident. Who was the missing man? Had he ever been found? Bessie had no idea and her diary was no help. The incident was never mentioned again, at least not in the books that Bessie had pulled out from the back of her wardrobe. She'd read the books dated from the late fifties through to the early seventies and hadn't found a single mention of any women who had gone missing. Even Emma Gibson didn't rate a note, although the turkey sandwich that Bessie had eaten on the twenty-fourth of April 1957, was recorded.

The entire exercise had been a waste of time, but it had filled the morning. Now, as the local paper was being delivered around the island, Bessie could start ringing her friends. Wanting to be certain that she wasn't getting ahead of herself, once she'd eaten lunch she walked up to the shop at the top of the hill to get herself a copy of the paper. The young man behind the till was a stranger to Bessie.

"Hello," she said brightly as she walked into the shop.

"Yeah," he replied, glancing up from his phone for a second.

Bessie frowned and then quickly made her way through the aisles, grabbing a few things she needed. When she got to the till, the shop assistant rang up her purchases without saying a word.

"How much, then?" Bessie asked when he was done putting every-thing into a bag.

"It's there," he grunted, pointing to the total displayed on the till.

"It's polite to tell the customer anyway," Bessie replied.

He blinked at her and then shrugged and read out the numbers. Bessie handed him a twenty pound note and waited for her change. When he gave it to her without speaking, she thought about requesting that he count it back to her, but decided it wasn't worth the bother. In the future, she'd try to avoid the shop and the disagree-able young man.

Back at home, she read through the entire paper. While she learned a few things about some recent government initiatives and found out all of the local sports scores, there was nothing different in the article about the skeleton in Peel from what Anna had told her. Dan Ross quoted the inspector as saying that the investigation was "active and ongoing," which sounded fairly meaningless to Bessie.

With that out of the way, Bessie settled in to get comfortable and picked up her phone. When she finally put it down several hours later, she had a list of four women who were possibilities. It didn't seem much for the amount of time and effort Bessie felt she'd put in, but it was the best she could do. She'd spoken to nearly all of her closest friends and acquaintances, including a few women who'd done nothing much with their lives beyond gossip. While she was tempted to start asking questions about the women herself, she knew that was a job for the police. Sighing deeply, she stood up and stretched slowly. What she needed now was a walk on the beach.

It was sunny but cold as she walked briskly away from Treoghe Bwaane. Having spent so many hours sitting down, her legs seemed to want to walk forever. She sped past the holiday cottages and Thie yn Traie, determined to keep going until she felt less restless. A short while later, the new houses that had been built less than a year earlier came into view. Bessie continued past them, not stopping until she'd reached the stretch of beach where another row of houses was about to be built.

The sign on the sand told her that only three plots remained unsold of the ten that were proposed. From where Bessie was standing, the site didn't look big enough to hold ten houses, but someone must have measured everything before the plans had been submitted. While the houses were meant to be detached, Bessie was certain that they'd end up being very close together, maybe even more so than the new houses that she'd just walked past.

While she was tempted to walk farther, Bessie was starting to get tired. Taking a deep breath of sea air, she turned and began to stroll back towards home. There were only a few signs of life in the new houses as Bessie approached them. She smiled and then waved when she spotted Grace at the sliding door at the back of the house she shared with Hugh and the baby.

"Aunt Bessie, how are you?" Grace called, having slid open the large glass door.

"I'm fine, but don't let the baby get a chill," Bessie replied.

"She's well wrapped up. We were just coming outside for a bit of fresh air," Grace explained. She stepped outside and then pushed the door shut behind herself. "I try to get her out every day, at least for a short while. Sea air is good for everyone."

"It's been good for me, anyway," Bessie laughed.

"I'm sure it's good for Aalish as well. She's getting so big so quickly."

Bessie looked at the baby. As far as Bessie could tell, Aalish didn't look all that different from the last time Bessie had seen her, but she didn't say that to Grace. "How are you doing, then?"

"We're doing well. I loved having Mum here, but I think it's better for all of us that she's back in Douglas now. She still visits nearly every day, but she isn't usually here when Hugh gets home from work."

"Do Hugh's parents visit much?" Bessie had to ask.

"His mum comes over at least once a week. I think she'd come more often, but she doesn't feel entirely comfortable here, even when Hugh is at home, and he isn't always able to be here when she visits. His father came once, but he didn't seem all that interested in Aalish."

"That's probably typical for men of that generation. What about your father?"

"Oh, Dad loves Aalish to bits, but he's busy with work and all of his other things. He comes up most Saturdays to spend a few minutes with us, but then he usually has plans to golf or has some sort of committee meeting or something."

"So you and Hugh are having to cope on your own for the most part."

"Which is how it should be, as Aalish is our baby. I'm really happy that I can stay home with her for now, but I have been thinking about going back to work, too. Staying home is, well, not quite what I expected."

"I imagine it's rather dull, really, even though Aalish is hard work."

"It is rather dull, if I'm honest. I love every minute with Aalish, but the cooking, cleaning, laundry, and whatever that take up all the rest of my time isn't any fun at all."

"Maybe you could do supply teaching and only work a few days a week come September. That might be the best of both worlds."

"I'd like that. I was talking to the head of the primary school here in Laxey about doing just that, actually, but he wasn't sure that he'd be able to use me all that much. He did say that a bad tummy bug went through the school a few years ago and he ended up having to bring in a supply teacher for two days each week as just about each teacher fell ill in turn. Am I a terrible person if I wish for another, similar bug?"

Bessie laughed. "Perhaps you could wish for something like a training scheme that takes each teacher out of school for a few days, one after another. That would be nicer than a tummy bug."

"You're right, of course, and I'm not actually certain that I want to go back to work anyway. In theory, it sounds good, but I'm afraid I'll miss Aalish too much if I actually try."

"Perhaps you should start by going out for a meal with Hugh. I'm sure he'd love an hour or two of your undivided attention."

"Did he tell you that?"

"Not at all. I'm not sure if the idea has even crossed his mind."

Grace made a face. "I have been neglecting him, of course, but Aalish is incredibly demanding."

Bessie looked at the tiny bundle curled up in her mother's arms. "I'm sure you're right, but at the moment she doesn't seem at all demanding."

"I fed her, changed her nappy, and put her in clean clothes just before we walked out of the house. I probably have another half an hour before she'll start wanting something again."

"She seems fascinated by everything."

"Yes, Mum reckons she doesn't sleep as much as other babies. Of course, Mum is convinced that she's going to be a genius, but she thought the same about me and my siblings, and we're all sadly normal."

"Normal can be quite a good thing."

"Oh, yes, of course. One of my friends just had a baby who has had all manner of complications. I'm ever so thankful that Aalish seems completely normal, at least so far. From my years of teaching, I'm well aware of the many differences between children and their abilities, many of which are invisible and some of which are difficult to diagnose. All Hugh and I can do is try our best to give Aalish the best possible start in life."

"I think you're doing a wonderful job so far," Bessie told her.

Aalish picked that moment to wrinkle up her tiny face. A second later, she began to cry, quietly at first, but with rapidly increasing volume.

"My goodness, what's wrong?" Bessie asked.

"She's probably just bored. She could be hungry, or she could need a new nappy. Maybe she's a bit cold or a bit hot or just ready for a nap," Grace replied with a sigh. "I do wish she'd hurry up and learn to talk."

Bessie chuckled. "You've a while to go yet before that will happen," she said. "I'm going to leave you to it. Good luck."

Grace nodded. "Come on then, pet," she said to Aalish. "Let's go back inside and see if we can work out what's bothering you."

Aalish's sobs got quieter as Grace turned and opened the door into the house. "She just doesn't want any less than one hundred per cent of my attention," Grace muttered as she stepped into the house.

Bessie grinned and continued on her way. As she reached the stairs to Thie yn Traie, she saw Maggie going into the last cottage in the row of holiday cottages. Maggie was the one person she hadn't yet rung about the missing women. Now was probably a good time to try to speak to her, actually.

"Hello?" she called as she approached the last cottage. Maggie had left the cottage's door wide open. "Maggie?"

"Who's that?" Maggie demanded, sounding nervous.

"It's Bessie. I was just coming back from a walk." Bessie stuck her head into the cottage and smiled at Maggie as she emerged from the short corridor that led to the bedrooms.

"Bessie, hello. You didn't half give me a fright. There's just something about this cottage that makes me anxious. I can't wait until we can get it torn down."

"I thought you said you'd already cleared it out."

"We did, and then I checked it again the other day. This morning, someone from the police rang to say that there were lights on inside the cottage. I met a constable down here and we checked the place over and didn't find anything out of place except one light that was switched on. After I got home, I started to worry that I'd forgotten to turn it back off, so I popped down here to double-check."

"And it was off."

"How did you know?"

"I walked past a while ago and didn't notice that there were any lights on inside the cottage. I would have noticed, too, as I've fallen into the habit of paying attention to this cottage."

"Haven't we all," Maggie sighed. "Anyway, yes, it was off. You can be my witness, actually, that all of the lights are off. If the police ring again, I'd love to have someone to back me up."

Bessie glanced around and then nodded. "Do you want me to check the bedrooms?"

"Would you mind? I'm certain that I switched everything off the last time I was here, but there was definitely a light on this morning."

It only took Bessie a moment to walk through the small cottage, checking all of the lights. Everything was turned off, as expected.

"If the police ring again, I'll know for certain that someone is breaking into the cottage again," Maggie said as she locked the door behind them.

"Who would do that?"

"I've no idea, but we both know it wouldn't be the first time."

"Yes, of course. Maybe you should have the power cut to this cottage."

"We've been considering that, actually. We'll have to have it done before we have it torn down, obviously. I suppose we haven't done it yet because we'd rather people broke into this cottage than one of the others."

"That makes sense, although it would be best if no one broke into any of them."

"Talk to Inspector Rockwell about that. He keeps promising to increase the patrols down here, but I haven't seen any evidence of it actually happening. I realise this cottage is the farthest from the road and that someone would have to actually walk down the beach to check that it was secure, but maybe if they had a constable do that for a day or two, whoever is breaking in would stop."

"Was there any evidence of a break-in this time?"

"No, but I'm certain I didn't leave the light on," Maggie said firmly.

Bessie shrugged. "Have you heard about the body from Peel Castle?" she changed the subject.

"Yes, a woman in her mid-twenties who died in the late sixties. Of course, I was a mere child in those days, but that doesn't mean I don't have some ideas as to whom you might have found."

"I've been ringing around, trying to make a list for the police. In a case such as this one, they need all the help they can get."

"It's that Inspector Lambert in charge, the one who used to work in Laxey. I didn't like her. I'm not sure I want to help her."

"First of all, Inspector Lambert is a very hard-working member of the constabulary who deserves our respect, even if we don't care for her as a person. Secondly, I'll do whatever I can to help anyone if it means tracking down a murderer. I hate the thought that someone was killed all those years ago and no one knew about it until this week."

Maggie nodded slowly. "I suppose you're right, although I'd still much rather help Inspector Rockwell than help Anna Lambert."

"You don't have to help," Bessie said. "I already have a short list of possible victims. I doubt you'll know of anyone else." Bessie knew Maggie wouldn't be able to resist that challenge.

"I don't know about that," Maggie snapped. "I have quite a few excellent sources, people even you don't know, people who live on the west side of the island."

"I suggested that it might be Emma Gibson," Bessie threw out the first name.

Maggie nodded. "She came up in more than one conversation I had today. Everyone seemed to feel as if she'd simply gone on holiday and vanished."

"That's how I remember it, too. What's odd is that I don't recall people talking about it at the time. No one seemed worried or upset when she didn't come back, which suggests that some sort of explanation was given by her family or friends if anyone asked." Bessie shook her head. "I simply don't remember enough about it all now."

"Her mother is still alive. I'm sure she'll be able to clear everything up without difficulty. She wouldn't speak to me when I rang."

"You rang Emma's mother?"

Maggie flushed. "When Emma's name first came up, I thought it would be easiest if I simply rang her mother and asked her what had happened to Emma. For some reason, Mrs. Gibson wouldn't speak to me. She said something about having enough problems with the local reporters, that she didn't want to have to deal with anyone at all."

"I'm sure Dan Ross got her name from one of his sources. No doubt he rang Mrs. Gibson and demanded that she tell him what happened to Emma. Maybe it isn't a very happy story. That could be why Mrs. Gibson never shared it with anyone."

"Surely we'd have heard if anything had happened to Emma."

"Maybe, but I believe it was easier to keep things quiet in those days."

"You may be right. Actually, you are right, because we've no idea what happened to Emma."

Bessie nodded. "What other ideas do you have?" she asked.

"I did wonder about Lauren Bell," Maggie replied.

Lauren was already on her list, Bessie thought with satisfaction. "I understand she left the island with a married man."

"She did, and then she came back, and then she left again, but no one seems to know when she left or where she went the second time."

"I was told that the married man she left with the first time is on the island."

"He is, which makes me wonder if she truly did leave again or if he killed her and hid the body."

"As I understand it, her parents disowned her when she ran away and refused to welcome her back when she returned."

"That's the story I heard as well," Maggie said. "So if she was murdered, there wasn't anyone around to report her missing."

"She must have had friends," Bessie speculated. "Maybe Inspector Lambert can find one of them."

"Hannah Butler left around the right time, too."

"She's on my list, but no one could tell me much about her."

"I never knew her, but one of my friends in Peel mentioned her name. Apparently, she was quiet and shy. Her parents were both killed in a house fire about a year before she disappeared. My friend is about the same age and had been at school with Hannah. She couldn't remember ever hearing anything about Hannah leaving, and she wasn't even certain of the year when it happened. She said she just realised one day that she hadn't seen Hannah for a few months or maybe even a year or more. She never saw her again."

"It's sad to think that people can simply disappear unnoticed," Bessie sighed. She hoped that someone would miss her when she was gone, but having lived alone her entire adult life, maybe she was being foolish.

"At least Thomas would miss me if I vanished tomorrow," Maggie said. "Probably not until he got really hungry, but at least he'd notice when his dinner wasn't ready for him."

Bessie wondered if Maggie actually cooked dinner for Thomas, but she didn't challenge the woman's words. From everything Bessie knew of the couple, it seemed more likely that Thomas did the bulk of the cooking at their house, but maybe that had changed since he'd been ill.

"I only have one other name on my list," Bessie said. "Joselyn Owens."

"I remember her. She came up while I was talking to my friends today, too. Even though she lived in Douglas, she was the talk of the island for a short while."

"Which is why it's odd that she disappeared without a trace."

"Her husband knew where she went. He just wasn't talking. He still isn't, as far as I know."

"You didn't ring him?"

Maggie blushed. "I may have, but he wouldn't speak to me, either."

"I don't blame him, all things considered."

"I suppose you're right, but he didn't have to be rude to me, anyway."

"I'm sure he's already been questioned by Dan Ross. No doubt Inspector Lambert won't be far behind, either. I feel sorry for the poor man."

"Unless he killed Joselyn and hid her body at Peel Castle."

Bessie nodded. "Did you hear any other names when you were ringing your friends?"

"Just one," Maggie said smugly. "Do you remember Meredith Houseman?"

Bessie frowned. "The name is vaguely familiar. She wasn't from Laxey, was she?"

"No, she grew up in Ramsey. That was where she was living when she disappeared."

"You'll have to tell me the whole story," Bessie sighed. "I don't remember it off the top of my head."

"She was Meredith Brown before she met Joe Houseman," Maggie said, clearly relishing the fact that she knew something that Bessie did not. "She was around twenty-two when they got married. They settled into married life in Ramsey and were just a boring, ordinary couple, as far as I know."

"But?" Bessie asked when Maggie paused.

"Oh, sorry, of course, you don't remember the story," Maggie said. "Joe was offered a job across, somewhere in the Lake District, I believe. They left together, even though her parents were opposed to the idea. They didn't want their daughter so far away. They'd been very protective of her and I don't think they cared for Joe Houseman."

"If she left the island with her husband, then she didn't disappear."

"That's just it. She left with her husband, but he came back to the island alone."

Maggie's words triggered something in Bessie's memory. "He came back about a year later, didn't he?"

"Yes, that's right. Her parents thought that he'd murdered Meredith and buried the body in the Lake District."

"What did Joe say to that?"

"At the time, he just laughed and said that Meredith was alive and well, living in the Lake District with some friends that she'd made while they'd been there. He never offered any reason as to why he'd come back to the island without her, though."

"Did her parents get the police involved?"

"They insisted that they were going to file a missing person report, but I don't know if they ever did. After a short while, the talk all died down and I never heard anything more about Meredith. Her father passed away in the eighties and I believe her mother died a few years later. Joe is still alive, though."

"Let me guess: he wouldn't talk to you."

"I didn't try ringing him. He was creepy and odd and I didn't want to speak to him."

Bessie nodded. Now that Maggie had mentioned it, she remembered some of the things she'd heard about Joe Houseman over the years. He had a reputation for being mean and for drinking too much. What she couldn't recall was whether he'd had the reputation before he and Meredith had moved away or if he'd earned it once he'd returned.

"I'm going to give all of the names to Inspector Lambert. She'll be able to track down the women in question, if they're still alive," Bessie said.

"I'll bet she won't find many of them," Maggie retorted. "Joe Houseman probably killed Meredith before they even left the island. All five women are probably dead now, otherwise they'd have come back, surely."

"Maybe they made new lives for themselves elsewhere," Bessie suggested.

"Maybe, but I doubt it," Maggie replied gloomily.

As Bessie finally made her way home, she realised that she was starving. It didn't take her long to put together a satisfying evening meal. While she ate, she read a few chapters in her latest book. After she was done, she added Meredith Houseman's name to her list for Anna. Bessie didn't think the skeleton was hers, but she wasn't entirely certain why. Maybe she just felt that way because Maggie was the one who'd come up with Meredith's name. Shaking her head at the idea, Bessie debated spending more time with

Onnee before giving into temptation and curling up with her book instead.

Bessie had been in the habit of grocery shopping every Friday, but she'd had to rearrange things while she'd been busy with Christmas at the Castle. Now that life was returning to normal, she still hadn't rescheduled her regular Friday taxi. When she woke up on Saturday morning, she realised that her cupboards were mostly bare. Keeping her walk short, she rang her taxi service as soon as she was home, requesting a ride into Ramsey.

"Hello, Bessie," Dave, her favourite driver, greeted her a short time later. "You never go into Ramsey on a Saturday."

"I may have done it once or twice before," Bessie laughed. "I do try to avoid it, though, as it's usually much busier than a weekday. I'm out of nearly everything, though, so I haven't much choice."

"It's still pretty early in the morning. The shops shouldn't be too busy yet."

"I just need the grocery shop today," she replied.

Her trip around the large shop seemed to take longer than normal, as nearly everyone she saw wanted to talk about the body at Peel Castle.

"I heard that all you could see were two skeletal arms, reaching desperately towards the door," one woman said.

Bessie sighed. "Not true."

"I heard that the skeleton was right inside the door and that there were scratch marks all over the door as if she'd tried to claw her way out," another told her.

"I didn't look at the back of the door," Bessie said, hoping the woman was wrong. "The skeleton wasn't near it, though."

As Dave loaded her shopping bags into the boot of his taxi, Bessie did a quick mental tally. Three people had insisted that the body had to be Emma Gibson's. Two had suggested Joselyn Owens, and one woman was convinced it was Lauren Bell. No one had mentioned either Hannah Butler or Meredith Houseman.

Back at Treoghe Bwaane, Dave helped her carry the shopping into the house.

"Sad what you found in Peel," Dave commented as he put her bags on the table.

"It was very sad," Bessie agreed.

"Have the police worked out whom you found yet?"

"Not as far as I know. It's very early days yet, anyway."

"Yes, I suppose so," he replied.

Bessie gave him a curious look. "What's wrong?"

"Nothing's wrong, exactly, I was just wondering if it could have been Lauren Bell. She's my wife's distant cousin and her name came up when the body was found, that's all."

"If the police don't already have her name on their list, I'll be giving it to them. It's come up several times when I've spoken to people about the body."

"My wife said she was rather wild, Lauren, I mean. She ran away with a married man, but then she came back. The family doesn't really talk about her, but my wife heard that she then ran off with a different married man a few months later. I don't know if that's true."

"No one seems to know exactly what happened to her. I believe the family has always been deliberately vague about her whereabouts. Hopefully, someone will have an address for her and the police will be able to cross her off their list."

"Her mother would have been the most likely person to have stayed in touch with her, but she passed away years ago. I'll ask my wife who she thinks might know where Lauren is now."

"That would be helpful. Let me know what you find out."

Dave nodded. "I'll ring you later."

Bessie nodded and then let Dave out. It only took her a few minutes to put the shopping away. Once that was done, she made herself some lunch and then did a quick tidy-up of the kitchen. Next, she rang Doona at home.

"I wasn't sure if you were working today or not," she told her friend.

"I am, but only for a few hours and not until the afternoon."

"I was just wondering how things were going with Sue."

Doona sighed. "No change, really. She rang last night, but she seemed very confused and only talked to John, not the children. He told me afterwards that she seemed to think that they were still married and that he was neglecting her by not being with her when she was ill. When he asked her about Harvey, she didn't seem to know whom he meant."

"Oh, dear."

"The police are still involved in some way, too. Harvey had words with John after he'd spoken to Sue. He's very unhappy and claims he's being treated like a criminal."

"I hope Sue is being treated at the best hospital available."

"Apparently there aren't any hospitals near where they are at the moment. Harvey keeps making vague promises about taking her to a proper city, but he keeps reminding John that he's rather busy saving lives at the moment."

"Maybe he should be more concerned about saving Sue's life."

"Yes, that's exactly what John told him. That was the end of that phone conversation."

Bessie sighed. "I wish I could do something to help."

"If you see John, I suggest that you don't mention any of this," Doona told her. "He's having to put it out of his mind during working hours."

Someone knocked on the door as Bessie put the phone down.

"My goodness, it isn't every day that I get two police inspectors here at the same time," Bessie exclaimed as she opened the door to John and Anna.

Anna made a face as John shrugged. "Two heads are better than one," he replied.

CHAPTER 6

"How are you?" Bessie asked John as she ushered the pair inside.

"I'm holding up," he replied. He glanced at Anna and then back at Bessie. "Today's visit is not personal," he added.

Bessie nodded. If Anna didn't know about John's problems, she wouldn't hear about them from Bessie. She must know that something was wrong, though, as John looked unwell. He was thinner than usual, his brown hair needed a trim, and his gorgeous green eyes were bloodshot. He looked gaunt and exhausted.

"And how are you?" she asked Anna.

"I've been better," Anna replied. "It seems the chief constable doesn't trust me to do my job properly." Unlike John, she didn't look unwell, just angry.

Bessie raised an eyebrow. "Oh, dear."

"It isn't that at all," John said. "He knows I've worked with Bessie on several cases in the past and he didn't want you using one of my best sources without my involvement. If you'd prefer to speak to Bessie privately, I've plenty of other things I could be doing."

Anna shook her head. "I'm happy for you to be involved. You're one of the best investigators I've worked with in my career. I simply resent being told that I have to include you in my conversations with Bessie."

"How do you feel about all of this?" John asked Bessie. "The chief constable has asked Anna to include me in any conversations she has with you about the skeleton that was found at Peel Castle."

"Anna and I have already had one conversation about the skeleton. I'm not sure I understand why the chief constable wants you included, but I've no objection. If you weren't here, I'd probably ring you later and talk you through the whole case anyway. I'm simply used to doing that when it comes to cases."

John nodded. "Anna, if you feel that I'm in the way, just let me know and I'll go."

"Thank you," Anna said. "I may be a touch oversensitive at the moment."

"Tea? Biscuits?" Bessie asked.

"Yes, please, to both," John replied as he sat down at the table.

"Can I help in any way?" Anna asked.

"Oh, no, sit down and relax," Bessie replied. "It won't take more than a minute to get the kettle on and put some biscuits on a plate."

The two police inspectors talked quietly while Bessie made the tea. She couldn't hear what they were saying, but it sounded serious. The conversation stopped as she put the plate of biscuits on the table. When the tea was ready, she served them both before joining them at the table with her own cup.

"Thank you," John said.

"Yes, thank you so much," Anna added.

Bessie smiled and took a sip of her drink. As she selected a biscuit and put it on the small plate in front of her, John cleared his throat.

"As far as I'm concerned, this is Anna's case. I'm just an interested observer."

Anna nodded. "Let's start at the beginning, then. I told you before that the skeleton belonged to a woman in her mid to late twenties and that she passed away in the late sixties. We've learned nothing to contradict that since we last spoke."

"I have a list of five women who may have disappeared about the right time. They were mentioned by various friends of mine," Bessie told her.

"We've been through the missing person reports from nineteen sixty to the present and haven't found one that matches our skeleton," Anna said. "I have a constable going through missing person reports from across and further afield, but that's a good deal more time-consuming and complicated."

"It sounds complicated."

"You mentioned Emma Gibson when I was here last. Is she one of the five?" Anna asked.

"Yes. No one with whom I've spoken seems to know what happened to her."

"Tell me about her," John invited.

"She was a primary schoolteacher in her mid-twenties. She was unmarried. I remember her as being rather pretty, but I don't know that that matters. All of my friends and acquaintances said much the same thing. She went on holiday one day and simply never came back to the island."

"I have an appointment to speak to her mother," Anna told her. "She seemed quite reluctant to see me. Any idea why?"

"None at all. I had a nodding acquaintance with the woman, but not much more than that. It was her mother, Emma's grandmother, who most often used to bring Emma to play on the beach. I believe Emma's mother used the time to do some shopping or run other errands that needed doing. I haven't seen or spoken to her in years."

"I'm going to see her on Monday," Anna said. "I'm hoping we might be able to cross Emma off our list after that. What other names have you been given?"

"Maggie Shimmin reckons it might be Meredith Houseman," Bessie said.

"Tell me about her," Anna invited.

"She was Meredith Brown before she married Joe Houseman," Bessie replied. "She was in her early twenties when they married, and a few years later they moved to the Lake District. He came back to the island about a year later, alone."

"And no one rang the police?" Anna sounded incredulous.

"Her parents said they were going to file a missing person report, but I don't know if they ever actually did. Meredith was the talk of the island for a few days, but then something else happened and everyone seemed to forget about her. I always assumed that she'd chosen to stay in the Lake District. Otherwise her parents would surely have done something."

"I know Joe Houseman," John said in a low voice.

"Why?" Anna demanded.

"He drinks too much at pubs in Ramsey and then tries to drive himself home. He's been picked up for drink driving at least half a dozen times in the past two years. He's banned from driving, of course, but that doesn't seem to stop him."

"He won't stop until he kills himself or someone else," Anna muttered.

"The last time he was stopped, he went to prison for six months. I'm told that he's doing much better since he's been out," John told her.

"I hope so. I'm going to have to talk to him about Meredith. Are her parents still alive?" she asked Bessie.

"No, they both passed away years ago."

"Did Joe have a drinking problem before they moved to the Lake District?" Anna asked.

Bessie shrugged. "I don't remember either of them very well, not well enough to answer that question, anyway. Someone told me that Meredith's parents didn't like Joe, but I don't know why."

Anna made a few notes and then looked up at Bessie. "Meredith seems less likely to me than Emma. If Joe did do something to her, surely he would have left the body in the Lake District. He had no reason to bring it back to the island."

"Unless they fought on the ferry on the way back here or something similar," Bessie offered. "I do remember that everyone was surprised when Joe returned, though. I'd have expected Meredith to ring her parents and let them know if they were coming back together."

"Why didn't she ring them anyway, to let them know that Joe was returning?" Anna wondered.

"That's something you'll have to ask Meredith if you find her," John said.

Anna nodded. "Who's next?" she asked Bessie.

"Lauren Bell," Bessie replied.

"Her story, please," Anna said.

"I can't tell you much, except that she left the island with a married man. Less than a year later, they were back. He went back to his wife, although why she allowed it is another matter. A few months after that, Lauren disappeared again."

"And no one knows where she went?" Anna asked.

"I took a taxi into Ramsey this morning and my favourite driver, Dave, drove. His wife is distantly related to Lauren. He's promised to try to find out if anyone in the family knows where she is now."

"That would be helpful," Anna said. "I'm assuming we'll be able to track down most of the women with a little bit of effort."

"That was what happened with Hugh's case last year," Bessie replied. "He was able to find everyone except the man who turned out to be the victim."

"It's difficult for people to truly disappear," John said. "It gets increasingly difficult every day, as well. The world keeps getting smaller and more connected all the time."

"Is there anything else you can tell me about Lauren?" Anna asked.

"Dave remembers hearing that she ran off with another married man, but he didn't know any more than that. As I said, he's going to ring me later."

"Please let me know what he says when you speak to him, even if he can't help," Anna told her.

Bessie nodded.

"That's three of the five. Who else do you have?" Anna asked.

"A woman called Hannah Butler may have disappeared about the right time," Bessie replied.

"May have?"

"No one seems to remember what happened to her. She was single and she worked as a shop assistant in Kirk Michael at the village shop there."

"And that was thirty years ago, so the staff has probably changed a dozen or more times since then," Anna sighed.

"At least," Bessie agreed. "She lost both of her parents in a house fire, probably about a year before she disappeared."

"Did she have any other family on the island?" Anna asked.

"Not that I'm aware of, but she may have. You might have better luck with family than with former work colleagues, though. I can't imagine anyone she used to work with still being employed there," Bessie said.

"And the last one?" Anna asked after she'd written several notes.

"Joselyn Owens," Bessie replied, spelling the woman's rather unusual Christian name.

"As you saved her for last, do you think she's the most likely candidate?" Anna asked.

Bessie flushed. While she did think the skeleton was mostly likely to be Joselyn, she hadn't necessarily wanted the inspector to know what she was thinking. "Hers is the strangest story," she replied. "All things considered, I can't quite believe that no one knows what happened to her."

"Tell me the story, then," Anna said, sounding impatient.

"Joselyn was pretty and fun-loving. Her father, Clifford Caine, owned an import and export business on the island. It was very successful and they lived well. When Joselyn was around sixteen, her father hired a young man right out of university. Sam Owens was handsome and smart and from what I've heard, he swept young Joselyn off her feet. Her parents insisted that they wait until Joselyn was eighteen to marry, and they ran off to Gretna Green on her birthday to do just that."

"I didn't realise girls from the island ran away to Gretna Green," Anna said.

"Not many did, but Sam was from Scotland, and I think Joselyn thought it would be exciting and romantic. She had her parents' permission to wed at eighteen anyway, so they didn't need to run away, but they did."

"And she never came back?" Anna asked.

"Oh, no, she came back. They both came back. Her father bought them a small house in Douglas and they settled into married life together. Sam travelled a good deal for work, often spending several months at a time in China or America. Joselyn usually went with him. She was nominally employed by her father's company, but she never had to worry about taking time off from her job."

"I assume this is all going somewhere," Anna said impatiently.

"Sorry, yes, it is going somewhere. In early sixty-seven, Sam went away on an eight-month trip to Southeast Asia. When he returned to the island, Joselyn was six months pregnant."

"Ah," Anna said. "So she had an affair while he was gone."

"It certainly seemed that way. The entire island was talking about it, of course. There were a number of different rumours as to who the father might be, but no one seemed to know for sure."

"I'll want a list of everyone who was named as a possibility," Anna said.

Bessie shook her head. "At one time or another the list probably included just about every man on the island, from Joselyn's own father to the eighty-five-year-old man who cleaned the windows at Joselyn's house. From what I can recall, there were lots of rumours and speculation, but no one name ever seemed more likely than any of the others. Joselyn wasn't talking, of course."

"And then what happened?" Anna asked as Bessie took a sip of tea.

"About two months later, when Joselyn would have been about eight months along, she left the island. As far as I know, she never came back. No one that I've spoken with has any idea what happened to her."

"What did her parents say?" Anna asked.

"They refused to discuss the matter, as did Sam, who still worked for Joselyn's father."

"He did?"

"Oh, yes, in fact, he worked for the man until Clifford retired in the early nineties. He sold the business and gave Sam a generous early retirement package. Sam wasn't even fifty yet, I don't believe. He's never worked again."

"He's still on the island?"

"Yes, he still lives in the same house that he and Joselyn moved into when they were newlyweds."

"What about Clifford?"

"He passed away about a year after his retirement. I believe he knew his health was failing. That may be why he was so generous to Sam. Clifford's wife, Kathleen, had passed away about ten years earlier and Clifford ended up leaving everything he had to charity. It wasn't all that much, really, I suspect because he'd already given Sam the bulk of his fortune."

"Did Sam remarry?"

"No. I believe he and Joselyn are still married, unless she's dead. I've never heard any gossip linking him with any other woman, though."

Anna made a few more notes. "That one seems simple enough. Sam must know what happened to his wife."

"You'll just have to hope he'll talk to you," John said.

Anna nodded. "If this were a straightforward murder investigation, I could push people a good deal harder. As it is, I'm asking them about events that happened over thirty years ago and that might have nothing to do with the skeleton that was found."

"Do you even know for certain that the woman was murdered?"

"No, we don't," Anna sighed. "We also aren't certain if the body was moved or not after death. It's possible, although it would be odd, that she simply died of natural causes. What she was doing at Peel Castle and why it's taken so long to find the body are questions that need answering still."

"What sort of natural causes kill a woman that young?"

"Cancer, maybe," Anna replied. "Although young people do sometimes have heart attacks or strokes. She may have had heart problems or some other life-limiting condition that can't be determined from the remains."

"Even if she did die of natural causes, surely someone would have reported her missing?" Bessie asked.

"You'd expect so. It's unusual for a woman so young to not be missed, but maybe we aren't looking in the right place for the missing person report. Maybe she was reported missing in Devon or Belfast or wherever she actually lived. Perhaps she was simply on holiday here, visiting the castle as a tourist."

Bessie shook her head. "There are simply too many possibilities."

"It does feel that way at the moment," John replied "Your list gives Anna a starting point, anyway. By the time she's tracked down those five women, you may have come up with a few other names for her to try. Alternatively, the searches that are being done through old missing person reports across might yield some positive results. I find it difficult to believe that no one missed our victim."

"Did she appear to have been in good health?"

"The coroner couldn't tell us much," Anna said. "He's sending the skeleton to experts in London so that more testing can be done. That could take quite some time, though."

"If you had to pick one name off your list for Anna to focus on, which would it be?" John asked.

"Joselyn," Bessie replied.

"Why?" Anna demanded.

"Her disappearance bothers me. I feel as if we should know what happened to her, but we don't. Sam should be able to tell you where to find her, which would take her off the list quickly, but if he won't talk about her, then I think there must be more to her story than we know," Bessie explained.

"He kept working for her parents, which suggests that whatever happened, they didn't blame him," Anna said.

"Yes, I always wondered about that," Bessie said. "The whole situation was odd, but they were all perfectly pleasant people. Clifford and his wife did a lot of charity work. Sam was on a fundraising committee at Noble's for a great many years. When Joselyn first left, it was strange, but over time people stopped talking about her. I hadn't thought about her in years before the skeleton was found. Was there any sign that the woman was pregnant when she died?"

"None," John replied.

Anna made another note and then looked at Bessie. "Which woman do you think is the second most likely, then?"

Bessie sipped her tea while she tried to think. "Lauren Bell, maybe. She and Emma Gibson both seem equally likely in my mind, although I'm not sure I can explain why."

"And the other two seem less likely, why?" Anna wondered.

"I simply don't know enough about Hannah Butler to have an opinion on her," Bessie admitted. "As for Meredith Houseman, Maggie was the only one who mentioned her name. It doesn't feel right, but I'm not sure why."

Anna nodded. "I'm going to start with Joselyn. You said she wasn't left anything in her father's will?"

"No, she wasn't mentioned at all. Everything went to charity. Her mother didn't leave her anything, either."

"Was there anything else?" Anna asked John.

"Not on this case, anyway," John replied. "I do need to talk to Bessie about some other issues, but that can wait until you're finished."

Anna nodded slowly. "I'll go and get started on the list, then. Please ring me if you get any additional names, or hear anything else about any of these women. I'll probably come back to see you again in a few days, maybe Tuesday."

"I'm usually here, but if you ring first, you'll know for certain," Bessie said.

"I'll try to ring first, then," Anna said as she got to her feet. Bessie walked her to the door and let her out.

"I can't believe the chief constable is having you work with her on this. She's a trained inspector," Bessie said as she sat back down next to John.

"And she's a very good one, at that, but there have been issues," he replied.

"Oh, I know all about the issues. Some man treated her badly, and now she's being treated badly by the chief constable, too."

"The chief constable is doing what he can to help her," John argued. "I know she resents my involvement, but it's entirely possible that he'd have called in an additional inspector for this case anyway. We're digging through thirty-year-old missing person reports from all over the world. It's a big job for two people, let alone just one."

"And none of this is your fault," Bessie added. "I'm sorry. I don't even like Anna, but I'm finding myself feeling sorry for her."

"She'd hate that, if she knew."

"Yes, I know."

"I don't want you feeling sorry for me, either."

Bessie patted his arm. "Are you okay? You look as if you haven't been eating, and you only ate one biscuit since you've been here."

"I haven't had much of an appetite lately."

"I'm happy to listen if you want to talk about anything."

John shrugged. "I told myself I was going to limit today's conversation to the body at Peel Castle. I don't want to bother you with my problems."

"Sometimes we all need someone with whom to share our problems."

Bessie got up and switched the kettle back on. "More tea, or would you prefer coffee?"

"If it isn't too much trouble, coffee would probably help."

"What did you have for lunch?"

"Lunch? I don't know that I had lunch." John glanced at the clock. "I should have, really, by now."

"Where are the children today?"

"They're both with friends for the day and overnight. I thought they needed and deserved a break from everything."

"And so do you."

"Sadly, as the adult, I don't get breaks."

"You're here now, at least."

"With my home phone forwarded to my mobile," he sighed.

Bessie was tempted to tell him to switch the phone off for half an hour, but she knew he wouldn't agree to the idea. "I don't know the whole story, but it seems to me as if there's very little you can do from here," she said as she got out bread and sandwich meat.

"There's nothing I can do from here, except get increasingly frustrated. Harvey won't tell me anything definite and when I talk to Sue she doesn't usually make sense. If I didn't have the children to worry about, I'd fly to Africa myself and find out what's really happening down there."

"The children need you here."

"Yes, they do. Doona and I have talked about it for hours and hours and we keep reaching the same conclusion. Whatever is happening in Africa, I have to put the children first. They may well be losing one parent. They need me."

"How are they doing?"

"Better than I am, really," John sighed.

Bessie put a ham and cheese toastie on the table in front of him. "Coffee will be just a minute longer," she said.

He nodded. "I'm not really hungry."

"But if you don't eat, you won't have the energy to keep going. As you said yourself, the children need you."

After a long sigh, he took a bite of the sandwich. Bessie made herself a cup of tea and then poured coffee for John. After putting both cups on the table, she sat back down.

"What can I do to help?" she asked.

"This is helping," he replied, nodding towards the half-empty plate. "I believe it's the uncertainty that's making it so difficult. Things have been up in the air since she and Harvey left, with them changing their return date over and over again. That was difficult enough for all of us. This is worse, of course."

"Have you spoken to Sue's mother at all?" Bessie asked.

John nodded. "She rang me a few days ago. We hadn't spoken since, well, since Sue moved back to Manchester. She's upset and anxious and she wants me to do something."

"Something specific?"

"She wants me to go to Africa and bring Sue home," John sighed.

"She'd do it herself if she could, but she has too many health issues. She got angry when I told her I wouldn't go."

"What did she expect you to do with the children?"

"She offered to have them stay with her, an idea they both hated, I should add."

"They're in school. They can't simply go and stay in Manchester in the middle of the school year."

"That's what I told her, but she disagreed. She's Sue's mother, so obviously her concerns are for Sue over everything else, even her grandchildren. I understand that, but my priorities are different."

"I don't suppose she knew anything more than you do?"

"No, if anything, she knew less. I don't think she's been asking Harvey the number of questions that I've been asking. She hasn't spoken to Sue in several weeks, either, even though the children speak to her nearly every day."

"I wonder why."

"Apparently Harvey always rings her when Sue is asleep. I'm not sure why he'd choose to ring her when Sue is asleep and ring us when Sue is awake, but that's something she'll have to discuss with Harvey if she wants an explanation. I simply told her that we've spoken to Sue fairly regularly."

"Was she upset?"

"Less so about that than about my refusal to go to Africa. She was also angry that I'd asked the police to get involved. Harvey saved her life, or so she believes. She won't hear a negative word about him."

"Maybe that's why he has Sue talk to you. You're less likely to believe what Harvey says."

"Maybe, but I'd rather he didn't, really."

"Oh?"

"She's incredibly confused," John explained as he pushed his empty plate away. He took a biscuit. "She sometimes talks to the children as if they were much younger than they are, for instance."

Bessie frowned as John began to nibble on his biscuit. "That must be difficult for the children."

"It is, obviously, but it's also difficult for me. A few nights ago she started talking about our honeymoon and how much fun we'd had. She kept telling me that she loves me." He stopped and swiped angrily at his eyes.

Bessie patted his arm. "How sad."

"I'm sure it's difficult for Harvey to listen to, as well. When she left me, she told me that she'd never truly loved me. That was difficult to hear. Now, listening to her babble on and on about how much she loves me and how happy being with me makes her, well, that's almost worse. I don't know what to believe any longer."

"You should believe whatever makes you feel better."

"I want to see her so badly," he said angrily. "I want her well again, too. I never wanted anything bad to happen to her. The children need her, if nothing else."

"Surely things can't go on this way for much longer."

"I've been ringing everyone I know and asking for a lot of favours. A colleague that I worked with years ago has connections in Nigeria, with the police there. He's going to get someone to talk to the police where Sue and Harvey are staying. Maybe I'll get more information that way, as the police aren't really telling me anything when I ring."

"I wonder if Andrew could help," Bessie said.

"Andrew? Do you mean Andrew Cheatham? I never thought of ringing him."

Bessie had met the former police inspector when she and Doona had been on holiday in the Lake District. He'd been helpful to them when Doona had been suspected of murder, and he and Bessie had stayed in touch ever since. Andrew had recently visited the island, and together the pair had solved two cold cases.

"He was pretty important in Scotland Yard, wasn't he? He may have some international connections. If he can't help, I know someone who knows someone who works in the government," Bessie replied.

John raised an eyebrow. "Should I ask?"

Bessie shook her head. Her friend, Janet Markham, had some sort of relationship with a man who claimed to work for a top-secret government organisation. Bessie had never met the man in question and had no idea whether he'd told Janet the truth or not, but she was prepared to do whatever she could to help John, even if that meant asking Janet to ask Edward Bennett for assistance.

"I'm not certain I want to ring Andrew," John said. "I hate asking for favours, and I've been doing it a great deal lately."

"I'll ring him. I hate asking for favours, too, but only for myself. I'm happy to do it for you and for Thomas and Amy."

John ate another biscuit in silence. Eventually, he nodded. "If you can ring him, I'd really appreciate it."

"I can't promise he'll be able to help, but if he can't, maybe he'll be able to suggest someone else who can."

"Let me know what he says," John requested as he got to his feet. "I need to get home. The house is a disaster area. The kids are almost always at home, sitting by the phone. No one has dusted or vacuumed in weeks. I'm afraid to go into the kitchen. Dan Ross would love to write about me being attacked by my own dirty dishes."

Bessie chuckled. "He just loves gripping headlines."

"Thank you for your time. I feel better for having talked with you."

"I'm always here if you need to talk. I'm here if the children need to talk, as well. I know they have you and Doona, but they might benefit from a chat with me or even a trained counsellor."

"Doona suggested the same things, both you and a counsellor. I've made an appointment for them both next Friday afternoon with a highly recommended counsellor. I may take you up on your offer as well."

"You know where to find me."

"I do. Thank you again."

Bessie walked John to the door and gave him a tight hug before he left. She watched from the doorway as he drove slowly away. After shutting the door, she sighed. She didn't really want to ring Andrew Cheatham, but she'd promised.

CHAPTER 7

"*B*essie, what an unexpected pleasure," Andrew's voice came down the line.

Feeling surprised that he'd actually answered, when she'd been expecting a machine, Bessie blinked and then took a deep breath. "I hate to bother you, as I'm sure you're busy."

"Not at all. I mean, I am busy, but you aren't a bother. I was just talking about you yesterday, in fact, but that's a conversation for another day."

"Is it?"

"Yes, indeed. Maybe for the spring, but probably for the summer. I'm going to have to come back and see you in order to have a proper conversation, as well."

"Whatever do you mean?"

Andrew chuckled. "Not a thing, really. All will be revealed when the time is right, if that time ever comes. What can I do for you, though?"

"I was hoping for a favour for John, actually," Bessie said, firmly pushing everything Andrew had said out of her head. If he wanted to talk in riddles, she wasn't going to let it bother her.

"John? John Rockwell, do you mean? I'm happy to do him a favour if I can. He's a very fine man and an excellent police inspector."

"It's a rather more personal problem, though," Bessie said. "I don't know how much you know about John's marriage or his former wife?"

"To avoid confusion, pretend I know nothing and tell me everything."

"I don't know how they met or how long they were together before they married, but I do know that not long after they were married Sue told John that she was still in love with her former boyfriend, Harvey."

"Oh, dear."

"Yes, well, her confession was complicated by the fact that she was already pregnant with Thomas, her and John's first child together. Apparently, after much discussion, the couple decided to try to make things work, even with Harvey's shadow looming over the relationship."

"Was she seeing Harvey at all?"

"I don't believe so. Sue and John had a second child, but I understand they were having some difficulties when they moved to the Isle of Man. Sue hated it here, which I'm certain didn't help."

"That must have been difficult for John. From what he's told me, he likes everything about the island."

"Yes, he does. Anyway, around the same time as their move, Sue's mother fell ill. To cut a long story short, her oncologist just happened to be Harvey."

"My goodness. I take it he wasn't now happily married to someone else?"

"I believe he was single. Whatever, once they saw each other again, Sue decided to end her marriage to be with Harvey. I'm probably oversimplifying what was undoubtedly a difficult decision for her, but I've never met Sue, so I'm not terribly sympathetic."

"I assume Harvey was in favour of the idea."

"He must have been, because they got engaged before the divorce was finalised and were married last July."

"My goodness, that quickly?"

"Yes, that quickly. Sue was living with the children in Manchester by that point anyway, but as soon as the children's school term finished, they came over to the island to stay with John while Sue and Harvey went on their honeymoon."

"This is all sounding quite familiar now," Andrew said. "Didn't they go to Africa so that Harvey could use his medical training to help there?"

"They did. They were meant to be back in September, but they kept pushing their return back, week after week."

"Which left John having to make all sorts of decisions about schooling for them. We did talk about this when I was there."

"Yes, I'm sure we did. Anyway, just before Christmas, Harvey informed John that Sue was ill. At the time, Harvey didn't think that she had much time left, and he had John gather the children almost immediately for what he said might be their last chance to speak to their mother before she died."

"Those poor children."

"Now, here we are, several weeks later, and it seems that Sue is still holding on, although Harvey insists that she's beyond treatment."

"Which hospital is treating her and what's their official diagnosis?"

"That's just it, she isn't in a hospital. They're somewhere rather remote and Harvey doesn't want to leave because he feels his work is too important to interrupt."

"His work is more important than his wife's health?" Andrew sounded angry.

"From what I hear, yes, although this is all second- or third-hand information. John has spoken to the local police and they're meant to be investigating, but no one seems to be able to give him any solid information. He talks to Sue occasionally, but she seems somewhat out of touch with reality."

"And Harvey is only telling John what he wants John to know," Andrew sighed. "Where are they exactly?"

Bessie told him what John had told her about their location. "I'm not sure I could find that on a map."

"I could. If I were John, I wouldn't waste any more time or effort on working with the local police. They're most likely for sale to the highest bidder and I imagine that Harvey is paying them enough to keep them quiet, whatever they may have found."

"He could get away with murder?"

"It's difficult to say for certain, but maybe, especially if he truly is saving lives there."

"I was wondering if there was anything you could do, if maybe you had any connections in that part of the world."

"I have connections everywhere," Andrew laughed. "Let me ring a few people and see if I can get any more information." He asked Bessie a dozen questions about Sue, most of which she couldn't answer.

"I wish I knew more. You should ring John," she said in the end.

"I may do just that, but not today. For today, I'm going to start the ball rolling in Africa. It sounds as if it might be urgent."

"It might," Bessie agreed.

"Before I go and start ringing people, tell me how you are, though," Andrew said.

The pair chatted for several minutes about everything that had happened to each of them since they'd last seen one another.

"After a thorough investigation, the police have determined that Oliver was pocketing three-quarters of the money that his charity raised each year," Bessie told him as she finished telling Andrew about the last murder investigation in which she'd been involved. "He's going on trial for both murder and fraud."

"I do miss policing," Andrew said. "I don't miss spending my time with men and women who are happy to steal from cancer victims, though. Let me see what I can do for John. I'll ring you in a day or two with an update," Andrew promised.

"Thank you," Bessie replied.

She made dinner on automatic, her mind racing. As she was clearing away the dishes, someone knocked on her door.

"Bessie?" the woman on the doorstep asked, frowning at her.

"Yes?"

"My goodness, you look a good deal older than I remember," her visitor blurted out.

Bessie frowned. She'd stopped counting her age when she'd received her free bus pass, but she knew she was a good few years away from receiving a telegram from the Queen. The woman at the door looked to be of a similar age, anyway. "I'm afraid I don't recognise you," she said stiffly after a moment.

"Oh, goodness, of course you don't. I've grown old, too, haven't I?" she laughed. "I'm Evangeline Gibson. My mum lived up the road from here and we used to bring my daughter Emma to play on the beach sometimes."

Bessie nodded. "I remember you, but I don't think I would have recognised you." You're much older than I remember, she added to herself.

"We're all getting older," Evangeline said. "I hope I haven't come at a bad time. I needed to talk to someone and you were the only person I thought might listen."

"Come in," Bessie invited. "Have a seat while I put the kettle on."

"It's exactly the same," Evangeline marvelled as she looked around the cosy kitchen. "I was only in here once or twice, when you invited Mum and Emma and me in for tea and biscuits, but it looks exactly the way I remember."

"I suppose most people would have put in a new kitchen by now, but this one suits me, and everything works."

"I had a new kitchen fitted twelve years ago and I still regret it. It still feels as if everything is in the wrong place, and none of the new things work as well as the old ones did, either. I'd had my old cooker for thirty-seven years, you know. I've had to buy three in the past twelve years now, as each one breaks after it runs out of warranty."

Bessie put biscuits on a plate and set it on the table. "They don't make things to last these days. People want new things all the time, so they don't need to make things that last."

Evangeline sighed. "I'm afraid you're right about that."

A short while later, with tea on the table, Bessie sat down opposite her visitor. "What's on your mind, then?" she asked.

"Emma, of course. The entire island is talking about her, aren't they?"

"I don't know about the entire island, but her name has come up a few times recently in connection with the skeleton that was found at Peel Castle."

"Emma isn't dead."

"I'm happy to hear that."

"Can you simply tell the police and that horrible man at the newspaper that she's alive and well? Will they all leave me alone if you do?"

"I can tell them all that you've told me she's alive and well, but I'm not certain that they'll believe me any more than they'd believe you. The police will want proof as they are investigating an unusual death. Without any proof, the reporter will probably simply speculate wildly."

Evangeline frowned. "I don't want any more wild speculation. I just want it all to go away."

"If you tell the police where to find Emma, they'll go away, anyway."

"I don't want to talk to the police."

Bessie sighed. "Whatever Emma did or whatever trouble she may have been in or caused, the police just want to be sure that she isn't their skeleton now. Whatever happened in the past is ancient history."

Evangeline shrugged and took a biscuit. While she ate it, Bessie drank some tea and tried to imagine what the other woman was hiding. Maybe Emma had been pregnant when she'd left.

"If I tell you where to find her, can you ring her and talk to her and then tell the police she's fine?" Evangeline asked eventually.

"They aren't likely to take my word for it. It's their job to investigate and they have to be absolutely certain before they can cross her name off their list," Bessie replied, even though she was fairly sure that if she told John she'd spoken to Emma, he'd cross her off the list of possibilities.

"She doesn't want to talk to the police."

"That's understandable, but in this case they aren't interested in anything more than verifying that she's alive."

"That's all? They aren't going to ask her why she left the island or what she's been doing since she's been gone?"

"They might, but she doesn't have to answer. As long as she can give them enough information to verify who she is, they should be satisfied."

Evangeline blew out a long breath. "That should be fine," she said softly. "What sort of questions will they ask, do you think?"

"Just whatever they have to ask in order to prove her identity. If she has a passport or a driver's license, those can probably help prove who she is."

"She has both," Evangeline said. "I thought the police would be able to track her down through them, actually."

"If it were a murder investigation and they had a solid reason to believe that the body was hers, they might be able to search for such things, but I don't believe they can do so without a good reason. There are probably dozens of Emma Gibsons in the UK, too. It would take them a long time to track them all down."

"Yes, I suppose so," Evangeline sighed. "I'm going to go home and ring Emma. I may tell her to ring you, if you don't mind. Maybe you could set her mind at rest about everything."

"I'm happy to speak to her if you think it would help."

"It might," Evangeline said. "That will be for Emma to decide."

She got to her feet and headed for the door. "Thank you for your time," she said formally as she opened the door.

"It was nice to see you again," Bessie replied.

"Yes, thank you," she replied absentmindedly as she exited.

Bessie walked over and shut the door behind her. It had been a very strange conversation. She thought about ringing Anna or John to tell them about the chat, but decided to wait and see if Emma herself rang.

Assuming she truly is still alive and well, Bessie added to herself. Was it possible that Evangeline was going to ring and pretend to be Emma? Bessie wondered. The phone interrupted her thoughts.

"Bessie? It's Dave. I'm afraid I'm ringing with rather bad news. My wife couldn't think of anyone who might have contact information for Lauren. She even rang all of her relatives on that side of the family, well, most of them anyway. No one talks to Uncle Gus, but regardless, none of them were able to help."

"Never mind. It was kind of her to try. I'll pass the information along to Inspector Lambert. She may want to speak to your wife. Maybe she'll even want to talk to Uncle Gus."

Dave laughed. "Trust me, she doesn't want to do that."

Bessie put the phone down wondering what was wrong with Uncle Gus. She was still tidying the kitchen when the phone rang again.

"Bessie Cubbon? This is Meredith Houseman. I know you know everyone on the island, so could you please tell them all to stop talking about me?"

"I'm afraid I don't have that much power," Bessie replied.

The woman on the other end of the phone laughed. "No one can stop Manx skeet once it starts. I remember it well. That, and far too many other things, too. I don't miss it, you know."

"The island?"

"The island, the people, the weather, the skeet, the TT, all of it, any of it. I never felt as if I belonged on the island and once I got away, I was certain I didn't."

"You need to ring Inspector Anna Lambert of the Peel Constabulary. She'll need to verify that you are indeed Meredith Houseman."

"Oh, I talked to her first," Meredith replied. "She got my number from Joe and rang me. Once I heard what was happening, I knew everyone would be talking about me again. When I spoke to Joe, he suggested ringing you. He said you could stop the gossip if anyone could."

"You still talk to Joe?"

"We're still married, which suits us both." Meredith sighed. "I wasn't going to tell you the whole story. I don't think anyone needs to know the story, really, but I told the police inspector enough of it to satisfy her. I may as well do the same for you."

"I'd appreciate that. When you're done, you'll have to tell me which parts of the story you don't mind my repeating to others."

"For Joe's sake, I'd rather you didn't tell anyone anything. The police have the story, or enough of it to keep them happy. I don't want anything about me in the local papers. I'm only telling you because I believe I can trust you to keep my secrets."

"As long as the police know everything, I won't repeat what you tell me to anyone."

"Excellent." There was a long pause and then Meredith laughed again. "I'm making it all sound incredibly dramatic, but it's really quite a boring story. I suppose that's why I'd rather you not repeat it. I'd much prefer if people were imagining that I'm off having a fabulous life somewhere."

"And you aren't?"

"It's okay, but it isn't fabulous. Here's the thing, I got married way too young to a man that I didn't really love. Joe's a great guy and we had some fun together, but it was never a great romance. For what it's worth, Joe didn't really love me, either, he was just hoping for regular sex. We did okay for a while, and then he was offered a job in the Lake District. He didn't want to take it."

"He didn't?"

"No, he loved the island, a good deal more than he loved me, as it turned out. I managed to persuade him to take the job anyway. I promised him that we'd give it a year and then, if he wasn't happy, we could move back to the island."

"And a year later, he moved back."

"Exactly. I fell in love with the Lake District. It's beautiful here, and it doesn't rain nearly as much as it does on the island. When we first moved across, I found a little job that I loved, working in a local antique shop. The owner and I, well, we had an affair. It wasn't a great romance either, but it was a good deal more exciting than life with Joe had been. Anyway, when the year was up, Joe wanted to go back to the island and I didn't. We didn't even argue about it, really. I told him to go, but that I was staying, and he didn't object."

"Why didn't he just tell everyone that when he got back to the island?"

"He told me that that's exactly what he did tell everyone. Is he lying?"

Bessie thought for a minute. "I gather he told everyone that you'd stayed behind with friends."

"Yes, that's exactly right. I moved in with the antique shop owner for a few months, but that didn't work out, so then I got my own little place."

"I was told your parents wanted to file a missing person report."

Meredith sighed. "You remember that list of things that I didn't miss from the island? You can put my parents at the top of that list."

"My goodness."

"They were incredibly overprotective and they were also very demanding. Even though I was married, they still wanted me to visit them at least three or four times a week. Every visit, they had a list of jobs that needed doing, as well. I was there almost every day, moving furniture, painting, decorating, taking them places they needed to go, and running their errands for them. They used to make Joe do a lot for them, too. It was exhausting. I think they were the main reason why Joe was willing to try the Lake District for that year, actually."

"Did he go back to helping them once he returned?"

"Oh, no, he was smart enough to get angry when they threatened to file a missing person report. He stopped speaking to them after that. I deliberately didn't ring them for a few weeks to spark the argument, actually."

"You're fortunate they never filed the report."

"If they had, Joe could easily have given the police my number. There's no law that says daughters have to ring their parents regularly."

"That's true," Bessie conceded.

"Anyway, I've been living over here perfectly happily for the past thirty-four years, with no plans to come back to the island. Joe has made rather a mess of his life, but that's his problem, not mine. We stay married mostly for his benefit, because he has terrible luck with women. If they get too attached, and the ones he goes for nearly always do, he just tells them that he's married. That usually gets rid of them."

"And you don't mind?"

"I walked down the aisle to get away from my parents, not because I wanted to be married to Joe. Now that I'm free, I can't imagine any reason why I'd want to marry anyone else. I've had the same man in my life for the past twenty-two years. We each have our own house and we see each other when it suits us both. Marriage isn't on the cards and he couldn't care less about my past or about Joe."

"Are you happy?"

"What does that have to do with anything?"

"Nothing. I'm just being nosy, really," Bessie told her. "I have a list of five women who are possible candidates for the skeleton that was found at Peel Castle. Someone told me that they believed that all five women would be dead and that even if they weren't, none of them were going to be alive and well. I'd love to be able to tell her that at least one of the women is living happily elsewhere."

"I don't know that I'm happy, at least not all of the time, but I'm content. I've had a good life, really, since I got away from my parents. Joe and I might have stayed together, if he'd have remained over here, but I've never missed him. As I said, I have a man in my life, but only occasionally, which is how I prefer it. On balance, I suppose I'm happy, or at least not unhappy."

"I'm glad to hear that."

"And now I must go. That man I was telling you about is going to be here soon. We're going out for a night on the town."

"I hope you have fun."

"I'm sure we will. Thank you for listening. What are you going to tell people about me now?"

"That I spoke to you and that you're absolutely fine, nothing more."

Meredith giggled. "That will drive some people absolutely crazy, won't it?"

"Yes," Bessie said with satisfaction, "it will."

She put the phone down and glanced at the clock. It was far too late for a walk on the beach. Even if she took one, the likelihood of seeing Maggie Shimmin tonight was slim. Unless there were guests in the cottages that needed something, Maggie rarely came to the beach in the evening hours. Now that the idea of a walk was in her head, though, Bessie couldn't stop thinking about it.

Sighing, she pulled on a jacket and slid into some shoes. The night air was crisp and cold, but she simply pulled her jacket more tightly around herself and strode quickly towards the sea. At the water's edge, she turned and began a fast walk to Thie yn Traie. She was only about halfway there when the skies opened and a heavy rain began to fall. Sighing deeply, she turned around and headed for home.

"That was a bad idea," she told her reflection in the mirror of the ground floor loo. Her short grey hair was dripping wet and her coat was soaked through. She hung it in the bathtub and then went up the stairs. It wasn't worth changing. She might as well simply get ready for bed, she decided.

In her nightgown, with her face washed and teeth brushed, she curled up with a book featuring a pair of very intelligent cats. After a few chapters, even though she was enjoying the story, she found herself yawning after every paragraph.

"You'll have to solve the murder tomorrow," she told the animals before sliding a bookmark into the book and putting it on her night-stand. She was asleep almost as soon as her head touched the pillow.

When she woke up the next morning, the fictional murder she'd been reading about dominated her thoughts. For the first time in a very long time, she was tempted to forgo her morning walk in favour of reading her book. After a shower and some breakfast, she reminded herself that she still wanted to see Maggie. Desire to share a bit of interesting news with Maggie won out over her eagerness to discover the resolution to the imaginary crime.

The cold air and threat of rain kept her walking briskly as she got farther from home. She walked past Thie yn Traie and then turned around as the first fat raindrops began to fall. The holiday cottages were all dark as Bessie walked rapidly past them. She was fumbling to use her key with icy cold fingers when she heard her name being called.

"Bessie, how are you this morning?" Maggie shouted across the sand.

"I'm wet and cold. If you want a chat, come over," Bessie called back. She switched the kettle on before she'd even taken off her coat. Maggie knocked a moment later.

"My goodness, what a horrible morning," Maggie exclaimed as Bessie let her into the cottage. "I'm glad Thomas stayed at home. The cold wouldn't have been at all good for him."

"It feels as if it wants to snow, rather than rain," Bessie replied. "We haven't had snow in a while."

"I came down to start making lists of the work that needs doing in each cottage before spring, but considering the weather, I think I may just go home and leave that job for another day."

"It isn't a day for going between the cottages, I wouldn't think. You'll just end up tracking wet sand into each of them in turn."

Maggie nodded. "You're right. I shall enjoy my cuppa and then go home."

Bessie made them both tea and then they sat down together at the table.

"How is the case going?" Maggie asked after a moment. "Have the police found any of the missing women yet?"

"They have, actually. Meredith Houseman rang me last night to let me know that she's alive and well."

"She did?" Maggie looked stunned. "I was sure the skeleton was hers. I never did like that Joe Houseman. Are you certain it was truly her and not someone Joe paid to pretend to be her?"

"She didn't say anything that made me doubt her. She seemed to know the island and her own life story perfectly."

"So where has she been and what has she been doing for all these years? Why didn't she ever come back, not even for her parents' funerals?"

"When Joe came back, he told everyone that she'd stayed behind with friends. That's exactly what she told me, as well."

"But what friends? Did they divorce? Did she remarry? I want to hear the whole story."

"Sadly, I don't know the whole story, nor do I have Meredith's permission to repeat any of the things she told me last night. All I can tell you is that I spoke to her and so have the police. As long as they are satisfied that she is who she claims to be, she'll be crossed off the list."

"But what else did she say? She must have told where she's been and why she didn't come back to the island."

"You don't like Joe Houseman. Surely you can imagine why she might have chosen not to come back here with him."

"He was her husband. Yes, I think she made a bad choice, but he was still her husband."

"And he may still be her husband. My only interest in Meredith was in finding out whether she was our skeleton or not. It seems she is not."

Maggie took a deep breath and then drank the rest of her tea. "I can't believe you won't tell me everything she said. It isn't as if I'd repeat it."

Bessie hid a smile behind her teacup. Maggie was incapable of keeping secrets. "It isn't my story to tell, though. If you really want to know what happened, maybe you should ask Joe."

"I may just do that," Maggie said, getting to her feet. "Now that I know he didn't kill her, I'm far less afraid of him."

"If you do decide to talk to him, make sure you do it somewhere public," Bessie said quickly. "He may not want to discuss Meredith, and he has been known to get violent when angry."

Maggie shrugged. "The only place I'll ever find him is at the pub, anyway. I wonder if Dan Ross knows about Meredith."

"She's spoken to the police. I doubt they'll tell him anything, though."

"I should ring Dan, then," Maggie said as she headed to the door. "He's always so very grateful when I share news with him."

Which is why I don't share anything with you, Bessie thought as she let Maggie out. She shut the door behind her and then sat back down with her tea. Maybe Dan could talk to Joe and get enough of the story to satisfy both himself and Maggie, she thought.

The tea hadn't created enough washing-up for Bessie to bother with, even though she hated leaving dirty things in the sink. She'd wash them when she washed the lunch dishes. That was a better use of her hot water supply. Frowning, she left the room so that she didn't have to look at the offending cups any longer. Grabbing her book, she sat down in her favourite chair and began to read.

The book wasn't a particularly long one, and it seemed only minutes later when Bessie found herself reaching the climax. She turned the page and read about the knock on the door. The cats were racing around, shouting, as the protagonist walked towards the door. Bessie turned the page as her telephone rang. She thought about ignoring it, but then she remembered that Emma Gibson was meant to be ringing. That was worth interrupting her reading for, she decided, if only just.

"You'd better not be selling double glazing," she said before she picked up the phone.

CHAPTER 8

"Miss Cubbon? Or should I say Aunt Bessie? It's Emma Gibson," the voice on the phone said.

"Emma, it's good to hear from you," Bessie exclaimed. "How are you?"

"I'm fine, thank you," she said after a short pause.

"You don't sound certain."

"This is just, I don't know, odd. The idea that people think I might be dead is strange, for a start."

"If it makes you feel any better, no one was worried about you until the skeleton turned up at Peel Castle."

"It doesn't make me feel better at all. It's horrible that someone has been lying there, dead, for all these years. I can't imagine how the poor woman got stuck in there or why no one found her until now."

"The police are trying to answer both of those questions."

"It seems to me that they're much busier harassing my mother than answering those questions."

"Have they been harassing her?" Bessie asked, surprised.

Emma sighed. "Probably not nearly as much as she thinks they have. She regards anyone who asks anything about me as troublesome, though."

"As long as you are alive and well, the questions will stop. You simply need to let the police know that you're fine."

"I've already spoken to an Inspector Anna Lambert. She was the one who was bothering Mum. I believe she's satisfied that I'm perfectly fine."

"They'll be happy to be able to cross you off the list."

"And you'll be able to stop the rest of the gossip, won't you?"

"I've no control over the island's gossip," Bessie chuckled. "You should remember, from when you lived here, that the island thrives on skeet. I'm sure people will get bored with talking about you in another day or two, though."

"Skeet," Emma laughed. "I haven't heard that word in a long time. You're right, of course, there isn't much else on the island for people to do besides gossip. And yes, in another twenty-four hours something far more exciting will happen and I'll be forgotten again. I just hate to see my mother so upset, that's all."

"Your mother should be happy that you are alive and well," Bessie suggested.

"She is, of course, but she's also worried that people will find out why I left the island."

"I won't ask, as it isn't any of my business unless it had something to do with the dead woman at Peel Castle."

Emma laughed again. "My goodness, my life isn't anywhere near that interesting. I left for my own reasons, not ones that I'm embarrassed about, but ones that make my mother uncomfortable."

Bessie nodded. "And those reasons keep you from visiting, as well. Do you miss the island?"

There was a long silence at the other end. Bessie worried that she might have upset the woman. She opened her mouth to apologise, just as Emma spoke.

"I do miss the island, actually. We've been talking about visiting one day, but my mother would prefer if we didn't. She's as supportive as she can be, but she still finds it difficult."

It took a great deal of effort, but Bessie managed to swallow all of the questions that sprang into her head. "If you do visit, you're welcome here for a cuppa," she said after a minute.

"You truly mean that, don't you? Even though you've no idea why I left the island or what I've done since."

"I remember you when you were six. You were playing on the beach with a few other children and one of them, a much older lad, started throwing rocks at the seagulls. You got incredibly angry and shouted at him. Do you remember?"

"I do. He pushed me over into the water and I started to cry. His mother made him apologise and then took him home. I was with Granny, and she brought me to your cottage so that I could get out of my wet clothes and dry off. I sat in your kitchen, wrapped in a towel, and told you the whole story about the rocks and seagulls while Granny went home to get me dry things."

"You were a lovely child with impeccable manners. I'm sure you've changed a lot in the last thirty-odd years, but I believe you can tell a lot about what sort of adult a person will be if you get to know him or her as a child."

"You're probably right. I'm awfully glad I made a good impression on you all those years ago, anyway. I still get upset when I see people mistreating animals or other people."

"For what it's worth, the young man who pushed you into the sea is now a secondhand car salesman with a reputation for being less than honest about the cars that he sells."

Emma laughed. "That doesn't surprise me in the slightest. He's still on the island?"

"Oh, yes. He's been married three times and has four children. Three of them work for him, and I wouldn't buy a car from them in an emergency."

"What about the fourth child?"

"The youngest boy, Trevor, is an environmental activist. He works for a charity in the UK, raising money to protect wildlife. He and his partner, Doug, have been together for twenty years, but his father still doesn't approve of the relationship. He doesn't seem to mind when his other children get married and then divorced over and over again, but then, as I said, he has been married three times himself."

"Do Trevor and Doug visit the island?"

"They do. They stay in a hotel rather than with Trevor's parents, but they do visit. He loves the island, and he does some fundraising over here on a volunteer basis when he can."

"Interesting."

"Is it? Are you involved with wildlife good causes?"

"No, not at all. It's interesting because I'm involved with another woman."

Bessie chose her next words carefully. "Is that what your mother wants to keep secret?" she asked.

"Yes, of course. I may as well tell you the whole story, now that I've told you the only interesting part."

Bessie chuckled. "If that's the only interesting part, I'm not sure I want to hear the whole story."

Emma laughed. "You probably don't, but I'd like to tell you anyway, if you don't mind."

"I don't mind. I assume you don't want me to repeat any of it, though."

"I don't really care what you repeat, but it would probably break my mother's heart if people on the island found out about me. She's been keeping it a secret for such a long time. Please don't tell anyone my story. I didn't even tell the police all of this, because they didn't need to know it."

"I'll simply tell people that you're alive and well," Bessie assured her, deciding that she'd have to avoid Maggie for a while. She didn't want to annoy her by again not revealing everything she knew.

"I was a teacher," Emma began. "I taught primary school for three years and that was more than enough time for me to realise that I didn't really care for children."

"Oh, dear."

"Yes, exactly. I also knew I was different in that I wasn't interested in men. Mum wanted me to get married and make her a grandmother, but that was the last thing I wanted to do. The only thing I really wanted to do was travel. I loved the island, but I knew there was a big world out there and I wanted to see more of it. I was still living at home, so I'd been able to save up some money. That summer, when school broke up for summer holidays, I went off to have an adventure."

"And you never came back," Bessie said after a long pause.

"No, I didn't. Neither did Janice, but no one is looking for her."

"Janice?"

"Janice Smith. She was another teacher at the same school where I was teaching. She was a comeover, though, not Manx. She'd done her teacher training and then decided to teach her way around the world. She was going to get jobs at schools in different places, a year or two at a time, until she'd been everywhere."

"That sounds fascinating."

"I thought so, too, except for the part about teaching. As I said, I don't really like children. Janice loves them, as long as they all go home at the end of the school day."

"So you left together?"

"We did. Janice had taught on the island for a year and had decided that that was enough. The island was too much like home, which in her case was Birmingham. She wanted to go to more exotic places and she invited me to come along. We were just friends at that point. I didn't really understand that I was a lesbian. Such things weren't really discussed in those days. I just thought I wasn't interested in men."

"I hope things are easier for children today."

"They seem to be. Anyway, I keep getting sidetracked from my story. Janice and I left the island, intending to be away for five weeks. Well, I was going to be gone for five weeks. Janice wasn't planning on going back to the island. She had a teaching job lined up in Canada for September. We took my car across to the UK and then took the car ferry over to France. From there, we just started driving, stopping to see whatever caught our fancy. By the end of the five weeks, I was madly in love and, luckily for me, Janice felt the same way."

"So you decided not to return here."

"I went to Canada with Janice. For the first year or two, we maintained the fiction that we were just friends, but over time we both came to hate lying about our relationship. I finally told my mother everything just before she was due to visit us in Canada. She opted not to come."

"I'm sorry."

"I understood. This was thirty years ago and attitudes were very different. Janice has lost jobs over our relationship, and we've had difficulties renting places to live, as well."

"You haven't been teaching?"

"No, I haven't. I'm a writer. I write romance novels for one of the large publishing companies, the type that put out dozens of new books every month. I write under several different pen names. The years that Janice and I spent travelling allow me to set my stories all over the world. I make decent money and I have the flexibility to go wherever Janice wants to go next. They don't care about my private life, either, as long as my stories are believable."

"I wonder if your mother is embarrassed about that, too."

Emma chuckled. "She may be, at that. I'm sure she would be if I were straight and happily married, but the whole lesbian thing overshadows everything else."

"But you and Janice are still together?"

"Oh, yes, we're like an old married couple now. We've travelled the world, though. She taught English in China, Japan, Russia, South America, and New Zealand. I could go on and on, but I won't. Suffice to say that we lived her dream of teaching just about everywhere. I got to see the world in ways I never imagined I would. My writing brought in little extras over the years, let us live a bit more comfortably than we might have on just one income. Now it's funding our retirement, as neither of us has much in the way of a pension."

"You're both retired?"

"Janice is retired. She burned out a bit near the end, but she'd taught for over thirty years in every imaginable condition. We spent a year in the Middle East where she taught at a very expensive private school. The class sizes were tiny and the children were so well behaved as to be slightly scary. She also taught for a year in India at a school that was nothing but a flat patch of earth in the middle of a village. No walls or roof, no furniture, no books, just her and a group of ten to thirty children, depending on what else was happening in the village at the time. Thirty years was enough."

"I should think so."

"We're in Birmingham now. Her parents are both gone, but her brother lives here and he's been very kind. He and his wife treat me as if I'm one of the family and their children and grandchildren are very special to us. Mum visits occasionally. I think about visiting the island, but I wouldn't do it if I couldn't bring Janice, and that would make Mum uncomfortable."

"Ideas are changing, even on the island. Maybe you'll be able to visit one day."

"I'd like to think so, but I truly don't want to upset Mum. If she'd rather we not come, that's fine, too. I've been all over the world. The island will always be home for me, but I've come to appreciate Birmingham. After everything we've seen and done, wherever Janice is, that's home, anyway."

"It sounds as if you've had an amazing life."

"It has been pretty amazing. It's funny, though, wherever we've been in the world, we always used to laugh about how the day-to-day chores remain the same. We still had to grocery shop and cook and clean, whether we were in a tiny house in India or a mansion in the Middle East."

"Where was your favourite place?"

"That's an impossible question. I enjoyed different things about different places. Some of how I felt about a particular place is also tied to where we'd been just before it, too. The first place we went after India felt incredibly luxurious, even though it wasn't really. Canada felt much like the UK because we went there immediately after we'd left here, but when we went to Canada again a few years later, after a stint in Europe, it didn't feel at all familiar."

"You should write a book about your travels."

"I've been trying to persuade Janice to write about her experiences, actually. She can talk for hours about the children she taught."

"If she ever does write the book, let me know. I'd love to read it."

"I'll tell her that. Maybe it will motivate her."

"I'm awfully glad that you're doing so well. I'm sure the police were happy to cross you off the list of possible candidates for the body from Peel, too."

"Inspector Lambert didn't sound very happy when I spoke to her," Emma replied. "She sounded a bit annoyed, really. I didn't tell her all the things I told you. I simply told her that I was alive and well. I gave her my passport number so that she could confirm that I'm who I claim to be, and that was pretty much the extent of our conversation."

"Whom do you think we found, then?" Bessie asked, wishing she'd thought to ask Meredith the same question.

"My goodness, how should I know?"

"Do you remember anyone else leaving the island in the year or so before you left? Someone who left and never came back?"

"I'm afraid I didn't pay that much attention to other people in those days. I was busy with work, of course. Mum used to talk about people. We were still living together, but I don't really recall anything specific. Let me think for a minute, though."

Bessie let her mind wander back to her book as she waited. Who was at the man's door? There were only two good possibilities, although there was a third that Bessie knew she'd find less satisfactory. She was frowning over the various different plot resolutions that she'd imagined when Emma spoke again.

"It's no use. I can't remember anyone's name or anything else. I'm sure Mum told me about various people leaving the island, affairs, and all manner of things, but it's all just a blur. I'm going to talk to Janice, though. She used to keep journals where she recorded various things. She may have made notes on some of the things that happened on the island. I'll ring you back tomorrow or the next day."

"I'd appreciate that," Bessie said. "At this point, the police need all the help they can get."

"What makes you so sure the victim was from the island? Surely she could simply have been visiting?"

"If she'd just been visiting, she should have been missed when she didn't return home."

"There are people who don't have anyone to miss them," Emma said. "Janice and I met a few of them over the years, people who could vanish tomorrow and not be missed. I hope your woman isn't one of those."

"I do, too."

She put the phone down and then stared at it. Both Meredith and Emma had told her that they'd already spoken to Anna, but she still felt as if she should share what she'd learned with the police inspector. After debating with herself for a minute, she picked up the phone and rang the Laxey station.

"Laxey Neighbourhood Policing, this is Suzannah. How can I help you?"

Bessie made a face. Suzannah was a fairly new addition to the station and thus far Bessie hadn't been impressed with the woman. She knew that Doona didn't care for her, either, which didn't make Bessie feel more warmly towards her. "Is Inspector Rockwell available, please? It's Bessie Cubbon," she replied. She didn't have a number for Anna, but John would be able to get Anna a message.

"I'm sorry, Mrs. Clubbon, but Inspector Rockwell isn't in the office at the moment. Would you care to leave a message?" was the unwelcome reply.

"What about Hugh?"

"Me? I'm here. I'm not sure I know what you mean."

"Not you, Hugh," Bessie sighed. "Constable Hugh Watterson."

"Constable Watterson isn't in the office either. Did you want to leave a message for him, too?"

Bessie took a deep breath. "Please ask John to ring me," she said.

"John?"

"Inspector Rockwell."

"To ring Mrs. Clorben, yes, of course."

"It's Cubbon. C – U – B – B – O – N."

"You've missed out the R, Mrs. Crubbon."

"There isn't any R in my name."

"No? Maybe you'd better spell it again."

"You know what? Never mind. It's a good thing there isn't a man standing over me with a knife. By the time you understood me, I'd be dead."

"For emergencies, you should ring 999. Do you want me to connect you?"

"No, I don't," Bessie said tightly. "I don't want you to do anything at all. Thank you anyway."

"What about the man with the knife?"

"There isn't any man with a knife," Bessie snapped before she put the phone down. She paced around the kitchen for several minutes, working off her frustration with Suzannah before she sat back down with her book. As she struggled to find her place, she heard sirens. Lots of sirens. Before she could investigate, someone began pounding on her door.

"Hugh? What brings you here?"

The young man stared at her for a minute and then pulled her into a hug. Bessie was sure she could see tears in his eyes as he released her. She looked behind him and gasped. There were four police cars, all with lights flashing and sirens blaring, behind her cottage.

"Whatever has happened?" she demanded.

"Suzannah said there was a man with a knife at your cottage," Hugh told her.

"You must be joking," Bessie exclaimed. "She couldn't get my name right, not once, but she managed to send the entire police department here because of a stupid remark I made?"

Another police car rolled to a stop. John Rockwell's car was right behind it. He'd barely shut off the engine before he was running towards Bessie and Hugh.

"Bessie's fine," Hugh said quickly.

John sighed with relief. "What happened to the man with the knife? Who was it? Did you recognise him?"

"There wasn't a man with a knife," Bessie snapped. "That woman is an idiot."

John pulled out his mobile phone and punched a number. "It's all good," he said a moment later. "Apparently Suzannah misunderstood something."

After a moment, he nodded. "Yes, I agree that isn't surprising."

He dropped the phone into his pocket. "Doona," he told Bessie. "She was notified too, and she wanted to come, but Amy is home because she's poorly, and Doona is sitting with her. I didn't want Amy left alone. It took some doing, but I managed to persuade her that I would be more useful against a man with a knife than she would."

Bessie didn't know if she wanted to laugh or cry. "You need to do something about Suzannah," she said after a moment. "I'll admit that I shouldn't have spoken as I did, but I was quite fed up with her inability to listen to me properly."

John turned around and looked at the row of police cars behind him. "One minute," he told Bessie before he walked over and spoke to each of the drivers in turn.

Hugh had to move his car, as he'd more or less abandoned it in the middle of the parking area. John drove his next to Hugh's now neatly parked car and then the pair walked into Treoghe Bwaane with Bessie as the others all drove away.

"Tell me everything," John said as he settled into a chair.

Bessie repeated the conversation she'd had with Suzannah. When she was finished, John put his notebook away and grinned at her.

"I don't blame you for being frustrated, but it's never a good idea to tell the police that there's a man with a knife at your house."

"I didn't tell her that."

"No, but she heard it that way and she panicked. She was able to get your address from our system and she sent every available car here as an emergency."

"She can get my information from your system?"

"Yes."

"Then why can't she get my name right?"

John frowned. "I'm not entirely certain how the system at reception works. I'm going to see what I can find out, though. What happened today was unacceptable."

"I am sorry," Bessie said.

"It isn't your fault," Hugh told her. "It also isn't the first time that Suzannah has sent everyone out on an emergency call that was simply a misunderstanding."

"I think I'd be more worried about the opposite happening and her not sending help when it's needed," Bessie said.

"If people need emergency assistance, they should ring 999," John interjected. "The reception staff at the station have very different training to the 999 staff."

"I'll bet they could take a simple phone message," Bessie muttered under her breath.

John chuckled. "But what did you want to talk to me or Hugh about? You now have both of us."

"I really just wanted a number for Anna. I've spoken to two of the women who were on our list and I wanted to be certain that she's crossed them both off now."

"I wish I'd known that," John told her. "I was actually in a meeting with Anna when I received the emergency notification. I should have brought her along."

"I don't really need to speak to her," Bessie said, feeling as if she'd much rather talk to John anyway, especially since he was already there.

"No?"

"Meredith Houseman and Emma Gibson both rang me, that's all. I spoke to each of them for several minutes and I'm satisfied that they were who they claimed to be, which means they are both alive and well."

John wrote the names down. "Anna was just telling me that she'd eliminated two women from the list, but she hadn't had time to explain."

"Where have they been and why haven't they been back?" Hugh asked.

Bessie flushed. "Neither of them wants their story repeated," she said. "Obviously, if Anna needs to know, then I'll tell her, but I don't believe anything either of them said is at all relevant to the investigation."

John nodded. "Unless they can suggest other possible candidates," he said.

"I forgot to ask Meredith about that, but Emma is going to talk to a friend of hers who was on the island at the same time to see if they can come up with any names for us."

"A friend who was on the island at the same time?" Hugh echoed. "She left with this friend?"

Bessie nodded. "Please don't ask anything else."

Hugh frowned and then shrugged. "I suppose I'm just being nosy."

"Which is a desirable trait in a police constable," John said. "In this case, though, I think we have to respect Ms. Gibson's right to privacy."

"Yes, sir," Hugh replied.

"If that's all, I need to get back to the office," John said, getting to his feet. "I have meetings all afternoon, and I believe I need to do some staff retraining, as well."

"Maybe you could simply replace her," Bessie said softly.

John smiled but didn't reply. Hugh followed him to the door.

"I'll get back to what I was doing, then," he said. "I'm glad it was a false alarm. I was really worried about you," he told Bessie.

She gave him a hug and then let both men out. It was nearly time for some lunch, but after her unusual morning, all Bessie could think about was finishing her book. She sat back down in her chair, determined to ignore the real world until she'd reached the end.

Twenty minutes later, she was sorry she'd bothered. The author's solution to the case was not one she'd considered, nor was it a satisfactory conclusion in her opinion. She put the book on top of the pile she intended to donate to charity and then went to get herself some lunch. As she ate, she rewrote the ending in her head until everything was just the way she wanted it to be. While she'd never tried her hand at writing, she was very tempted to write down her alternate ending to this particular book. She could print it out and add it to the book before she gave it away, giving future readers a chance to enjoy what she was sure was a better conclusion. Surely they'd be grateful, she thought.

As she did the washing-up, finally washing the cups from her tea with Maggie along with the lunch things, she thought about Emma and Meredith. They'd both had to leave the island to find happiness. What might have happened if she'd left the island? A knock on the door cut short her thoughts.

"I hope this isn't a bad time," Anna Lambert said.

"Not at all. Come in," Bessie replied.

"I wanted to hear about your conversations with Meredith and Emma. I've spoken to both of them, but I suspect they both told you a good deal more than they told me."

Bessie shrugged. "They both also requested confidentiality."

Anna nodded. "I won't take notes, but I'd be grateful if you'd give me a basic idea of what they've been doing with their lives since they left the island."

After a moment, Bessie decided that sharing the basics wouldn't hurt. "Meredith simply wanted to get away from her parents and Joe," Bessie said. "From what she said, she's been in the Lake District ever since."

"Why the secrecy, then?"

"I think she simply doesn't like the idea of being talked about."

"I can sympathise."

Bessie nodded.

"And Emma?"

"Went travelling and never came back."

"That's what she told me. I'm sure there's more to the story."

"She went travelling with another teacher, a woman called Janice. They've been together ever since."

Anna blinked and then nodded. "That would be what her mother wants to keep secret, then, and it explains why she didn't want to share much with me. Thank you for telling me."

"I trust you to keep it all confidential. Emma knows me, which is why she trusted me. I believe I know you well enough to do the same with you."

"Thank you," Anna said, flushing. "The secrecy aspect bothered me, but it makes more sense now, especially in Emma's case. That's two names off the list, anyway. Three more to go, unless you've any new ones to share with me?"

"I wish I did, but I don't. Emma is going to talk to the other teacher and see if together they can remember anyone else who left the island around that time. If they come up with anything, I'll let you know."

"Thank you. I'm working on the other three. They're proving more difficult to track down, but that isn't surprising."

"Sam Owens can't help with Joselyn?"

"Let's just say he won't help," Anna told her. "Maybe you can persuade him to talk. I didn't manage it."

"I don't think I've met Mr. Owens more than once or twice in my life. I can't imagine why he'd talk to me."

"Keep me informed if you do talk to anyone," Anna said sternly as she stood up. "I should say anyone else. Let me know if Emma has any ideas, too."

"I don't have a number for the Peel station."

Anna nodded and pulled a business card out of her pocket. She used a pen to write a number on the back. "That's my mobile number. Ring me anytime. You won't be interrupting anything important."

"Thank you. I'll ring you if I hear anything interesting."

"Ring me even if what you hear is boring," Anna replied. "Sometimes cases are solved by the most boring of details."

Bessie took herself for a long walk while she thought about what Anna had said. Her answering machine light was blinking when she got back home.

CHAPTER 9

"*I*t's Doona. Would you like to get dinner with me tonight? There's nothing to eat at my house and I'm too exhausted to shop," the message said.

Bessie rang her friend back at home. "I'd love to go out tonight. Where do you want to go?"

"How about the café in Lonan? I haven't been there in ages," Doona suggested.

"I never say no to going there," Bessie agreed.

Knowing that Doona was going to be there at half five gave Bessie some extra motivation to get some work done. She had a small pile of unpaid bills that needed sorting, and some correspondence to reply to as well. As she sealed up her letter to Janet Markham, Bessie wondered again if Edward Bennett could help John. She hadn't mentioned anything to Janet about Sue in her letter, but she could always ring Janet if Andrew was unable to assist. With those little jobs out of the way, Bessie pulled out Onnee's letters and began to work on the next one.

When Doona arrived, right on time, Bessie was ready.

"How are you?" she asked Bessie.

"I'm fine, I suppose," Bessie replied.

"What's wrong?"

"Onnee had her baby."

"Oh, dear. It didn't go well?"

"There were complications. The baby survived, but the doctors have told Onnee that she could lose the little girl at any time. The letter was full of so much pain that it was difficult to read."

"I am sorry."

Bessie nodded. "I know this all happened over fifty years ago, but I still feel incredibly sorry for Onnee. Her husband sounds quite dreadful, too. He's spending nearly all of his spare time with his former fiancée, as she's unwell. Onnee is on her own with the baby, feeling alone and friendless."

"Perhaps she needs to make more of an effort to find new friends," Doona suggested.

"She doesn't drive and apparently there isn't any public transportation in the small town where they live. She talks of walking to the local library, but apparently the only people she's met there are older. She needs to meet other new mothers."

"What's wrong with the baby?"

"She isn't specific, at least not in the letter that I read today, but there were problems with the delivery, whatever that means. She's been told that, even if the baby survives for a while, she won't ever be able to do much. It sounds as if they suspect brain damage."

Doona wiped a tear from her eye. "I can't believe I'm crying over something that happened so many years ago."

"You should read the letters. I've been in tears all afternoon."

"No, thank you. It's bad enough hearing about them from you."

Bessie shook her head. "Let's find other things to talk about over dinner," she suggested.

"Yes, and let's go. I'm starving," Doona replied.

The drive into Lonan didn't take long. The small car park for the café was already half full when they arrived. There was a sign on the door that read "Under New Ownership Beginning First of February."

"I didn't realise they'd sold the place already," Bessie said as Doona pulled the door open.

"I heard that Jasmina, from the café at the Laxey Wheel, was going to take over. I hope that's right, as she's wonderful," Doona replied.

"That is right," the girl at the door told them. "Jasmina is taking over on the first of February. She'll be doing her home-cooked specialties and puddings while Dan and Carol will be making their sampler plates at their new location in Onchan."

"Splendid," Bessie said. "I've loved having Dan and Carol so close to home, but they need more room, and so does Jasmina. She only has four tables in her current location."

"I know," the girl laughed. "I've been there loads. She's an amazing cook. I can't wait to see what she does with a proper kitchen."

"Will you be working for her here?" Doona asked.

"I will. She was kind enough to hire all of us, even though she isn't certain how successful she'll be here."

"We'll have to make a point of coming in regularly once she opens," Bessie said.

"Table for two tonight?" the girl asked.

"Yes, please."

"Right this way." She led them to a small table in the corner.

"What has Dan prepared today?" Doona asked.

"It's a celebration of pork today," she was told. "Our main course sampler contains a grilled pork chop, a serving of pork tenderloin wrapped in bacon, a pork sausage, and a slice of gammon. For pudding, he went with apple, as that pairs so nicely with pork. You'll get a tiny apple tart, half of a baked cinnamon apple, a portion of Eve's pudding, and a scoop of Dan's homemade apple and cinnamon ice cream."

"Yes, please, to all of that," Doona laughed.

"Me, too," Bessie added.

After taking their drink order, the girl walked away.

"How are you?" Bessie asked Doona as they both sat back in their chairs.

"I'm hanging in there. John is pushing the kids to try to get back to normal, or at least as much as they can, which means I'm spending less time with them. It's odd, because I find that I miss them."

"Any idea what is happening with Sue?"

"Not really. John said you were going to see if Andrew Cheatham could help at all."

"I've spoken to him. He's going to see if he can find out anything."

Doona sighed. "She should come home, sick or not. At least if she was in Manchester, we would know we were getting accurate information about her care."

"Is that a possibility?"

"I don't know. Harvey insists that she's too ill to travel. Maybe that's something that Andrew can find out."

Bessie nodded. "Maybe we should talk about other things."

"As Inspector Lambert is in charge of the Peel Castle case, I've not heard anything about how that's progressing. Have you been able to help at all?"

"I gave Anna a list of five women who disappeared from the island at about the right time. So far, two have turned up alive and well."

"Really? That's good news, I suppose, although I'm sure Inspector Lambert would rather work out who was found in Peel than find women who are alive and well."

"Probably," Bessie agreed. "She's very eager to solve the case."

"I never cared for her when she worked in Laxey, but I do think she's had a difficult time of it lately. I'm trying to be nice to her when I see her now."

Bessie smiled. "I'm doing everything I can to help her, which I never imagined I would."

"There are still three good possibilities, then?"

"I don't know how good they are, but there are still three possibilities. The longer I have to think about the case, the more likely it seems that the woman wasn't from the island, though. I keep thinking that she would have been missed if she'd been from here."

"Not if she was murdered and her killer told everyone that she'd chosen to leave. We've seen that happen before, after all."

"That's true," Bessie sighed. "Why are people so horrible to other people?"

"There's a conversation I'd rather miss," the waitress said as she delivered their drinks. "Your food will be right out."

"Thank you," Bessie said. She took a sip of her drink. "Let's find something pleasant to discuss over dinner," she suggested to Doona.

They were talking about the weather when the food arrived a few minutes later. Once they were eating, they found plenty to discuss as they enjoyed their meal.

"I've never tried wrapping pork tenderloin in bacon, but now I'm not sure I ever want to eat it any other way," Doona said when she finally put her knife and fork down on her empty plate.

"It was very good, but then, so was everything else."

Pudding was equally delicious. The two women were just finishing their last bites of that when Dan came out of the kitchen.

"I heard you were here and I had to come and say hello," he told Bessie.

"Hello," she laughed. "How are you? Are you looking forward to the big move?"

"Yes and no. We've done so well here, in a less than ideal location, that I'm worried that once we're more conveniently located, people won't bother coming."

"If you keep doing the same amazing food as you did tonight, you'll fill your larger dining room without any trouble," Bessie predicted.

"I hope so. We're going to be open fewer hours in the new location. Our goal is to make the same profit by working a bit less. We're going to do more catering to help make up the difference, too," Dan told her.

"Now I shall have to come up with a reason to have something catered," Bessie mused.

Dan laughed. "We're pretty well booked for catering for the next three months, actually. Elizabeth is keeping us pretty busy."

Bessie nodded. Elizabeth Quayle was the only daughter of Bessie's friends, George and Mary. They were the wealthy owners of Thie yn Traie, the mansion near Bessie's cottage. Elizabeth had dropped out of several different universities, unable to work out what she wanted to do with her life. She'd recently begun a party planning business on the island and Bessie was amazed and delighted that it had become a success almost immediately.

"I'll be doing a lot more on my own for the next several months," Dan added. "We're just now telling people. Carol is expecting our first child in late July."

"Congratulations," Bessie exclaimed. She knew that one of the reasons that the couple had moved to the island was so that they could start a family. Carol had stopped working at the café some months earlier and Bessie had been waiting for the good news ever since.

"It was more difficult than it should have been," Dan sighed. "We had to have some specialist treatment, but now that she's actually pregnant, we're both over the moon."

"I'm delighted for you both," Bessie replied.

"It does put rather more pressure on me to make a success of the new restaurant, though," Dan added. "Having another mouth to feed is worrying."

"You'll be fine. I'm sure, if the restaurant doesn't work out, that you could become a private chef for just about any family on the island," Bessie suggested.

He laughed. "Mary keeps offering me that very job at Thie yn Traie. I suppose that's something I could fall back on if things go terribly wrong."

"They won't, though. You're far too good," Doona said.

"Thanks for coming in tonight," he told them both. "I'd better get back in the kitchen. Those apples aren't going to bake themselves."

He gave Bessie a quick hug and then disappeared. After they'd paid the bill, Bessie and Doona walked back to her car.

"I feel as if I should walk all the way back to my cottage after eating all of that," Bessie said as she climbed into the passenger seat.

"I know what you mean, but it was all so good."

"I'll take a walk on the beach when we get back."

"I hope you don't mind if I join you," Doona said. "I don't really know what to do with myself at the moment. I've been spending so much time with the kids that I feel as if I should be doing your laundry and nagging you to do your homework."

"I haven't had homework in a good many years, but you are welcome to do my laundry, if it will make you feel better."

"That's fine. I have plenty of my own that needs doing, actually, but it can wait until we've walked off a few of those apple calories."

"I don't think the apples were the problem. The pastry and the cake, on the other hand..." Bessie trailed off.

Bessie changed into trousers and comfortable shoes before she and Doona set out across the sand. Doona had left a pair of trainers at Treoghe Bwaane some months earlier, so she changed into those before they headed out.

"It's a beautiful night," Doona said, looking up at the starry sky.

"There isn't any cloud cover. I feel as if I can see forever."

"My solicitor in the UK reckons things might be sorted soon," Doona said after several minutes of walking in silence.

"That's good news, isn't it?" When Doona's second husband had died, she'd been shocked to learn that he'd named her as his heir even though they were separated and Doona had filed for divorce. Charles had been a wealthy businessman, co-owner of hotels, restaurants, and a holiday park, among other things. The arrest of Charles's former business partner not long after Charles's death had complicated the inheritance. While the authorities tried to work out how much Charles had known about or had been involved with his former partner's illegal operations, most of the estate had been frozen. In spite of that, Doona had already received a few cheques for life insurance policies that had given her more money than she'd ever imagined having.

"It's good news. I want it all to be over, even though I'm afraid of what might happen next."

"What might happen next?"

"I could inherit a lot of money," Doona said gloomily.

Bessie couldn't help but laugh. "Most people would be delighted by that idea."

"I know, and I should be delighted, but I've already been given more money than I ever dreamed of having and I've no idea what to do with it all. What will I do with even more?"

"Quit your job and travel the world," Bessie suggested.

"Maybe, if things, well, depending on other things."

"How are things between you and John?"

Doona stopped walking and turned to stare at the sea. "I don't know," she said eventually in a very low voice. "He's so sad and worried about Sue that I can't possibly say anything to him about, well, about us. I don't think I'd ever realised how much he loved Sue. He still cares about her now, and that's difficult for me."

"You need to give him time."

"I have been giving him time. I'll keep giving him time, too, but I don't know how long I want to wait, either. As you said, I could travel and see the world. If my solicitor is right about how things are going to be settled, I won't have to work any longer. My life could be totally my own. If John asked, though, I'd stay right here and help him with the kids until they're both old enough to not need him any longer."

"You're in love with him."

"Sadly and rather desperately," Doona sighed. "I fought it for a long time. He was married and then he was going through an ugly divorce. When the kids came to stay, I thought that might push us apart, but mostly, it's brought us together. Or rather, it was bringing us together until Sue fell ill. That's driving us apart."

"All you can do now is wait," Bessie told her. "John has to work through his feelings himself. It's difficult for me to imagine how he must feel."

"I know. I keep reminding myself that this must be almost unbearable for him, but that just makes me want to do more to help. The more I try to help, the more he pushes me away, though."

"I wish I had wise words of advice for you, but I truly don't know what to tell you, except I'm sure it will all work out for the best in the end."

"I may end up owning half of a holiday park," Doona told her. "Maybe we should go for another visit."

"I wouldn't mind going to Lakeview again, actually. I quite enjoyed some aspects of the holiday."

"There were a few bright spots in between the murder and my spending a night in prison and all of that."

Bessie grinned. "The ice cream was good."

"And we played crazy golf," Doona replied. "The painting and drawing classes were good fun, too."

"I thought you were going to start taking some art classes," Bessie remembered.

"I was, but then I decided I wasn't ready yet. Maybe another round of classes at Lakeview will be just what I need."

"We should book something, rather than just talk about it."

"I agree, but I don't want to leave until this mess with Sue is resolved, one way or another."

Bessie nodded. "That's understandable."

They walked for a bit longer, but Bessie could tell that Doona's mind was elsewhere. "Let's turn around," she suggested when they reached the stairs to Thie yn Traie.

"I should get home and do that laundry I was talking about," Doona said a few minutes later. "I feel odd about not knowing anything about the Peel Castle case, though. I don't even know any of the names of the possible victims."

"Don't worry about it for tonight. If we get a chance, maybe we can have one of our gatherings in a day or two to discuss the case. A lot will depend on John's schedule, though."

"If we do get together, he'll probably want to invite Inspector Lambert to attend. It is her case, after all."

"Yes, well, I suppose I could live with that."

"I'm not sure I could," Doona muttered. She insisted on checking Bessie's cottage before she left.

"We've only been a few paces away. No one had time to break in and if they'd tried, we would have seen them, anyway," Bessie told her empty kitchen as Doona stomped around above her head.

"I'll ring you soon," Doona told her when she reappeared in the kitchen. "Maybe, if things don't get resolved with Sue, we should have a holiday regardless."

Bessie nodded, suspecting that Doona would never actually agree to leave the island until the circumstances changed. Feeling slightly at loose ends, she looked through her bookshelves, searching for some old favourite that might fill an hour or two before bedtime. The phone rang before she could find just the right thing.

"Miss Cubbon? It's Emma Gibson again. I hope it isn't too late to ring."

"It's only half eight," Bessie laughed.

"Yes, I know, but Mum always taught me that ringing anyone after eight was rude."

"I think you're fine until nine."

"Good. I was going to wait until tomorrow, but Janice and I are catching an early flight to Barcelona in the morning. We both feel as if we need to get away so we booked a last-minute holiday there. We'll be gone for a fortnight."

"How lovely for you. I hope you have a wonderful time."

"Thank you. I was ringing because I'd promised that I would. Janice and I had a long talk about the skeleton and who it might have been."

"Did you come up with any ideas?"

"I remembered a woman called Lauren Bell. Her nephew was in my class and some of the other children teased him about his aunt running away with the owner of the local chippy. He was married and his wife worked at the chippy with him. I remember them better than I remember Lauren, if I'm honest."

"Her name has been mentioned before."

"As I recall, they left and then came back. He went back to his wife, and she got her own little flat because her parents disowned her, or very nearly. She left again not long after that, but I don't remember anything else about her."

"Someone suggested that she left with a different married man."

"If she did, I certainly don't remember who he was," Emma replied. "Anything is possible, though."

"The police are looking for her."

"I hope they find her. Janice wondered about Hannah Butler."

"Her name has come up before, too. What does Janice remember about her?"

"She worked at the shop in Kirk Michael. Janice rented a room in Kirk Michael when she first came to the island. She'd taken the room, sight unseen, when she'd taken the position, without knowing anything about the island. Once she moved across, she discovered that Kirk Michael was a bit remote for her purposes and she relocated to Douglas. She was only in Kirk Michael for about two months, but she remembers Hannah quite clearly."

"What does she remember about her?"

"She was quiet and Janice thought she seemed depressed. Janice's mother battled depression her entire life, so Janice knows what she's talking about on that front. Anyway, she says she tried to talk to Hannah whenever she was in the shop, but she said Hannah was always monosyllabic and monotone. When Janice knew she was moving, she tried to suggest that Hannah talk to a doctor about how she was feeling, but she doesn't believe that Hannah was really listening."

"I wonder if anyone in Kirk Michael remembers any more about her," Bessie said, mostly to herself.

"Janice reckons that Louise Larkin will remember her, if she's still alive."

"Louise Larkin?"

"She runs the shop in Kirk Michael. If you've ever been in there, you'll probably have met her."

"Strange as it might sound, I don't believe I have ever been to that shop," Bessie said. "I don't know that I've ever done more than simply ride through Kirk Michael. If Janice knew Ms. Larkin, she may not still be working."

"If she is, she'll be able to tell you all about Hannah."

"I may have to try to track her down, then," Bessie said.

"If you do, tell her that Janice sends her best. According to Janice, Louise took a maternal interest in everyone who came into the shop, even if they only came in once or twice. She was nearly always there and she used to tell Janice to buy more vegetables and fewer chocolate bars whenever she saw her."

Bessie chuckled. "Now I'm looking forward to meeting her."

"Janice told me that she nearly decided to stay in Kirk Michael just because Louise made her feel so welcome. She didn't because one of the other lodgers at the house where she was staying wouldn't leave her alone, though."

"That's unfortunate."

"She was happier when she moved, anyway, and it was all a very long time ago."

"It was, at that," Bessie agreed.

She put the phone down and then paced back and forth across the kitchen floor. It seemed odd that she'd never heard of Louise Larkin if she'd been living on the island for so many years.

Feeling too restless to try to sleep, Bessie went out and sat on the rock behind her cottage. Breathing deeply, she let the sea air calm her spirit. When someone said her name, she jumped.

"Maggie? What are you doing down here so late?" she demanded, after her heart rate had returned to something closer to normal.

"The police rang that there were lights on in the last cottage again," Maggie sighed. "I don't know how, but the lights in one of the bedrooms had been switched on again. There wasn't any sign of a break-in, at least. I'm starting to believe that the cottage is haunted, though."

"It seems more likely that kids are getting in somehow," Bessie replied. "Whatever, it must be annoying for you."

"It is, rather, but I suppose it comes with the job," Maggie sighed. "Any more information on any of our missing people?"

"I spoke to Emma Gibson recently."

"Did you? Let me guess. She's alive and well and you can't tell me any more than that."

Bessie shrugged. "She's alive and well, yes. I don't know much beyond that, really."

Maggie sighed. "I'm too tired to push you for more information tonight," she said.

"Are you all right?" Bessie asked.

"I'm fine."

Bessie stared at her friend. The moon was doing its best to illuminate the beach, but it was too dark to see Maggie's expression.

"Sit down," she suggested, patting the rock.

"I should get home," Maggie replied.

"What's wrong?" Bessie asked softly.

Maggie took a deep breath and then walked over and sat down next to Bessie. "I'm worried about Thomas," she said in a whisper. "There, I've said it."

As Maggie began to sob, Bessie patted her pockets, searching for tissues. "I'm sorry," she said after a moment. She patted the woman's back, wondering if Maggie would notice if she dashed up to her cottage for tissues.

"I'm just tired of being strong all the time," Maggie said eventually. "He's been ill for months and he doesn't seem to be getting better. The doctors keep saying that we need to be patient, that he's older so it takes longer for his body to heal, but I'm not convinced. What if there's something more serious wrong? What if he's dying? I can't run the business on my own. I can't live on my own, either."

"Just because he's taking time to recover doesn't mean he won't. If the doctors aren't worried, you shouldn't be, either."

"Doctors don't know everything. My cousin's sister went to the doctor on a Monday and he said everything was just fine. She dropped dead on Tuesday without warning."

"What killed her?"

"The doctor said it was just one of those things. Her heart just stopped. It was her time."

"That's terribly sad."

"She was ninety-eight, of course, so a good deal older than Thomas, but still."

"If you aren't happy with his doctors, you can always ask to see someone else," Bessie suggested.

"I told Thomas that, but he's happy with his doctors, even if I'm not. He doesn't realise just how unwell he actually is, of course."

"I'm sure the cold weather isn't helping. Thomas will probably rally in the spring."

"He'd better. As I said, I can't live without him."

"You're stronger than you think you are."

"Let's talk about something else," Maggie said. "Tell me about the case. Surely there's something you can talk about to do with the case."

"Someone said I should talk to Louise Larkin about Hannah Butler."

"That makes sense. Hannah used to work for Louise back in the day. I'm sure, if anyone knows where to find Hannah now, it will be Louise."

"I'm sure I don't know Louise," Bessie said.

Maggie laughed. "You do, though. Everyone on the island knows her. You just know her nickname rather than her real name. She's LouLar."

"LouLar?" Bessie echoed. "I never realised that was short for Louise Larkin. I also never realised that she worked in the shop in Kirk Michael. I only know her because of her charity work."

"She's been raising money for the Wildlife Park since it first opened. It's something of an obsession of hers."

"Yes, that's exactly how I'd describe it," Bessie chuckled. "I haven't seen her in years, but the last time I saw her she spent half an hour trying to persuade me to adopt a pelican. We don't cross paths very often, luckily."

"She must be over a hundred years old," Maggie speculated. "The last time I saw her, which was probably five years ago, she was still working part-time in the shop and still raising money for the animals. She knows everyone on the island, of course, but she doesn't gossip."

Bessie nodded. She'd heard the same about the woman, although she'd have put her age at closer to eighty than a hundred. "I don't suppose you know when she works at the shop?"

"Goodness, no. As I said, I haven't seen her in years. She used to work every morning, but I'm sure she's cut her hours now. She may even have retired, for all I know. She's still alive, though. We'd have heard about it if she'd passed away."

The pair chatted for a few more minutes about nothing much. Eventually, Maggie got to her feet.

"I need to get home. Thomas needs his medication and then he needs to be tucked up to bed. I suppose I should get some sleep, too."

"Give Thomas my best," Bessie told her. "Tell him I'm looking forward to seeing him down here one day soon."

Maggie nodded. "I'll tell him, but I wouldn't count on it being soon, if I were you."

Bessie gave her an awkward hug. "I'm sorry," she said.

Maggie nodded brusquely. "I'm sure I'll see you around," she said gruffly before she walked back up the beach.

It was getting late and growing colder. Bessie got down off the rock and headed inside, feeling chilled. She was snuggled under the duvet for several minutes before she began to feel warm again. Her last waking thoughts were worried ones about both Thomas and Maggie.

A steady rain was falling when she woke up the next morning. It didn't seem to improve while she was in the shower. After toast with honey, Bessie pulled on her waterproofs and took herself for a short, brisk walk. When she reached the last of the holiday cottages, she turned back towards home. There were puddles everywhere and walking through the sand was difficult. She got back to Treoghe Bwaane feeling as if she'd walked a good deal farther than she actually had. After a brief internal debate, she decided not to ring Anna Lambert right away, telling herself that she'd have more to share with her if she spoke to LouLar first.

Her taxi service promised to have a car at her cottage within an hour, leaving Bessie pacing back and forth while she waited. The driver who knocked on her door forty-three minutes later was a stranger to Bessie. He kept her entertained all the way to Kirk Michael with stories from his days as a London taxi driver.

"Just leave me at the shop," she instructed him. "I don't know how long I'll be, but I can ring for another car when I'm done here."

CHAPTER 10

"*E*lizabeth Cubbon," a voice said from somewhere as Bessie walked into the shop.

She looked around and then spotted the woman that everyone called "LouLar" in a chair in a corner of the room. Her grey hair was thin, caught up in a loose bun at the back of her head. As Bessie walked towards her, she decided that Maggie might be right. LouLar might well be close to a hundred years old. She was wearing thick glasses, and when she smiled, there were several gaps in the teeth.

"LouLar," Bessie replied. "How are you?"

"Old," LouLar replied. "Same as you. At least you're still getting around, anyway. My knees have both quit working, so I spend all my time stuck in chairs, either here or in my house."

"I'm sorry to hear that."

LouLar shrugged. "I'm still alive, that's the important thing. I'm still raising money for the animals, too. It's been my life's work."

"You've done a great deal of good, too."

"I hope so. I always thought I'd get married and have children, but I never managed to find a husband. I had a near miss when I was nineteen, but then someone better looking came along and he took off." She laughed. "I think I made a lucky escape with that one, really.

Anyway, I've had a good long life on my own, working here and helping the Wildlife Park. My doctor reckons I should have passed on years ago, but then he's my third G.P. because the first two died on me."

Bessie smiled. She'd outlived a few doctors herself. "I can't believe you're still working."

"Oh, I'm not, not really. If you actually want to buy anything, I'll shout for Clara. She's in the back, pretending to take stock while she texts her boyfriend. She's meant to come out when the door buzzer rings, but she ignores it most of the time."

"I came to speak to you anyway."

"I thought as much. There are plenty of shops between here and Laxey. We don't carry anything special."

"I don't know that I've ever been in here before," Bessie said as she glanced around the small room. "It's very well laid out."

"It's tiny, which means we have to make careful use of every inch of space. I used to rearrange everything at least once or twice a year, but no one bothers now. I dare say the customers are happier that way, anyway, even if it's boring for me."

"It's always good to be able to find what I want easily in a shop."

"Yes, but it's boring for the staff," LouLar laughed. "I read the local paper every day. I assume you've come to talk to me about Hannah Butler."

"I have. Janice Smith suggested that you might know where she is now."

"Janice Smith? My goodness, I'd completely forgotten about her. Let me think for a minute."

Bessie took a short tour of the room as the other woman squeezed her eyes shut, muttering "Janice Smith" under her breath. It didn't take Bessie long to decide that LouLar had been correct. The shop didn't stock anything different to what she could find anywhere on the island.

"She was a teacher," LouLar said triumphantly. "She came over from across, Birmingham, maybe. This was in the late sixties, if I remember rightly. She took a room in Kirk Michael without seeing it and then discovered it wasn't at all convenient."

"There's nothing wrong with your memory."

"She stayed in Kirk Michael for about six weeks, maybe eight. She used to come in nearly every day. I think she simply needed to talk to another adult after a day spent with small children. I was sorry to see her go when she moved, but I knew it would be better for her to be somewhere else."

"What can you remember about Hannah Butler, then?" Bessie asked.

LouLar sighed. "I've been thinking about her ever since I saw her name in the paper. I never would have thought of her as a possibility for what you found at Peel Castle, but once I read her name, it made sense."

"Why wouldn't you have thought of her?"

"I don't know. She was quiet and shy and I suppose I simply couldn't imagine her getting herself killed and hidden at Peel Castle."

"It might not have been murder. The police haven't determined what happened to her yet."

"Really? Dan Ross made it sound as if it was a murder investigation."

"Yes, well, you can't believe Dan Ross about anything."

LouLar laughed. "Don't I know it. He's all about eye-catching headlines. The articles themselves are usually incredibly disappointing, though. He never seems to know very much and he seems to speculate a great deal. I thought that Harrison Parker did a better job, but I understand he's moved back across already."

"That's what I've heard, as well. He wasn't here for very long."

"No, but his articles were much more interesting than Dan's usually are. Harrison always made everything sound exciting, even things like council meetings and business mergers."

"Apparently he did such a good job of it that he was offered a job across."

"And now we're stuck with just Dan again," LouLar sighed. "He actually comes in here fairly regularly to try to get information from me about anything that happens in this part of the island. I never tell him anything, of course."

"Has he been in to ask you about Hannah?"

"Not yet, but I'm sure he will be soon, unless he doesn't realise she used to work here."

"How was she to work with?"

"As I said, she was quiet. I always thought she was shy and not very happy, either. She only worked a few hours a week, maybe ten or fifteen during the busier times of the year. That was all that she needed, as first she lived with her parents and then she inherited the house and some money when they died."

"Was the house here, in Kirk Michael?"

"It was a few miles up the road, sort of in the middle of nowhere. She sold it after a while and then moved into a room in a house in the village here."

"Which house? Does it still have the same owners?"

LouLar laughed and then gave her the address. "You could probably walk there from here, actually. It isn't far. It's been in the Quayle family for generations. That's the Kirk Michael branch of the family, of course. Rosemary will probably remember Hannah, if she's having a good day. Her memory comes and goes a bit these days."

"Is that the same Rosemary Quayle who used to have a stall at the farmers' market in Laxey?"

"Sure is. The family has farm acreage all over the island. George and Agatha had four boys and their wives used to take things to all the different markets, including Laxey. Rosemary didn't like farming much, so she lived in the house here rather than staying on one of the farms. That didn't get her out of helping out, though."

"She would have been living there when Hannah lodged there, then?"

"Probably. George passed suddenly, and money became an issue for a while. That was why they took in lodgers, just for a few years. I'm pretty sure Rosemary and Junior were married before George passed. She may even have had a few babies by that time."

"Do you remember when Hannah left? Did she say anything about where she was going?"

LouLar shook her head. "She just came in one day and said she wouldn't be back. I asked a lot of questions, but she wouldn't answer any of them. She was polite about it, but distant, if you know what I mean. Now that I think about it, I didn't ask that many questions. I asked a few and she made it clear that she didn't think it was any of my business, so I let it drop. We didn't discuss it again."

"I don't suppose you remember the date?"

"I wish I did. I can narrow it down to a year and within a few months, but that's the best I can do. It was after TT, the summer of sixty-eight, I believe. She'd been staying at the Quayle place for about three months by that time."

"What about friends or boyfriends? Did she have a man in her life?"

"If she did, she kept very quiet about it. During TT, when we had extra staff on, she worked with some of the other younger girls. They were always talking about men, but I don't remember Hannah ever joining in the conversation. I don't know if she was shy or simply didn't have anything to add."

"Maybe she wasn't interested in men," Bessie mused.

"I think she was, actually. There was a man who used to shop here in those days who was very kind to her. She used to blush and stammer when he spoke to her. I suspect she was quite infatuated, really."

"What happened to him? Is he still on the island?"

"I've no idea. He didn't live in Kirk Michael. I believe he actually lived in Douglas, but whatever he did for a job used to bring him out this way once or twice a week. He used to come in here for cold drinks in the summer and tea in the winter. His name was Robert. I'm not certain I ever heard his surname."

"And you never asked?"

LouLar laughed. "I wasn't as nosy in those days. I talked to every-one, but I rarely asked questions. Besides, I always used to try to let

Hannah take care of him when he was here. I thought it would be good for her."

"When did he stop coming into the shop?"

"Oh, before Hannah left. Maybe three or four months before. I remember him telling me that we wouldn't be seeing him again for a while, actually. He was getting married and moving to the south of the island. His fiancée's family had a business down there, if I'm remembering correctly."

"What did Hannah say when she found out he was getting married?"

"Not much, as I recall. She wasn't here the day he told me. I mentioned it to her the next time I saw her and she just kind of shrugged."

"Did he come in again after that when Hannah was working?"

LouLar stared at her for a minute. "You can't actually expect me to remember that," she protested. "I thought I was doing well with what I've told you so far."

"You've done brilliantly well. I suppose what I was really asking was whether you remember any sort of upset the next time Hannah saw him."

"I would remember if there had been any upset, so that suggests that there wasn't, at least not when I was in the shop. Contrary to popular belief, I'm not here every minute that the shop is open, and I wasn't in those days, either. In fact, I used to come and go even more frequently in those days, what with my fundraising efforts and time spent with friends and whatnot."

"If there had been any unpleasantness, you would have heard about it, though," Bessie suggested.

"Yes, definitely. I was in charge of the shop assistants in those days. Anything that upset any of our staff would have been reported to me."

"And he stopped coming in months before Hannah left?"

"That's how I remember it. It was a long time ago, though. You don't think he killed her, do you?"

"I've no idea. I'd like to find him and talk to him about Hannah, though, if he's still alive."

"Hannah would be close to sixty now, and he wasn't much older than she was, so he's probably still alive. I'm not sure how you'll find him without a surname."

"Did Hannah have any female friends?"

"She was friendly with a few of the other girls in the shop, at least superficially, but she never really talked about her life. There was a girl, let me think for a minute." LouLar shut her eyes again and began to mutter under her breath. "Abigail, Anne, Agatha, Bertha, Betty, Barbara, Claire, Candy, Darlene, Denise, Debby, no, it was a flower, I think. Aster, Rose, Daisy. It was Daisy," she told Bessie. "Daisy Evans. Her parents had a cottage in the village and young Daisy used to come in nearly every day for odds and sods. She was another quiet one, but she and Hannah struck up a friendship. They used to go for long walks together."

"Does Daisy still live on the island?"

"Oh, no, her parents moved across right around the same time we're talking about, maybe a bit before. Daisy wasn't going to go with them, but in the end she decided she didn't want to stay on the island on her own."

"So Hannah's parents were killed in a fire and less than a year after that a man she may have had feelings for married someone else. At the same time, her only friend moved across. Do I have that all right?"

"It sounds right, and terribly sad when you put it that way. Hannah was quiet and shy, but I hope she wasn't suicidal."

"So do I," Bessie told her. "Do you know where Daisy and her family went?"

"Leeds, I believe."

Bessie sighed. "Evans is far too common of a surname for the police to ever track her down there."

"Maybe Rosemary Quayle will be able to tell you more. She might know where Daisy went. Maybe Hannah went across to join Daisy wherever she was. I'd like to believe that's a possibility."

"At this point, everything is a possibility. Can you tell me anything else about Daisy?"

"As I said, she was quiet and shy, too, just like Hannah. Not entirely like Hannah, though, as she had a man in her life. I remember her laughing with Hannah one day, talking about him. He was very upset about her moving away. Apparently he'd suggested that she marry him and remain here. From what I could overhear, Daisy didn't think the man was at all suitable for marrying. She planned on ending things with him when she left, or so she said at the time."

"I should be writing all of this down. I'm going to go and see Rosemary next, but the police need to try to find Robert if they can, and they need to look for Daisy Evans, too."

"I hope the body isn't Hannah's. She was a sweet girl and I'd hate to think that something horrible happened to her."

"As I said before, at this point the police aren't certain how the woman died or how she ended up at Peel Castle. It's possible she died of natural causes while exploring the tower, for instance."

"If it is Hannah, I hope that's what happened. She was planning on leaving the island, though. I've always imagined that she ended up in Australia, living in the outback in a little house all on her own."

"You said she never told you anything about where she was going or why she was leaving. Did she seem happy about leaving?"

"I don't know that happy is the right word. She was anxious for a few weeks, jittery and not quite herself, and then one day she came in and said she was leaving. She was much calmer. I assumed she was relieved because she'd made the decision to go, or maybe a job offer had come through or something along those lines."

"How much notice did she give you before she left?"

"On paper, it was a fortnight, but she had some holiday pay due to her, so I don't think she worked more than once or twice after the day she told me she was leaving. I probably asked her a few more questions about her plans on those days, but if I did, I'm certain she refused to answer."

"I think I need to go and talk to Rosemary," Bessie said.

"Good luck with that. Her son and daughter-in-law live with her now. I'm sure they'll talk to you, but he wasn't much more than a baby all those years ago and she's from across."

"You said Rosemary's memory isn't good?"

"It comes and goes. I saw her at a fundraiser for the wildlife park about three months ago and she knew who I was clearly enough to try to avoid me," LouLar laughed. "Which reminds me, have you ever considered adopting an animal? We have three new capybara babies who need sponsorship."

"You'd have to talk to my advocate. He handles all of my charitable donations for me," Bessie told her.

"You've been telling me that for years, but I'm sure you have some say in what you support."

"I do have some say, and I have given gifts to the wildlife park over the years. I'm not certain I want to support capybaras, though. They're giant rodents, aren't they?"

"Yes, but they're adorable, really. You should go and meet them."

"Perhaps, one day," Bessie said, turning towards the door. "Thank you for your time today. I appreciate it."

"I hope I was helpful. I don't like to talk about other people, but in this case, I was prepared to make an exception. I'd like to know what happened to Hannah. I'll feel much better if you find out she's alive and well."

"I keep hoping the police will find all of the women whose names have come up in the investigation alive and well. So far, two of them have, anyway."

"Dan Ross had five names on his list. Which two have been eliminated?"

"Meredith Houseman and Emma Gibson."

LouLar nodded. "Emma left with Janice, of course. I saw them together once and realised they were a couple. Are they still together?"

"They are. They've lived all over the world and Emma told me that they're very happy together."

"Good for them. Meredith probably just wanted to get away from her parents. They weren't very nice, really. Not that that husband of her was anything to brag about. If I were her, I'd have stayed behind in the UK, too."

Bessie nodded. "Any thoughts on Lauren Bell or Joselyn Owens?" she asked.

"You should ask Harold Newman about Lauren."

"Harold Newman?"

"He ran off with Lauren once, leaving his poor wife behind. He came back eventually, and his wife took him back, as well. I never understood why. He wasn't a great catch before he ran off with Lauren." She began to laugh heartily. "He ran a chippy," she said, laughing again. "That's why I said he wasn't a great catch."

Bessie nodded and smiled. She didn't think the remark was all that funny, but clearly LouLar found it hilarious. "I had heard that he was still on the island."

"He is, although I lost track of him when he sold the chippy."

"What about Joselyn Owens?"

"I don't know that I ever knew her. Oh, I've heard of her, of course. The paragraph about her in the paper was actually quite funny. It made the point that Joselyn got herself pregnant while her husband was away, without coming right out and saying that in so many words. Her husband, Sam, is still on the island, anyway. If anyone knows where she is, surely he should."

"She seems the most likely candidate for the body, in my opinion," Bessie said.

"You may be right. Hannah did tell me she was leaving. Of course, Sam might argue the same about Joselyn. I'm sure the police have a difficult job working out whom they can trust."

"No doubt. I'm glad that's their job and not mine."

LouLar laughed. "And yet here you are, asking me more questions than any police inspector I've ever met."

Bessie flushed. "Thank you for everything you've told me."

"Again, you're welcome. As it's past midday, we should have lunch together," LouLar said.

Bessie glanced at her watch. She hadn't realised it was that late. "Is there anywhere to eat nearby?" she asked.

"No, but that doesn't matter. Clara can make us sandwiches. She makes me lunch every day when I'm here."

Although she was eager to get away and talk to Rosemary, Bessie didn't feel as if she could refuse the offer. Clara was called out from the back of the shop and told to prepare lunch for two. While they ate, the two women chatted about their lives on opposite sides of the same small island.

"Thank you for lunch," Bessie said an hour later. "Now I must go and try to find Rosemary."

"You're welcome here anytime, even if you didn't buy anything," LouLar laughed.

A light rain was falling as Bessie began the short walk through the village to the address that LouLar had given her. While she walked, she thought about everything LouLar had said. Was it possible that a depressed and lonely Hannah Butler had committed suicide? If she had, how had her body ended up at Peel Castle? Hoping that Rosemary might have some answers, Bessie made her way up the short walkway to a large house that had clearly been there for hundreds of years. As she knocked on the door, she wondered if she could find an excuse to walk through some of the house. She wanted to see every inch of it, really.

"Can I help you?" The woman who opened the door was not old enough to be Rosemary.

"I'm looking for Rosemary Quayle," Bessie replied.

"Are you a friend of hers?"

"Not exactly. I live in Laxey, so I didn't know Rosemary well, but I was talking with LouLar about a woman she and Rosemary knew many years ago. I was hoping I could ask Rosemary a few questions about the matter."

"You're Elizabeth Cubbon, aren't you?"

"I am, yes."

"So this must be to do with the body you found at Peel Castle."

I didn't find it, Bessie thought to herself. It seemed better not to say it aloud, and risk getting the door shut in her face. "It is, yes," she said instead.

"Mother read about the body in the paper. It upset her a great deal."

"I'm sorry to hear that. I don't want to upset her."

145

"She knew one of the women, Hannah something. Is that who you are interested in speaking about with her?"

"Yes, that's right."

The woman frowned. "I don't know what to say, really. Some of the things Rosemary told me about Hannah might be relevant to the case, but I'd rather not see her upset again. At the same time, I'd prefer that she speak to you, rather than the police. She talks about you all the time, whenever you're in the papers."

Bessie frowned. She hated when she was in the papers. "I'm surprised she remembers me."

"She usually does, on her good days. She only reads the papers on her good days, as well. When she's having a bad day, she tends to keep to herself."

"Who is at the door?" a loud voice called imperiously.

The woman made a face and then turned around. "It's Elizabeth Cubbon."

"Bessie has come calling? Why haven't you let her in?" the other woman demanded.

"You'd better come in," the first woman sighed. She shut the door behind Bessie and then led her down a short corridor and through the first door. The sitting room was large and all of its furnishing appeared to be expensive antiques. The woman sitting in the corner next to a window, slowly got to her feet. It took her several seconds to shuffle forward to greet Bessie. Her grey hair was very short. Her blue eyes looked clear and focussed as she studied Bessie.

"Miss Cubbon, I haven't seen you in a great many years," she said.

Bessie took the offered hand, giving it a squeeze before releasing it. "Mrs. Quayle, you're looking well."

The other woman laughed. "I'm not, though, not well or looking well, actually. I know I look my age and then some. I blame the children. I had six of them, if you recall, and they were all difficult."

The other woman made a noise. When Rosemary looked over at her, she flushed. Rosemary laughed.

"You've met my daughter-in-law, then," Rosemary said. "She married Harold, which was a very foolish thing to do, in my opinion.

He was the worst of the lot, really, although I shouldn't say that as he takes rather good care of me now."

"I'm Eloise," the woman told Bessie.

"Oh, yes, I should have said that. You must call me Rosemary, of course, and I'll call you Bessie, because everyone does."

Bessie nodded. "Everyone does," she agreed.

"Sit," Rosemary ordered. "None of the chairs are very comfortable, but they're all very valuable and I can't persuade Harold to change them for anything that people would actually want to sit on for any length of time."

"You know Harold wants the furnishings to be in keeping with the age and style of the house," Eloise said in a tired voice. It was clearly an argument that had been had many times.

Rosemary glanced at her and then shrugged. "Try the couch," she told Bessie. "It's slightly less ghastly than the chairs."

Bessie sat down as directed. The couch was uncomfortable, which made her wonder just how bad the chairs were.

"Eloise, we need tea," Rosemary announced.

"Oh, I don't want to be any bother," Bessie said quickly.

"It's no bother," Rosemary said firmly. "It isn't often we get guests, especially not important guests. We must treat them properly."

"I don't think I'm at all important," Bessie protested.

"You've been in the papers over and over again for the past year or more," Rosemary countered. "I know you work with the police now on all of their important investigations."

"That isn't exactly true. I do sometimes help the police, but only in a very minor way," Bessie told her.

"Eloise, tea," Rosemary barked.

The other woman shot Bessie a nervous glance and then left the room.

"I don't want to talk in front of her. She fusses over me far too much," Rosemary explained. "You want to know about Hannah. I got rather upset when I saw her name in the paper. The idea that the body you found might have been hers, that someone murdered her just when she was about to start a new life, well, it was a shock more than anything." She pulled a tissue out of her pocket and dabbed at her eyes.

"The police aren't certain it was murder."

Rosemary looked surprised and then sighed. "They think she killed herself and then locked herself in a tower at Peel Castle? That seems quite far-fetched."

"There are dozens of possible explanations, including that she was exploring the castle and simply died of natural causes in the tower."

"She was healthy as a horse," Rosemary scoffed. "Oh, she was sad and tended to mope around, but physically she was healthy."

"You remember her well, then?"

"I do. She was our first lodger, not long after my father-in-law passed away. Money was tight and we needed a bit extra to keep things going. Taking in a lodger helped us pay the mortgage here. Some of Junior's brothers wanted to sell this house. There were several farms, you see, but I didn't want to live in a farmhouse. I wanted to live here. Anyway, I had the idea that we could rent out a room or two here. There are twelve bedrooms, you know. We didn't need them all, or even half of them."

"Twelve?" Bessie echoed, now even more eager to see the rest of the house.

"My husband's mother had a room, but she moved from house to house all the time, wearing out her welcome at each place as she went. Junior and I had a room, and we'd just had Harold, so we had a nursery. That left plenty of extra room for lodgers."

"How did you advertise?"

"We didn't advertise. We simply told a few people, including that LouLar woman at the local shop. It wasn't long before she was sending us potential lodgers."

"And Hannah was the first."

"She was the second, actually, who came to see about the rooms. She was the first we allowed to stay."

Bessie was curious about the other candidate, but she didn't ask. It wasn't her business, and she probably wouldn't have cared for the woman's reasons for turning the other man or woman down.

"She was selling her childhood home at the time and hadn't worked out what she wanted to do next. Her parents had died in a house fire, one she'd only just managed to escape herself. Part of the house was badly damaged, but she was still living there. I know she didn't get much when it sold because of the damage."

"How long was she with you?"

"Three months, maybe four. Towards the end of her stay, she came and told me that she was leaving, but she paid me for an additional couple of months to make up for the short notice."

"What did she tell you about her future plans?"

"Absolutely nothing. I asked, of course, but she just said she had plans that she preferred to keep to herself. In retrospect, I should have pushed her harder, but at the time it would have felt rude."

"Did she have many belongings?"

"She sold all of the furniture that was salvageable from her house. By the time she moved in here, she had one small suitcase and another bag for toiletries and things, and that was all. I felt quite sorry for her, really. I even offered her a few things, clothes I didn't wear any longer and that sort of thing, but she always politely refused."

"She took her suitcase and bag with her when she left, then?"

"Yes, of course."

"And she didn't leave you any forwarding address?"

"She did, actually. She gave me the name of her friend who lived across. I was meant to forward any post that came for her to the friend."

"I'm sure you don't still have the friend's information, but do you remember her name?" Bessie asked, almost holding her breath in hope.

"I do still have the friend's information," Rosemary told her with a smug smile. "I wrote it in my address book and I'm still using that same book today." She got up from her chair and slowly crossed the room to a small desk in the corner. It only took her a moment to find the black book.

"Daisy Evans," she read out. Bessie copied down the address that Rosemary had been given.

"If the police can track down Daisy, they might be able to find out what happened to Hannah," Bessie said. "Did you ever have to forward any post to Daisy?"

"Not a single thing," Rosemary said sadly.

"Tea," Eloise announced from the doorway.

CHAPTER 11

The three women talked about how much the island had changed in recent times as they sipped tea and ate crustless sandwiches and tiny cakes.

"How did you manage to put all of this together so quickly?" Bessie asked after a while, as Eloise passed around a platter full of biscuits.

"We have tea every afternoon," Rosemary told her. "It's a family tradition."

The look on Eloise's face suggested that it was a tradition that wasn't going to be continued once Rosemary was gone.

"Everything is delicious," Bessie added.

"Eloise does an adequate job," Rosemary conceded. "She's my favourite daughter-in-law, even if Harold is far from being my favourite child."

Eloise choked violently, presumably on words she couldn't say to her mother-in-law. She sipped her tea and then gave Bessie what appeared to be a fake smile. "I hope you and Rosemary enjoyed your chat."

"We did. She remembered quite a lot about Hannah. The police may want to talk with you as well," she added to Rosemary.

"How exciting. I've never spoken to the police before. Aside from the chief constable, of course. He's a family friend. I've never been questioned in a murder investigation, anyway."

"As I said, it may not have been murder," Bessie reminded her.

Rosemary waved a hand. "It sounds much better to say that I'm going to be questioned in a murder investigation than anything else. That's what I shall tell all of the children when I speak to them next."

Eloise rolled her eyes and took a large bite out of a biscuit. Bessie hid a grin behind her teacup.

"Can you tell me anything else about Hannah?" Bessie asked as she nibbled on the last of her tiny cakes.

"She was very quiet, the perfect lodger, really. She was home every night quite early, although she did sometimes sneak out."

"She did?" Bessie asked in surprise.

"Yes, it seemed out of character for her, but when I asked her about it she told me that she suffered from insomnia, so she often went for long walks when she couldn't sleep. She thought that was preferable to walking around the house and risking waking us or Harold, who was usually up in the middle of the night anyway. That child never slept, which is why I discovered that Hannah was sometimes sneaking out, you see."

Bessie nodded. "Do you think she was sneaking out to meet someone?"

Rosemary looked surprised by the idea. "Hannah? Whom would she have been meeting? The girl didn't say boo to a goose. It could only have been a man at that hour, in secret in that way. I can't imagine Hannah sneaking out to meet a man. She wasn't the type."

"Maybe she was meeting Daisy somewhere," Bessie suggested.

"Oh, no. I met Daisy on a handful of occasions. The girl was bright and sensible. I guarantee she wasn't sneaking out of her house at all hours to do anything. She worked very hard in a solicitor's office every day from eight to six. Hannah didn't work very many hours at all. That meant, if she needed them, she could have lazy days where she didn't get out of bed until ten or eleven."

Bessie nodded. "As I said, the police may want to speak to you. I should be going."

"Must you?" Rosemary asked. "I'm enjoying our conversation. I haven't felt this good in years."

"It's getting late and I need to ring Inspector Lambert and tell her what you've told me before she goes home for the night."

"Inspector Lambert?"

"She's an inspector at the Peel Constabulary," Bessie explained.

"Oh, dear. I don't want to talk to a woman," Rosemary said. "I've seen photographs of your Inspector Rockwell. He's lovely. I want to talk to him."

"The case is Inspector Lambert's to investigate."

Rosemary made a face. "I'm sure she's good at her job, but I'd much prefer talking to a man, especially a handsome young man. If Inspector Lambert comes, you must tell her that I'm unwell," she told Eloise.

Eloise gave her a stiff smile. "If you say so."

"I do say so. Tell her that I'm only prepared to talk to Inspector Rockwell because Bessie said he was the best."

"Don't drag me into this," Bessie protested. "I'm trying to help Inspector Lambert."

Rosemary shook her head. "At my age, I can be just as stubborn as my two-year-old granddaughter. Young, attractive men don't even notice me any longer. If I can get one hanging on my every word for half an hour, I'm going to do it."

Bessie chuckled. Rosemary clearly knew what she wanted. Too bad Bessie was the one who was going to have to explain the situation to John and Anna.

"I'll see you out," Eloise said as Bessie got to her feet.

"Thank you for your help," Bessie told Rosemary. "I've enjoyed talking with you."

"Likewise. You should visit more often."

"You're always welcome to visit me on Laxey Beach."

Rosemary grinned. "That's an invitation I might just take you up on, actually. I've never been to Laxey Beach, but I've heard a great deal about it. If I do come, you'll have to show me where you found your first body and then show me the holiday cottage where everyone keeps getting murdered. I could see the stairs to Thie yn Traie, too. I've read about them in the paper many times. Can you see much of Thie yn Traie from the beach?"

"Just the wall of windows at the back of the great room."

"That's a shame, as I probably wouldn't make it up the stairs," Rosemary sighed. "Eloise, when you come back from showing Bessie out, we must check my schedule and see when we can go to Laxey."

Eloise nodded and then led Bessie out of the room.

"I'll do everything I can to discourage her from visiting," Eloise said as they reached the front door.

"She's more than welcome, as are you," Bessie replied.

"That's kind of you, but Rosemary rarely leaves the house. She isn't as strong as she wants you to believe. Her memory isn't as good as it seems, either. It's possible she hasn't remembered things exactly right."

"It will be up to the police to work out what to believe. They're experts at dealing with witnesses."

"If they do want to speak with her, please have them arrange it through me so that I can be present when they're here. She did well today, but sometimes talking about the past upsets Rosemary."

"I'll see what I can do," Bessie promised.

She headed out the door. When she reached the street, she pulled out her mobile. Her favourite taxi company didn't have anyone in the area.

"It'll be about half an hour, maybe a bit longer," the dispatcher told her apologetically. "There's a taxi rank near the shop there. Maybe you can find a taxi there."

Bessie thanked her and then walked back to the shop. There were two taxis at the rank and Bessie happily climbed into the first one. When she gave the driver her address, he stared at her blankly.

"Treoghe Bwaane? Never heard of it."

"It's on Laxey Beach."

"I can find that," he promised.

He did find it, but by the most circuitous route that Bessie thought she'd ever taken. She didn't complain when he told her what she owed him for the journey, because she'd seen parts of the island along the way that she thought she'd never seen before. That had to be worth something, she reckoned.

At home, she rang Anna Lambert to tell her about her day.

"If you could have John speak to Rosemary Quayle, I think he'd get better results," she concluded.

"I can arrange that," she replied. "What are you planning to do next?"

"I thought I might see if I could find Harold Newman."

"I've spoken to him and to his wife. She wasn't best pleased, talking about Lauren Bell, but they both denied having any idea what happened to her."

"Any idea where I might find him?"

"He has a small café in Onchan. It does tea and coffee and cakes and not much else. He told me he got tired of fish after so many years, but he wasn't ready to retire. His son really runs the place, but he works there a few mornings a week. His wife works there as well, but she doesn't work every day. She won't be there tomorrow, or so I was told."

"So if I were to go in for a cuppa tomorrow morning, he would probably be there, but she wouldn't. That might be for the best."

"I'm sure it would. It's been thirty-odd years since her husband's affair, but she still hasn't forgiven him."

"I don't blame her, really, although I do wonder why she took him back if she was that bothered about the affair."

"She gave me her version of events. It more or less matched his. We can discuss it further after you've spoken to them," Anna said.

"I don't expect to speak to her," Bessie replied. "What's her name?"

"She's Angela, and you may end up wanting to speak to her."

"I'm intrigued now. I'm definitely going for a cuppa tomorrow."

"Thank you for everything you've shared with me. I'm going to have someone interview Louise Larkin for me and if I can, I'll have John talk to Rosemary Quayle and her daughter-in-law. Hannah seems unlikely to me, but we've already eliminated two of our five candidates."

"Tracking down Daisy Evans might be useful," Bessie said.

"I'll have one of my counterparts in Leeds get to work on that. If she got married and moved away, we might not be able to find her, but maybe we'll get lucky."

"I hope so. She may well be the key to finding out what happened to Hannah."

Bessie put the phone down. There were still a few hours to go before dinner, and she found herself feeling restless. What she really wanted to do was find Harold Newman, but Anna had said he worked mornings at his café.

A short walk in the rain didn't improve her mood. Back at home, she headed up to her office and pulled out Onnee's letters. She was already feeling inexplicably cross with the world. Finding out that Onnee's baby had died couldn't make her feel much worse.

An hour later, she had two more letters carefully transcribed. Now she sat back and read through them. When Doona rang, she couldn't help but tell her what she'd discovered.

"I was just ringing to see how you are," Doona said.

"I've just been working on Onnee's letters. Did I tell you that she'd had her baby, but things went wrong in the delivery room and the doctors told her that the baby wasn't going to survive?"

"Yes, and if the baby died, please don't tell me."

"The baby didn't die, at least not yet," Bessie said happily. "In fact, the baby seems to be doing incredibly well. Onnee reports that she's feeding well and has begun smiling at her when she talks to her. The letters were cautiously optimistic, anyway. Clarence is still spending all of his spare time with Faith, but Onnee's too busy with the baby to care at the moment."

"That's good news. I wish we could get some good news."

"Nothing new on Sue?"

"Not really. She rang last night and talked to John for half an hour. He said she was completely lucid. She apologised for being ill and for not returning as scheduled, but insisted that she'll be back soon and that the children will have to return to Manchester with her as soon as she returns."

"Oh, dear."

"John pointed out that they're in the middle of the school year and can't just drop everything to move back to Manchester, but she refused to discuss any other alternative. She told John that Harvey is completely behind her decision and that he'll use every penny he has to drag John through the courts if he fights them."

"My goodness. Did John talk to Harvey at all?"

"No. Harvey is angry that the police are investigating. It's still an active investigation, as well. John got the impression that something was happening behind the scenes there, but he couldn't work out exactly what."

"Maybe Andrew has done something."

"That was John's thought, too. Anyway, I've told John that I'm prepared to use every penny that I have to help him fight back. I've no need for the money and I'd love to see it get put to good use. He's insisting he won't take my money, but I'm sure he'll change his mind if it means keeping his kids where they belong."

"Do the kids know about any of this?"

"Luckily they weren't home when Sue rang. John told them both, after the conversation, that their mother was hoping to take them back to Manchester when she returned. They both told him that they don't want to go."

"What a horrible mess. I'm glad John has you on his side."

"I just hope Sue truly is recovering and is actually going to come home soon. Even if there's a long and horrible legal battle over the children, that's better than all this uncertainty."

"Surely the children are old enough to have some say in where they go?"

"We believe so, but John is worried that the courts will feel that Manchester is better for them, as that was their home for most of their lives. They have family there, and history."

"Their father is here. That has to count for something."

Doona sighed. "Until Sue gets back, there doesn't seem to be much we can do. John is meeting with Doncan in a few days to talk through his options. We want to be prepared for whatever Sue does."

"Good for him. I'm sure Doncan will be able to help." The advocate was one of the smartest men Bessie knew. If anyone could help John win custody of the children, it was Doncan.

"Let's talk about other things. What did you do today?"

Bessie told Doona all about her trip to Kirk Michael. "Tomorrow I'm going to visit the café in Onchan where Harold Newman works," she added at the end.

"I have the morning off. If you're going in the morning, may I come along? They have cake, I know they do."

Bessie laughed. "You're more than welcome, of course."

They agreed that Doona would collect Bessie around nine before Bessie put the phone down.

Another short walk and a light dinner filled the next hour. After that, Bessie curled up with a book of logic puzzles and spent a few happy hours solving several of them. When she put the book down, she sighed.

"You've done all the easy ones now. Next time you'll have to try a more difficult one," she told herself in a low voice.

Grabbing the mystery she was halfway through, she went upstairs and got ready for bed. She read until her eyes refused to stay open any longer and then switched off her light and went to sleep.

It was another rainy day when she got up the next morning. Frowning, she made herself porridge for breakfast, which only darkened her mood. As she ate her way through the bowl, she reminded herself that porridge was good for her. That didn't make it taste any better, though. As she washed her breakfast dishes, she wondered how porridge with chocolate sauce would taste.

"Hello, Bessie," Thomas Shimmin called from the back of the very last holiday cottage as Bessie walked past.

She stopped and then walked up the beach to join him on the cottage's patio. As she approached, she did her best to hide her shock. The man was a shadow of his former self, looking gaunt and drawn as he leaned on the sliding door while he waited for Bessie.

"How are you?" she blurted out as a greeting.

He chuckled. "I'm actually better than I look," he assured her. "I've battled my way through pneumonia, a secondary infection, the flu, and a few other things I can't even remember. I know I look horrible, but I'm actually feeling better than I have in months."

"That's good to hear."

"I feel horrible about leaving so much for poor Maggie. She's been working all the time, and you know Maggie, she never complains." His words were accompanied by a knowing wink.

Bessie laughed. "I have seen a great deal more of her than is typical. She said something about having to paint the cottages."

"That's why I'm here. We're storing all the paint in this cottage. It's good for storage, even if we can't rent it out any longer."

"I thought you were having it torn down?"

"We are, eventually, but for now, it's going to hold all the cans of paint and brushes and rollers and everything. We're having security systems fitted to every cottage, including this one, as well."

"Since this is the one that keeps getting broken into, that seems sensible."

"We got a good price on the systems, so adding an extra one didn't add much to the bottom line. We thought if we put security on all of them except this one, it would simply encourage people to break in here even more."

"You're probably right."

"Anyway, I brought down everything we need to paint and I'm very slowly moving it into this cottage. The men from the security firm are starting tomorrow, so if you see them around, don't worry."

"Thanks for letting me know."

Thomas nodded. "I'd better get back to work. Maggie will worry if I'm gone too long."

"I'm surprised she isn't helping you."

"She was going to help, but she's put her back out. The doctor has her on bed rest for twenty-four hours and she isn't allowed to lift or move anything for a week. It will probably drive her to distraction."

"Good luck," Bessie said.

"I'm going to need it," Thomas laughed.

Back at Treoghe Bwaane, Bessie only had a few minutes to get ready before Doona was due to arrive. It took some effort, but Bessie managed to keep the conversation away from Sue for the entire drive into Onchan. The small café had an equally small car park. Doona parked in the only empty space.

"I hope it isn't too busy," Bessie said. "I want a nice long talk with Harold Newman."

When she pushed open the café's door, she smiled to herself. There were only two other customers, a couple sitting in one corner talking intently with one another.

"Have you ever been here before?" Bessie asked Doona as Doona headed for a table near the back of the room.

"Several times. I lived in Onchan for a short while. I haven't been here in many years, though. They used to do wonderful cakes."

Bessie sat down across from Doona and looked around the room. Everything was clean and tidy, but the place looked tired and in need of freshening up. The door in the back wall swung open and a man walked out.

As he approached their table, Bessie studied him. She would have put his age at about sixty-five, maybe seventy. The little hair that he had left was grey and his shoulders were stooped. He shuffled a bit when he walked, but his smile was bright as he greeted them.

"Good morning. It's nice to see some unfamiliar faces for a change. We tend to get nothing but regulars in here," he said.

"I used to be something of a regular," Doona told him, "before I moved to Laxey."

"And you're Elizabeth Cubbon." The man nodded at Bessie. "I've seen your picture in the paper a great deal. Everyone knows about Aunt Bessie, anyway, but the pictures let me put a face to the name."

"It's nice to meet you," Bessie said.

He grinned. "I'm Harold Newman. I'd be willing to bet that you've come in especially to see me."

"I wouldn't mind having a word with you, actually," Bessie told him. "I'm sure you know that the police are trying to track down Lauren Bell."

He nodded and then looked nervously towards the kitchen. "If I suddenly change the subject, it will be because my son is in earshot. If he hears that woman's name, he'll ring my wife and she'll come down."

"And that's a bad thing?" Bessie asked.

Harold gave her a tight smile. "I'd just rather not upset her again."

"What cakes do you have today?" Doona changed the subject.

Harold rattled off a short list that made Bessie's stomach growl.

"I'll have the chocolate gateau," Doona said. "It's a bit early in the day, but it's never a bad time for chocolate, really. And a cup of tea, too, please."

"Victoria sponge for me," Bessie added, "and tea."

Harold nodded. "I'll get that sorted for you and then we can chat."

As the women waited, the couple across the room got up and left.

"And you were worried it would be busy," Doona said softly.

"We'll just have to talk very quietly so Harold's son doesn't ring his mother."

"Here we are," Harold said a moment later, delivering tea and generous slices of cake to the table.

"This looks lovely," Bessie exclaimed.

"I've told Herman that you used to be a regular and that I was going to join you for a chat as it isn't busy," he said as he sat down between the women.

"Herman?" Bessie asked.

"My son. He runs the café. I just work here. We try to treat it as if we aren't related, so this chat will constitute my official morning break."

"Which probably isn't too long. We should talk fast," Doona suggested.

"Oh, Herman won't care if we talk for hours, as long as there aren't any other customers in here. He'd do the same with any employee, not just me."

"What can you tell us about Lauren Bell, then?" Bessie asked before taking a bite of her cake.

"She was the biggest mistake of my life," Harold replied, shaking his head. "I was married to a wonderful woman. We had the chippy and we'd worked really hard together to make it a success. Harold was a baby and we were talking about having another child. Then, one day, Lauren walked into the chippy and I lost my mind." He stopped speaking and stared off into space.

"This is very good," Bessie said after a long pause.

"The cake? Thank you. My wife bakes them all herself," Harold said. "She didn't even know she enjoyed baking until we got rid of the chippy and bought this place. Turns out she's great at making cakes, and now she's starting to try her hand at pies."

"Pies? Maybe next time," Doona said.

"But you were saying," Bessie said encouragingly.

"Oh, I was admitting to being an idiot," he sighed. "I met Lauren and I forgot about everything that matters. It only took her a few weeks to convince me to run away with her. She was just desperate to get off the island, of course. She didn't really care about me at all."

"I'm sorry," Bessie said.

"Thank you, but your sympathy is misplaced. I deserved everything I got for leaving Angela and Herman as I did. We went across and I thought we were going to start a new life together, but she wasn't interested in working. She wanted to keep moving around, living off of the money I'd been saving for other things. Sadly, it took me a few months to realise that I was being used. By that time I'd spent about half of my savings. There was no way I could come back to the island under those conditions, so I found myself a job and I worked every single hour that I could until I'd replaced every penny that Lauren had spent. Then I came back and begged Angela to forgive me."

"What happened to Lauren?" Bessie asked.

"We split up when I realised what she really wanted from me. We were in Milton Keynes at the time and she stayed there for a short while." He blushed and then leaned forward towards Bessie. "She stayed in the flat I rented for another month or two, but only because she didn't have anywhere else to go. We weren't still together by that point." He sat back and sighed.

Bessie took a sip of her tea. "Where did she go next?"

"I'm not sure. One day she came back to the flat and told me she was leaving. She said she'd found herself a real man with real money and that she was off to travel the world. I wished her good luck. I didn't think I'd ever see her again."

"But you did?" Doona asked.

"When I finally got back to the island, I was surprised to learn that she was already back here. Apparently we moved back within a few days of one another. My wife didn't want to believe me that we'd split up months before, but in the end, she took me back anyway."

"Lauren didn't stay on the island for long, though," Bessie remarked.

Harold shook his head. "She was only here for a few months, maybe not even that long. Then she left again."

"Do you know why she left?" Bessie asked.

He glanced around the room and then shook his head. "I never spoke to her again, not after I got back to the island," he said in a rush.

Bessie glanced at Doona. Harold was lying, she was sure of it.

"Can you imagine how she might have ended up in the tower at Peel Castle?" Bessie asked.

Harold looked shocked. "I know that's why you're looking for her, but there's no way that skeleton was her."

"How can you be so certain?" Bessie wondered.

"She left of her own accord," he replied.

"That may be what you were told, but if you never spoke to her, you can't be certain. Maybe she got involved with another married man and he killed her and left her body at the castle."

"I'm sure she got involved with another married man, but they left the island together," Harold said.

"How can you be sure? Do you know the man's name or where they went?" Bessie challenged.

Harold flushed. "No, of course not. That was just Lauren, though. She hated the island and she was oddly attracted to married men."

"Maybe she chose the wrong one to get involved with this time," Doona said. "If the man she was having the affair with didn't kill her, maybe his wife did."

"I don't think so," Harold said stiffly. "I'm sure she's absolutely fine, living somewhere in the UK with whomever she ran away with all those years ago."

"Given her track record with relationships, I'd be very surprised if she's still with the same man," Bessie said dryly. "If she was absolutely fine, why hasn't she stayed in touch with her family?"

"They disowned her because of me," Harold said sadly. "They were very religious, her mother and father. When she came back, they wouldn't see her or even speak to her on the telephone. She ended up staying with some distant cousins for a short while until she left again."

"If she left again," Bessie said softly.

Harold opened his mouth and then snapped it shut. "I should go and see if Herman needs any help in the kitchen," he said, getting to his feet.

"He's hiding something," Doona said as the kitchen door swung shut behind him.

"He stayed in touch with Lauren after their relationship ended. That's the only thing that makes sense," Bessie replied.

"He knew all about what happened to her once she got back to the island, even though he claimed he didn't even know she was here."

"Exactly, and he's far too confident that she's alive and well. He must know where she is now."

"We just have to find a way to get him to tell us," Doona sighed.

"Maybe not. Maybe we can get him to get Lauren to ring Anna. That might be easier for everyone."

"Maybe. The cake is wonderful, anyway."

"It's excellent. I'm going to have to start coming in here more often."

"It's just a bit too far from home to be convenient, and I don't often visit Onchan."

"No, I don't, either," Bessie agreed.

"The park is nice. I brought the kids down for a round of crazy golf the other day. We had fun."

Bessie nodded. She opened her mouth to reply, but stopped when the outside door swung open. The woman who walked into the café glanced around and then frowned at Bessie. She crossed the room and then dropped into the chair that Harold had vacated.

She looked to be of a similar age to Harold. Her grey hair was pulled into a tight bun on the top of her head, and her eyes were red-rimmed as if she'd been crying. She stared at Bessie for a moment and then sighed.

"I'm Angela Newman. I understand you've been talking to Harold about that woman I shall not name."

CHAPTER 12

*B*essie nodded slowly. "The police are trying to determine if she might be the woman whose skeleton was found at Peel Castle."

"I should be so lucky," Angela snapped. "There's no way that woman is dead. Evil doesn't die."

"Angela? What are you doing here?" Harold demanded as he walked out of the kitchen.

"Herman rang me. He said you were talking about that woman again."

"You know how Aunt Bessie is always getting involved in these things. She came in especially to ask me about Lauren."

Angela stiffened. "We had an agreement."

"I'm sorry," he replied quickly. "I didn't mean to say her name. I was just discussing her with Bessie, that's all."

"You're Laxey's Aunt Bessie?" Angela asked.

"Yes, I am."

"You look older in your photographs."

Bessie wasn't certain how to reply to that remark.

"What has Harold told you, then?" Angela asked after a moment.

"I told them the whole miserable story," Harold replied. "They were really only interested in where she is now, though. Of course, I couldn't help them."

"Couldn't? Or wouldn't?" Angela shot back. "You know exactly where she is, don't you?"

Harold flushed. "You know I haven't spoken to her since we split up thirty-odd years ago."

"It was thirty-three years, three months, four days, and," she glanced at her watch, "four hours ago, based on what you told me when you came back to the island."

"There you are, then," Harold said, staring at the ground.

Angela looked over at Bessie. "You never married, did you?"

"No, I did not."

"What about you?" she asked Doona.

"I've been married twice, but I'm single now," Doona replied.

"You're both smarter than I am," Angela said. "I was foolish to get married in the first place. I had a bit of money. My parents both passed away in the same year and they left me a small house and a few bank accounts. I suddenly found that I was considerably more attractive to men."

"It wasn't like that," Harold protested.

"He was the most persistent," Angela said, nodding at Harold. "I thought he meant all the pretty words he said. We used my inheritance to buy the chippy. He didn't have a penny to his name when we met."

"That's not fair. I'd worked hard and I'd saved some money before I met you. I spent most of my savings courting you, remember?"

Angela laughed harshly. "And I spent every penny I had setting you up in business." She glanced at Bessie. "I fell pregnant almost immediately. That hadn't been in the plans, but I was pleased. He wasn't."

"I wanted to get the business up and running before we started our family. That was what we agreed on when we got married," Harold said.

"He nearly left me when I told him about the baby. I should have let him go. I had the idea, though, that I needed him," Angela sighed.

"I needed you," Harold said.

Angela looked at him for a minute and then shook her head. "He needed my money and he needed me working at the chippy so that he didn't have to hire anyone else. I worked there until the week before Herman was born and went back to work when Herman was ten days old. We had a cot in the corner and I used to feed him in between customers."

"I did try to find someone to take your place so you could stay home with Herman," Harold protested.

"But you never did. Instead, you left," Angela retorted.

"How many times do I have to apologise for that?" Harold asked. "I'm sorry. Laur, er, that woman mesmerised me, put me under some sort of spell or something. I've told you a million times that I'm sorry and that she was the biggest mistake of my life. I'm sorry."

"We never talk about her," Angela told Bessie. "I hadn't even thought about her in years, really. Now, with the body at Peel Castle, she's all over the papers and I can't stop thinking about her."

"If the police can find her, they'll cross her off the list and she'll fade back to obscurity," Bessie suggested.

"I know Harold knows where she is now. He's been lying to me for years, but I know he's kept in touch with her. Tell them," she said to Harold.

"I don't know what you're talking about," he muttered, staring at the wall.

"Look at me," Angela commanded. After a moment, he looked up and met her cold stare. "You lied to the police, just the same as you've been lying to me for all these years. If you tell Bessie what you know, at least I won't have to see her name in the papers any longer."

"I told you I haven't spoken to her in years," he protested.

"That's a conversation we can have later," she replied. "I'm looking forward to listening to you try to explain why you've kept in touch with her and why you've lied to me about it for over thirty years."

"I haven't kept in touch, exactly," Harold said slowly. "I truly haven't spoken to her in many years, but I do know a bit about where she went and where she might be now."

"Tell Bessie," Angela said.

"She left the island with a man called Liam Pearce. He was over here on a short-term work contract, just for six weeks or so. It wasn't long enough for him to bring his wife and their three children along."

Angela inhaled sharply. "She took a man with three children away from his wife?" she asked angrily.

"Yes," Harold replied softly. "I don't know the whole story, just bits of it, really. I did my best to avoid Lau, er, that woman, but sometimes she'd come into the chippy when she knew that I would be alone there."

Angela made a noise. "The nerve," she snapped.

"Yes, I told her not to come in, but she never listened to me. She used to bring Liam in with her. I think she wanted to flaunt him in front of me for some reason. He was a very senior executive with his company. He had a fancy car and expensive suits, where I always smelled of fish and chips."

"Nothing wrong with that," Angela interjected.

Harold shrugged. "She came in alone one day to tell me she was leaving. She said that she didn't have anyone else on the island to tell, as her family wouldn't talk to her anymore, but she wanted someone to know where she'd gone. I believe she thought that, in spite of everything, that she might inherit her parents' money one day. She wanted to be sure that someone would be able to find her if she did."

"She could have left an address with her parents' advocate," Angela said.

"She could have, but she didn't," Harold shrugged. "She told me that she was going with Liam and that he was going to set her up with a flat in London."

"Behind his wife's back, of course," Angela interjected.

"I believe so," Harold replied.

"Have you heard from her since?" Bessie asked.

"She sends odd notes and postcards," Harold admitted, glancing at Angela and then looking away, his face beetroot red.

"To where?" Angela demanded.

"To the chippy," he replied. "I haven't had any in a while, but the new owners used to ring me whenever anything turned up."

"The police will want to see the notes and postcards," Bessie said.

"I don't keep them," Harold said quickly. "I can remember the address she gave me, though, where she said I could write back to her." He gave Bessie an address in London. She wrote it down carefully.

"How often do you write to her?" Angela demanded.

"I don't write to her," he replied.

"You have the address memorised," she said. "That only happens if you use it repeatedly."

He flushed. "I sent her a note now and then, years ago," he said after a moment. "It seemed rude not to reply when she was writing to me, you see."

"I don't see. You promised me that you wouldn't have anything to do with that woman ever again."

"I never meant to hurt you. As I said before, she cast a spell on me, one that still affects me even now," he replied sadly.

Angela nodded and got to her feet. "Tell the police what Harold has told you," she said to Bessie. "I hope they find her alive and desperately unwell." She turned and swept out of the café. Bessie and Doona watched the door close behind her.

"How was everything?" Harold asked after a minute.

"Good," Bessie replied. She took out her wallet and pulled out a twenty pound note. "This should cover it, I hope," she said.

"Let me get you some change," Harold replied.

"Not necessary," Bessie said. She got to her feet and walked to the door, with Doona on her heels. They were back in the car before Bessie spoke again.

"I'm sorry about rushing out in that way, but I didn't want to spend another minute with that man. I'm not certain I could have been polite to him."

"I can't believe he stayed in contact with Lauren and lied to his wife about it," Doona replied.

Bessie sighed. "I think Angela was correct. I feel fortunate that I've never been married."

The drive back to Laxey didn't take long. Bessie rang Anna immediately.

"Why didn't he tell me all of this?" she demanded after Bessie had repeated everything that had been said in the Onchan café.

"He thought he could get away with lying," Bessie suggested. "I don't think he would have told us if his wife hadn't confronted him."

"I interviewed them separately," Anna sighed. "That's usually the best way to get one half of a married couple to tell his or her secrets."

"Never mind. I just hope you can find Lauren Bell so we can cross her off the list," Bessie said.

"The list is getting shorter and shorter. I have a lead on Daisy Evans, by the way. If I've found the right woman, she's Daisy Eckles now."

"That just leaves Joselyn to track down. Surely Sam knows where to find her?"

"He refused to speak with me," Anna told her. "He's a man of some wealth and influence on the island, so I have to tread carefully. I made an appointment to see him, and he was perfectly polite, right up until I mentioned Joselyn. He seems to think that I should take his assurances that she's fine as fact, even though he's not prepared to provide any proof."

"I'm going to have to see if I can find a way to talk to him," Bessie mused. "I wonder if Mary knows him."

"If you're talking about Mary Quayle, I believe she knows everyone," Anna said.

Bessie chuckled. "You could be right about that."

She put the phone down and then picked it up again, dialling the number for Thie yn Traie from memory.

"The Quayle residence." The man who'd answered the phone had a deep voice that sounded authoritative.

"It's Elizabeth Cubbon. I was wondering if Mary was available?"

"Aunt Bessie?" The voice changed completely. "How are you, my dear? I saw in the papers that you'd found another body. How awful for you."

"It was pretty awful, but at least this one wasn't recently murdered," Bessie replied. "But how are you, Jack?" she asked.

Jonathan Hooper had grown up on the island, and to Bessie he'd always be "Jack," the young boy with the ginger hair who'd scraped his knees on Laxey Beach daily throughout the summer months. As the butler at Thie yn Traie, he was known as Jonathan, and he had the necessary accent and proper training to go along with the position. Bessie knew that Mary thought he was the best butler they'd ever employed. Bessie was just delighted that he was back on the island after several years of living across.

"I'm very well, thank you. Mr. and Mrs. Quayle have very kindly offered to send me for some additional training at their expense. I'm quite looking forward to that, although it isn't for some months yet."

"What sort of training?"

"It's a course in modern security and technology. Mr. and Mrs. Quayle employ an outside firm to handle security here and at the Douglas house. That will continue, but the course should give me a better understanding of how the systems work. Additionally, the family is hoping to integrate more technology into the household, including the use of wireless networks and household servers."

"I didn't understand most of that," Bessie laughed.

"I'm not sure that I do, but I will once I've taken these classes."

"When do you go?"

"We haven't booked the course just yet. Mum hasn't been well for a few weeks, so we're waiting to be certain that she's on the road to recovery before I go away."

"I shall have to go and see her," Bessie exclaimed. "Is she well enough for visitors?"

"I'd say so. She's bored to bits, actually, stuck at home. She'd been battling a cold all winter, and that turned into flu and then pneumonia. She's been on antibiotics for a fortnight now, though. I'm sure she'd love some company."

Bessie made a note to go and visit the woman. "I'll try to get to see her this week," she promised.

"And after all of that, Mrs. Quayle isn't even home," Jack laughed.

"Just ask her to ring me when she has a minute. It isn't anything important."

"Is it about your body from Peel Castle?" Jack asked.

"It isn't my body," Bessie said tightly.

"Of course not. I didn't mean it that way at all."

"I was wondering if she knew someone who is tangentially tied to the investigation, that's all."

"I shouldn't ask, but if you don't mind telling me, in whom are you interested?"

"Sam Owens."

"Oh, him," Jack replied. "Mrs. Quayle does know him, or rather, he's been to the house, but I don't think she's very fond of him. You'd be better off talking to Mr. Quayle about Mr. Owens."

"Really?"

"They did some business together years ago. It must have been reasonably successful because they still get together for golf at least three or four times a year, or so I understand."

"Interesting."

"Should I have Mr. Quayle ring you, then?" Jack asked.

"Yes, please, if you think he might be able to help."

"Actually, I may have an even better idea, but leave it with me for a short while. I'll ring you back, or someone will."

"What does that mean?" Bessie demanded as the phone went dead in her hand.

Sighing, she replaced the receiver and then made a face at it. When that did nothing to improve the situation, she made herself an early lunch. A brisk walk on Laxey Beach in a strong wind made her feel better. She walked past Thie yn Traie, intent on walking as far as the new houses, but the wind kept pushing her back, as if it wanted to blow her home. Eventually, she conceded to nature and turned back around.

"Bessie, I knew I would find you out here," a voice called from somewhere above her as she was pushed back down the beach towards home.

She stopped and looked up at the stairs to Thie yn Traie. "Elizabeth, my dear, be careful on those stairs in this wind."

"It's fine," Elizabeth replied carelessly. She dashed down the last few steps and then jumped down onto the beach. "It is quite the wind, though, isn't it?"

"Come back to Treoghe Bwaane with me so we can both get indoors," Bessie suggested.

"I will, thank you," Elizabeth replied. She tucked her arm into Bessie's and they walked back to Bessie's cottage together. Inside the cottage's door, Elizabeth finger-combed her long blonde hair and then pulled it all back into a quick ponytail.

"I should have done that before I went out," she laughed.

Bessie put water in the kettle and then switched it on. "Biscuits?" she asked.

"I shouldn't," the girl replied, wrinkling her nose. "I've put on nearly a stone since I've been seeing Andy and it doesn't seem to be coming off, even though he's away at the moment."

Bessie grinned. Andy Caine was away at culinary school, learning everything he was going to need to know in order to open his own restaurant. It was his lifelong dream, and a substantial and completely unexpected inheritance had made that dream possible. He and Elizabeth had only recently started seeing one another, but they seemed well suited as far as Bessie was concerned. Andy's difficult upbringing made him appreciate the money that he now had, and he seemed to be teaching Elizabeth to realise just how privileged her own upbringing had been.

"I thought he was due back soon," Bessie said.

"He's taking an extra class, which means one more month away," Elizabeth sighed. "It's on dealing with difficult staffing issues, like terminating someone who isn't doing his or her job properly. I know Andy needs the class, because he's far too nice and won't ever want to get rid of anyone, but I really wish he'd come home."

"You may not feel that way when he's here all the time," Bessie pointed out.

Elizabeth frowned. "My mother says that all the time. I know you're both right, but I hate thinking that all we had was a brief romance. I really care for Andy a lot and I'm hoping we might have a future together."

Bessie was surprised to hear Elizabeth put those thoughts into words. She knew the girl cared for Andy, but she hadn't realised that Elizabeth was that serious about the man. "You're both still young," Bessie reminded the girl, who was in her mid-twenties. "Take your time and make sure you're certain before you do anything permanent."

Elizabeth nodded. "Andy keeps saying that we can't even talk about marriage until we've been in the same place together for at least a year. He's far more sensible than I am. I'd marry him tomorrow if he asked."

And be divorced before that year was up, Bessie added to herself. "Did you want to talk to me about Andy?" she asked as she made tea.

"Oh, no, not at all," the girl laughed. "I wanted to talk to you about Sam Owens."

"Oh?" Bessie replied as she set a plate full of biscuits on the table.

Elizabeth grabbed one and took a big bite before she replied. "Jonathan said you wanted to speak to him."

"I do, yes, but I don't think he wants to speak to me."

"Too bad for him," Elizabeth giggled. "He's coming to Thie yn Traie at eleven to talk to me. You should be there."

"Why is he coming to talk to you?"

"He wants to have some sort of party, although that might be too grand a word for what he's planning. Really, he just wants to have a few people at his house for drinks and snacks. He's no idea how to plan that, though."

"So you're going to plan it for him."

"Exactly. I won't even charge him much for my time as it will only take a few minutes to arrange everything."

"You should charge him less if you're setting him up for a conversation he doesn't want to have, as well," Bessie suggested.

Elizabeth laughed. "Maybe I will, at that."

"I don't want to upset him to the point where he decides not to use your services."

"I don't mind in the slightest if he does. As I said, I wouldn't be charging him much anyway, and I don't much like him, either."

"Why not?"

"I should have known better than to say that to you. I should have known you'd want to know why and I'm not sure I can tell you. There's just something about him that I don't like. He's cold. Maybe that's the best word for him. Haven't you ever met him?"

"I'm sure I have, once or twice, but I don't really remember anything about him."

"I'm sure he'd be delighted to hear that. I think he prefers to go through life as anonymously as possible."

"The situation with his wife must be very upsetting for him, then."

"I didn't even know he has a wife," Elizabeth told her. "He and Daddy are business associates, so I've known him for years, and I never once heard anything about a wife. It was only when the papers were full of the story that I found out."

"I'm sure Sam isn't very happy about that."

"He's furious. Apparently Dan Ross has been pestering him for a statement, and he said something about some nosy old woman ringing him out of the blue and demanding to know where Joselyn had gone. I know that couldn't have been you. You're much more subtle."

Even if I'm just as nosy, Bessie thought. "I suspect it was Maggie Shimmin."

"That makes sense," Elizabeth nodded. "She would do that."

"I'm not sure there's any point in my trying to talk to him, then," Bessie sighed.

"Of course there is. People always tell you everything."

"I don't know about that."

"Whatever, it's still worth a try. Come back to Thie yn Traie with me now. You can chat with Mum for a short while until Sam arrives."

"I'm sure your mother has other things to do."

"She's redecorating the master bedroom. I'm sure she'll be happy to be interrupted."

"I thought the master bedroom was redecorated before you moved into Thie yn Traie."

"It was, but Daddy decided that he didn't care for the wall colour when he had to see it every day. It's now being painted a shade that is just fractionally different to what was there before, but that means all of the bedding has to be changed as well. Since they're changing all of that, Daddy thought it would be a good time to get some new furniture, too."

Bessie sighed. Many years ago, more than she'd care to remember, she'd decided to paint her bedroom a nice bright, cheery pink. The colour had turned out to be a good deal brighter than she'd expected, but she hadn't had the money in her budget to cover over it right away. All these years later, she was still hoping that she might grow to like the colour, as she put off repainting again and again.

"Do you need any bedroom furniture?" Elizabeth asked. "Mum doesn't know what to do with the things they just bought last year. Daddy said she can't put anything else into storage because they already have so many units full of stuff."

"I don't need anything, and I doubt very much that anything they had in their bedroom would fit into my cottage."

Elizabeth blinked a few times and then looked around the snug kitchen. "I never thought about how small your cottage is," she said softly. "It feels so comfortable and warm that I never even considered the size. It's quite tiny, really, isn't it?"

"I suppose so. I've added to it twice, so it's considerably larger than it was originally."

"Goodness," Elizabeth exclaimed. "I think your entire cottage would fit into the great room at Thie yn Traie."

"It probably would," Bessie agreed.

"I can't imagine you living anywhere else, though."

'No, I can't, either."

"But let's get going. I don't want to be late for my meeting with Mr. Owens. Or rather, I do want to be late so that you can have a quick chat with him. What I don't want is for you to be late."

Bessie shook her head at the girl's ramblings and then stood up.

"Just let me freshen up," she said. "I'm not dressed for visiting Thie yn Traie."

"You look fine," Elizabeth said carelessly.

"I'm still going to change," Bessie replied firmly.

She was only gone a few minutes, just long enough to change into a skirt and jumper and comb her hair, but by the time she returned there was a man in the kitchen with Elizabeth.

"I didn't hear anyone at the door," Bessie exclaimed.

"This is Charles, our new driver," Elizabeth replied. "I rang him to come over and collect us."

Bessie smiled at the middle-aged man in the black uniform. "It's nice to meet you," she said.

"Likewise, Madam," he replied.

"You must call me Bessie. Everyone does."

He looked surprised, but then he nodded.

"Ready, Bessie?" Elizabeth asked.

"Yes, let's go," she replied.

Charles opened the door and then waited to follow until Bessie and Elizabeth had exited. He then had to wait while Bessie locked the door behind them. When they got to the car, he opened the rear door for them. Bessie climbed in after Elizabeth.

"This feels odd," Bessie whispered as the car began the short journey to Thie yn Traie.

"The car and driver? I'm quite used to having them at my disposal. I'm not sure why I bothered to learn to drive, really, except it's quite fun when the weather is nice and I can drive with the top down on my car."

"If you say so."

"I should teach you how to drive. It would be fun."

"Thank you, but I think I'm better off not worrying about that at this point in my life."

Elizabeth looked as if she wanted to argue, but just then the car pulled into one of the vast garages at Thie yn Traie.

"Here we are," Charles said as he opened the door next to Bessie.

She let him help her from the car and then stood back to let Elizabeth lead the way into the house.

"Mum is probably in the great room. Can you find her on your own while I go and do something with my hair?" Elizabeth asked.

"Of course," Bessie agreed.

She walked down the long corridor, only just resisting the urge to look into every open door. She'd been to the huge mansion many times, but she never grew tired of seeing all the different spaces around the house. The huge great room was far too large to feel comfortable to Bessie. She found Mary sitting on a couch, staring out at the sea.

"Bessie? I didn't know you were here," she said, jumping to her feet as Bessie walked into the room.

"Elizabeth invited me to come over so that I could have a word with Sam Owens when he comes to see her this morning."

Mary nodded, a frown on her face. "I read in the paper that his wife is one of the possible candidates for what you found at Peel Castle."

"Yes, that's right. Do you know him well?"

"I don't. He and George play golf together occasionally, but George would play golf with Satan himself if he could get eighteen holes in."

"Oh, dear. You sound unhappy."

Mary shook her head. "Just a bit frustrated, really. We were done with the redecorating here, aside from this room. I was excited to finally get started in here, as the room is too large as it is. I was hoping we could find a way to divide the space without losing any of the amazing views. Anyway, just before our designer started working on the plans for here, George decided that our bedroom needed to be completely redone. He has a million different ideas, most of them impossible, impractical, or unattractive. The designer has been here all morning, but George is off playing golf, leaving me to make all of the decisions."

"It's awfully windy to try to play golf."

"Oh, I'm sure they aren't actually playing. They'll be sitting in the clubhouse, watching the wind and hoping it will die down enough for them to fit nine holes in before it gets dark."

Bessie sighed. "I'm sorry."

"It's fine, really. I'm just feeling rather badly done to because it's all been dumped into my lap, that's all. I should be grateful that we have the money to do whatever we'd like and that George is happy to redecorate this house and isn't still trying to persuade me to move back to Douglas."

"I thought you were going to sell the Douglas house."

"So did I. George is now talking about giving it to one of our sons, although they both have perfectly lovely homes of their own. I don't know. He simply can't seem to let that house go."

"As long as you get to stay at Thie yn Traie, I suppose it doesn't matter."

"You're right, of course. You didn't come to listen to me complain, though. Let me think. Maybe I can tell you more about Sam Owens."

Bessie sat silently next to Mary as the woman shut her eyes and frowned.

"I'm afraid I don't know much," she said eventually. "I didn't even know he was married until I saw the article in the paper. I'd always thought he'd been a lifelong bachelor."

"How long have you known him? Since you moved to the island?"

"Oh, longer than that. He and George worked together on something years ago. They used to golf together once a month at the club George belonged to in Manchester when we lived there."

"So you knew him when he was younger. You never saw him with a woman?"

"He used to bring his secretary to special events," Mary replied. "She was at least twenty years older than he was and she was very happily married, as well."

"Interesting," Bessie said thoughtfully.

Jonathan Hooper walked into the room. The man who walked in behind him glanced around and then frowned at Bessie. He had a full head of grey hair and was dressed in a very expensive-looking suit.

"Mr. Samuel Owens," Jonathan said. He bowed and then turned and left the room.

CHAPTER 13

"Sam," Mary said warmly as she got to her feet. "Do come in."
She waited until the man had crossed the room to join
her before she spoke again. "You know Bessie Cubbon, don't you? I
always assume that everyone knows Bessie."

"We've met," Samuel conceded with a tiny nod at Bessie.

"It's lovely to see you again," Bessie said.

He gave her a thin smile. "I'm here to see Elizabeth," he told Mary.

"Yes, of course. She said something about planning a small gath-
ering for you. Let me go and find her. You can chat with Bessie while
I'm gone."

Sam looked as if he wanted to protest, but Mary didn't give him
the opportunity to do so. She was out of the room before he had a
chance to speak.

"Please, have a seat," Bessie invited.

He shrugged and then sat very carefully in the chair opposite hers.

"I haven't seen you in years," Bessie began. "It seems odd, on an
island this small, that we haven't seen more of one another."

"I never travel to Laxey. I assume you usually spend your visits to
Douglas in the town centre. I don't believe we have friends or
acquaintances in common."

"Aside from Mary and George."

"Yes, of course."

"How have you been?" Bessie asked.

"I'm fine. How are you?"

"Fine, thank you." After a long pause, she spoke again. "Aside from finding dead bodies nearly everywhere I go, of course."

He winced. "It is rather odd, that."

"It's also rather sad."

"I suppose it must be."

"You know people are speculating that the body could be Joselyn's," Bessie said softly.

Sam stared at her for a minute and then shrugged. "I'm not really interested in what people think."

"The police are concerned as well."

"They shouldn't be concerned about my wife. She's fine."

"I hope you were able to provide the police with proof of that."

He scowled at her. "They should take my word for it, as should you. The weather today has been interesting."

"It's been quite windy," Bessie agreed. "I suppose we should expect as much in the winter months."

"Yes, perhaps."

The mantel clock ticked slowly as Bessie stared at the sea. Samuel had made it clear he wasn't going to answer any of her questions, but she still felt the need to ask more. "I'm glad Joselyn is well," she said eventually. "She seemed sweet, the few times I met her."

"She was, er, is a very sweet person," he agreed.

"It was odd, her just leaving the island the way she did."

"She had a good reason for leaving and has several good reasons for staying away now. None of this is any of your business, of course."

"No, of course not. I truly don't mean to pry. Finding the body was quite upsetting, though."

"I'd have thought you'd be used to that by now."

"I'm not certain that I'll ever get used to any such thing. There are a tremendous number of unanswered questions with this body, though. The police aren't even certain if the woman was murdered or not."

"If she wasn't murdered, how did she end up at Peel Castle, tucked away in one of the tower walls?"

"I wish I knew. Maybe she died in an accident or even of natural causes and someone simply wanted to hide the body."

"That doesn't make sense. She must have been murdered."

"It will be easier for the police to work out what happened to her once they know whom they've found."

"I suppose so. They haven't found Joselyn, anyway."

"They won't cross her off their list until they have proof of that. You do realise that, right?"

"They shouldn't need proof. My word should be enough."

"You'd lie, though, if you'd killed her."

He looked shocked. "If I'd killed her," he echoed. "What an appalling thought."

"You must know that's why the police have questioned you."

"No, I didn't know that," he said. "It's such a ridiculous notion that it never crossed my mind. Why would I kill Joselyn? I had no reason to hurt her."

"She fell pregnant while you were away," Bessie said softly.

"Maybe I came home for a weekend in the middle of my trip."

"Did you?" Bessie asked, wondering why such a possibility had never been mentioned before.

"No, but that's not the point," he replied. "I'm not discussing this with you. It's all ancient history."

"Let's hope the police work out the woman's identity quickly. Once that happens, they'll leave you alone again."

"I just hope that horrible man at the newspaper leaves me alone, too. He's been ringing my house every day since that body was discovered."

"Dan Ross can be very persistent."

"He isn't the only one, either. Some woman rang and demanded that I tell her how to find Joselyn. People have been pointing and whispering when they see me in the streets. It's all very unpleasant."

"I'm sure it was worse when Joselyn first disappeared."

"I don't know about that. Her parents supported me. They knew where she'd gone, of course, so they didn't have any worries about what might have happened to her. People respected privacy a good deal more in those days, too. It wasn't polite to be nosy." The look he gave Bessie suggested that he was putting her firmly in the "not polite" category.

"Maybe Dan will manage to track Joselyn down himself. As I said, he's very persistent."

"I can't allow that," Sam said. "What must I do to stop him?"

"I don't believe you can stop him. He's simply doing his job."

"Sticking his nose into things that don't concern him. Surely I have a right to keep my private life to myself."

"I'm sure Dan would argue that the public has a right to know the truth, especially during a murder investigation."

"The body isn't Joselyn's. That's all the public needs to know."

"Tell Inspector Anna Lambert where to find Joselyn. Once she's confirmed that Joselyn is alive, she'll tell Dan Ross that Joselyn has been eliminated from consideration. That should be enough to stop Dan from investigating any further."

"Are you quite certain?"

Bessie shook her head. "I'm not going to lie to you. If Dan has decided to find Joselyn, he isn't going to be put off by anyone or anything. You just have to hope that he's more interested in discovering who was found in Peel than anything else."

Sam frowned. He slid down in his chair and stared out the window, breathing in and out in a controlled manner. After several minutes, he looked at Bessie.

"I assume you know Inspector Lambert?"

"I do, yes."

He nodded and then pulled a small notebook out of his pocket. He jotted something on the first sheet and then tore the sheet out and handed it to Bessie. "Tell her she can find Joselyn there."

Bessie looked down at the note. "Lakeside Lodge," she read.

Sam sighed. "You aren't going to be happy until you hear the whole story, are you?"

"You don't need to tell me anything," Bessie assured him. "I'll give this to Anna Lambert. She'll take care of it from there."

He shook his head. "I've never talked about Joselyn. Her parents didn't want anyone to know anything, and that was fine with me. I still don't want to talk about her, but I'd rather tell you than read about it in the paper."

"As long as Inspector Lambert can find her, that's all that matters."

"We were happy. She was very young when we fell in love, but we waited until she was eighteen to get married. Her parents wanted us to wait longer. Later, after she was gone, they told me that they were worried about her fragility, but they never mentioned that at the time. They just said they wanted to make sure we were both certain as to what we were doing."

"You don't have to tell me this."

"I was sure, so very sure," he continued as if Bessie hadn't spoken. "Joselyn insisted that she was sure, too. We ran away to Gretna Green. It seemed romantic and a bit wild, just like my wife. I'd have done anything to make her happy. I still will."

Bessie glanced at the door. Where were Mary and Elizabeth? Surely one of them should have come back by now.

"I worked hard for her father and he gave me more and more responsibilities. I travelled all the time, but I didn't mind. I usually took Joselyn with me, which was wonderful. We saw the world together. She loved travelling more than I did. She had such a huge sense of adventure."

He stopped and looked at Bessie. "To my mind, things were just about perfect, but Joselyn, well, she wanted one more thing. She wanted a baby."

Bessie nodded. She'd guessed that that was where the story was headed.

"I told her we'd talk about it when I got back. I was going away for six months and I didn't want to leave her behind pregnant and alone.

She didn't want to come with me. It was the first time she hadn't wanted to come along. She said she was going to stay home and decorate the nursery." His voice caught. "I would never have gone if I'd known."

Sliding forward in her chair, Bessie patted his arm. "You truly don't need to tell me any of this."

"It's cathartic, talking about it," he replied. "Maybe I should have done it years ago. Maybe it would have made a difference to someone somewhere."

"Secrets get harder to give up the longer we keep them."

Sam nodded. "I'm sure you think you've heard the next part of the story. When I came back, Joselyn was five months pregnant. I'd been gone for six months, so the baby wasn't mine. That's what you've heard, isn't it?"

"Yes, that's the story the I've heard."

"We decided, her parents and I, that that was a better story than the truth. I didn't mind if people thought Joselyn had cheated on me. Her parents thought that was preferable to people finding out just how ill she actually was."

"Ill?" Bessie echoed.

"She wanted a baby. Over time, it became something of an obsession. I didn't notice the changes in her. They were subtle, happening slowly over weeks and months. It was obvious, when I came back, but by that point it was too late."

"Mentally ill," Bessie guessed.

"Very badly mentally ill. As I said, her parents told me well after the fact that they were concerned about her mental health before we got married. They would have told me more, I believe, over time. They weren't expecting us to run away to Gretna Green."

"I'm sure the rest of the story is difficult for you," Bessie said sympathetically. "Coming home and finding her pregnant must have been incredibly hard."

"That's just it," he sighed. "She wasn't pregnant, she just thought she was pregnant."

Bessie stared at him for a moment and then shook her head slowly.

"But I remember seeing her in the shops one day. She was laughing and talking with a friend about getting ready for the baby."

"She was over the moon about the baby. When I asked her who the father was, she insisted that she'd been faithful, that I was the father. When I suggested that the dates didn't work, she simply ignored me. She hadn't been to see a doctor, not once, while I'd been away, so I made her go, insisting it was for the baby's health. He couldn't find a heartbeat."

Bessie blinked back tears. "That poor girl."

He nodded. "I had my suspicions by that point. Her refusal to see a doctor worried me. I could never feel the baby moving, either, although she kept insisting that she could. When the doctor suggested that she might not be pregnant, she became hysterical and had to be sedated. Her parents, her doctor, and I agreed that we'd simply let her continue with the fantasy for the time being. There wasn't anywhere on the island that was equipped to deal with her at that time."

"I'm not sure there is now."

"Probably not. It's a very specialised form of mental illness. I had a difficult job finding a place in the UK that could treat her. Her parents insisted that we tell no one where she was going. She was told that it was a specialist birthing centre."

"What happened to her?" Bessie asked.

"She's received the best care that I can afford, but her mental health is still incredibly fragile. When the nine months were up, they gave her a baby doll, and she remains devoted to that baby to this day. She's lost touch with the passage of time. As the baby hasn't aged, she assumes she's still in her early twenties. I had to stop visiting a few years ago as she refused to believe that I was her husband. We talk on the phone every night. Fortunately, my voice hasn't changed. She tells me all about what the baby is doing and I make up stories about her parents who simply can't seem to find time to ring but are thinking of her."

Bessie gave up on trying to hold back her tears. She dug around in her handbag and found a tissue. "I'm sorry, but it's all terribly sad."

"Don't be sad for her. She's completely unaware of reality. To her,

187

life is just about perfect. She has her baby and I'm going to come and collect them both as soon as the baby gets a little bit bigger. Then we're all going to live happily ever after as a family."

"I'll be sad for you, then," Bessie told him. "You've missed out on so much of life, having to deal with all of this."

He shrugged. "I had options. There were more aggressive treatment plans that might have snapped her out of her fantasy world and dragged her back to reality. I couldn't bring myself to try them, as they also carried risks that included permanent brain damage. Her parents left those decisions to me, although we discussed them regularly."

"Did they want to try more aggressive treatments?"

"They were terrified to try anything," he sighed. "She'd had problems when she was very small. They called it an unfortunate episode. They didn't like to talk about it, but from what I could determine, she'd decided that her parents weren't really her parents but that she'd been stolen from her real family. They ended up taking her to a hospital in London where she was heavily medicated for several months. When they brought her back to the island, it was some time before she began to behave normally again. I believe they worried that the medication she'd taken then might have led to her problems when she was older."

"Doctors need to focus on mental health the same way they do on physical health," Bessie suggested.

Sam shrugged. "Her parents actually urged me to divorce her. At first I refused because I was sure she was going to get better. I thought I'd be willing to try anything and everything to cure her. I truly believed that the doctors would be able to find some combination of drugs and therapy that would turn her back into the woman that I'd married. The reality of the situation didn't hit me for several years, actually."

"I can't even imagine."

"When I used to go to see her, the doctors would sit me down and give me a rundown of alternatives we could try. They'd tell me about the success rates they'd had with other patients or how well some drug had done in clinical trials, and then they'd tell me about possible side effects. After a while, I came to believe that Joselyn was better off where she was, in her own world, than she would have been in ours, possibly so brain-damaged as to be unable to walk or talk."

"I'm sure you're right."

He shrugged. "I've given up trying to work out if I've done the right thing or not. In some ways, it seems as if her life has been wasted, but if I had it to do over again, I'm not sure I'd do anything differently."

"You'd still stay with her, even knowing that she was never going to get well?"

"I promised her that much on our wedding day. I was desperately in love with her and I meant every word I said."

"You're a good man, Sam Owens."

"I don't know about that. I'll never stop wondering if I made the wrong choices along the way. Maybe, if she'd been given the right drugs, we could have been happy together again."

"You wouldn't have wanted to have children, though."

"No, you're right about that. I can't imagine she would have been happy without them, though." He sighed. "If I had a time machine, I'd go back and try every possible thing, from not marrying her in the first place to agreeing to having a baby with her before I went on that long trip. Maybe, if I did things differently, she could have had a happier life."

"I think she's had a happy life," Bessie told him. "You've made certain of that."

"You can tell your police inspector friend that if she wants to talk to Joselyn herself, she'll have to arrange it with the nursing staff. Joselyn doesn't like to talk to strangers. She's afraid everyone she meets wants to take the baby away. It all goes back to an early treatment plan, maybe twenty-five years ago. If the inspector would prefer, we can try to find a way for her to listen into one of my conversations with Joselyn. A few minutes of talk about how the baby is eating more now and getting stronger every day should convince your police inspector that I'm telling the truth."

"I'm sure someone from the care facility will be able to reassure Inspector Lambert," Bessie said, hoping she was right.

"I should finish the story, really," Sam sighed. "Joselyn's doctors rang me a few weeks ago. She has a brain tumour. They don't think it's anything to do with her mental health or with the various medications she's been on and off over the years, but they don't really know anything for sure. Or rather, the only thing they know for sure is that it's going to kill her, probably in the next three months or so."

"I'm sorry," Bessie said.

"I've already mourned for her and for the life we should have had together. I'm afraid that when she dies, I'll feel nothing but relief."

"I doubt that. You may be surprised by how much you grieve."

"I didn't intend to tell you all of that, but I feel, I don't know, lighter somehow now that I have. I didn't talk about it for years and people had stopped asking. In a way, I'm glad I've had a chance to tell her story. When she's really gone, maybe I'll tell more people."

"If people talked about mental health more, perhaps there would be less of a stigma attached to it."

"Yes, I know you're right. We'll see. For now, tell Inspector Lambert and anyone else with the police who needs to know. I think I need to go home and lie down for a short while. Please tell Elizabeth that I'll ring her another day."

He got up and marched out of the room without looking back. Bessie wiped away another tear and then swallowed the lump in her throat.

"What happened?" Elizabeth demanded as she bounced into the room a minute later. "Mum and I were standing at the end of the corridor, waiting for one of you to come looking for us. Instead, Sam simply walked out."

"He told me a few things and gave me some information for Inspector Lambert," Bessie replied. "I need to go and ring her."

"I'll have Charles take you home," Elizabeth said.

Bessie didn't argue. She wanted to get home as quickly as possible. Once back at Treoghe Bwaane, she rang Anna.

"It's a terribly sad story," she said at the end.

"Yes, it is," Anna said. "It was particularly difficult for me to hear."

"I'm sure it was."

"I think we need to talk," Anna continued. "I know you usually have dinner with John and Hugh and Doona in the middle of investigations. Can you do that tonight, and can I come along, too?"

"If you can arrange it, everyone is welcome here," Bessie replied. "Do you want to bring food, or shall I cook?"

"I'll bring something. We'll be there at six, or at least, I will be," Anna told her.

Bessie put the phone down and glanced at the clock. She'd missed lunch, but she wasn't feeling especially hungry. Sam's story had been heartbreaking. After pacing around the kitchen for several minutes, she headed for the door. Strong winds meant that it was raining sideways. Bessie stared at the rain and then sighed. There was no way she was going out in that.

She found a book and began to read, but found it difficult to concentrate. Eventually, she dug out some old magazines and flipped her way through them, simply marking time until her friends were due to arrive.

"I hope pizza will do for dinner," Anna Lambert said when Bessie opened the door to her a few minutes before six. "This place was on my way here from Peel."

"It smells wonderful," Bessie told her.

"I got four pizzas and some garlic bread. I hope that's enough."

"How many people have you invited?"

"Just John and Doona and Hugh, but as I recall, Hugh counts at least twice and maybe three times."

Bessie nodded. "You're right about that."

John and Doona arrived a few minutes later.

"How are you?" Bessie asked John as she pulled him into a hug.

"I've been better, but the children are both staying with friends tonight, which gives me less to worry about."

"And how are you?" Bessie asked Doona.

"I'm great," Doona replied, her smile not reaching her eyes.

Bessie studied her for a moment. She thought about pushing for more information, but Hugh's knock on the door interrupted.

"I'm probably late," Hugh said. "I thought I would just walk over, but the wind is terrible. I was going forward two steps and then blowing back one. I finally gave up and got the car."

"Everyone get food while it's hot," Bessie said. "Then we can talk."

They chatted about the windy weather and baby Aalish while they ate.

"What's for pudding?" Hugh asked as Doona and Anna cleared away the dirty plates.

Bessie looked at Anna. "Did you bring pudding?" she asked.

Anna flushed. "I didn't realise you had pudding at these gatherings."

"We don't always," Bessie said, lying to be polite. "I have boxes and boxes of biscuits. Those will do nicely with tea."

She switched on the kettle and then filled a plate with a selection of biscuits. When everyone was back at the table, Anna cleared her throat.

"I'm not sure how these things usually go," she said awkwardly. "I assume everything that is said here is strictly confidential."

"Yes, although I never repeat anything that I was told in a police interview to Bessie and Doona. They're civilians, after all," John said.

"Good, so we all understand one another," Anna said. "Obviously, I won't be repeating what I was told in interviews either. It seems as if Bessie knows more than anyone else anyway."

Bessie flushed. "I don't know about that. People do seem to tell me things, even things I don't want to hear."

"Originally, there were five possibilities for the woman at the castle," Doona said. "Some of them have been eliminated, though, right?"

"Thanks in no small part to Bessie, we've found Meredith Houseman and Emma Gibson. Today I spoke to Liam Pearce. He's the man with whom Lauren Bell took up after she and Harold Newman ended their relationship. After our chat, he had Lauren ring me."

"I don't suppose you can tell us anything she said," Bessie sighed.

"I'll tell you that she told me enough to make me confident that she truly was the Lauren Bell who left the island thirty-three years ago. She's had an interesting life, really, and an unconventional one. She wasn't able to suggest any additional names for the body from Peel Castle, either."

"That's another name off the list, then," Bessie said. "I found out where Joselyn Owens is, too. Her husband said that I could share the story with anyone in the police who needed to hear it. I believe you all qualify, therefore, but the story isn't to leave this room."

Doona was crying, and even John and Hugh looked sad when Bessie finished telling them what Sam had told her about Joselyn.

"I think I feel most sorry for him," Doona said after she'd wiped her eyes. "She sounds happy enough."

"She is happy enough," Anna said. "I spoke to her just before I came here. Again, she said more than enough to confirm her identity when we spoke. It was an incredibly strange conversation, but it was enough to satisfy me as to who she is."

"That just leaves Hannah Butler," Bessie said. "You said you'd found Daisy. Have you had a chance to speak to her yet?"

"We talked very briefly. She was on her way out, going to a doctor's appointment, she said. She's going to ring me back tomorrow morning. I told her about the body and mentioned Hannah's name. She didn't have time to talk at all, though, as her taxi arrived before I'd had a chance to finish speaking," Anna told her.

"If we eliminate Hannah Butler, is there anyone left?" Hugh asked.

"Not on the short list," Anna sighed. "I have a few other names, of women who disappeared from various places around the world, but they're all unlikely candidates. It's almost impossible to imagine how someone from India could have arrived on the island and then died at Peel Castle, for example."

"So if it isn't Hannah, it's someone who was never reported as missing," John said. "Perhaps someone who was alone in the world."

"Or someone like the women we've been discussing. None of them were ever reported missing, but they all disappeared from the island," Bessie said.

"It was more difficult to stay in touch with people in those days. No one had mobile phones or email. If someone moved away, you had to wait for them to write to you in order to get their new address," Anna said.

"But we're talking about a fairly young woman. Surely she would have had family and friends who would have noticed that she'd gone," Doona said.

"We could start ringing other constabularies and asking them to make lists in the same way that Bessie made our list for the island," John said. "No doubt the police in Liverpool could come up with at least a dozen names of women who'd moved away at around the right time, women that no one has seen since. It would be an endless job, though, trying to track them all down and then moving on to the list from the next village, town, or city."

"So, if it isn't Hannah, do we just give up?" Hugh asked.

"I'm not giving up," Anna said. "I'll start in Liverpool and see if anyone there can come up with the sort of list John suggested. Travel was more expensive and more difficult in those days. It seems most likely that she came to the island by ferry. That suggests some ties to Liverpool, or maybe Dublin."

"I know someone in Dublin who would probably enjoy helping with the case," John said. "He loves trying to solve impossible cases."

"If Daisy can't help, I'd be grateful if you could ring him," Anna said.

John nodded. "We need national newspaper coverage, as well. Maybe Dan Ross can try his hand at writing an article about our mystery woman that could get picked up and published in some of the bigger cities across. I'm sure hundreds of people would ring in with tips if the story was carried in a London paper."

"I'm not sure we want hundreds of tips," Anna said with a sigh. "I'm working on my own on this case, aside from all of the help you've given me," she added, nodding at John.

"Let's see what Daisy has to say," John suggested. "We can have another meeting after that to work out what to do next."

Anna nodded. "On that note, I suppose I should go. I haven't done laundry all week and I'm nearly out of clean clothes. My flat looks as if a bomb went off in the sitting room, as well. I need to spend some time with my vacuum cleaner and a duster."

Bessie walked the inspector to the door. "I don't feel as if we've been any help at all tonight," she said.

"I appreciate your time anyway," Anna replied. "Good night."

As she shut the door behind Anna, Bessie blew out a long breath. The atmosphere in the cottage seemed to lighten as Bessie turned back to her friends.

"I still don't like her," Doona said emphatically.

"Let's not worry about that for tonight," John said. "I'm afraid she's taken on an impossible job with this case. That skeleton could be anyone."

"I'm more interested in how the skeleton got into the tower wall at Peel Castle," Hugh said.

"She must have been murdered, and then the killer hid the body there," Doona said. "He or she has been very lucky up to this point, what with the body not being found for all those years."

"If it is Hannah Butler, I don't believe anyone had a motive for killing her," Bessie interjected.

"Maybe she was out taking one of her late-night walks and someone accidentally ran her over," Doona said. "Maybe they were drunk or somewhere they weren't meant to be, so they hid the body at the castle."

"That's one possibility," John said. "We could spend all night making a long list of possibilities, though. The only limit is your imagination. I believe we'd be better served waiting until we have more information."

"What if we never get more information?" Doona demanded.

"Then the case will remain unsolved," John replied.

CHAPTER 14

*D*oona made a few other suggestions for ways that the body could have ended up where it was found, but they grew increasingly implausible as she talked. When she mentioned aliens, Bessie had had enough.

"I don't think it was aliens," she said firmly.

"I'm just babbling," Doona sighed. "It seems preferable to admitting that we may never know whom you found or how she got there."

"I didn't find her," Bessie said flatly.

"I know, sorry," Doona told her. "I think we're all just out of sorts because we didn't get any pudding."

Everyone laughed.

"I should have made an apple crumble or something," Bessie said apologetically. "That would have taken time, though, and I was oddly eager to get through everything we needed to discuss."

"You don't feel the same way now that Inspector Lambert is gone, do you?" Doona asked.

"I always enjoy spending time with you three," Bessie told her. "I do think that this case has been a sad one from the very beginning, though. I've been told too many unhappy stories and I'm not antici-pating hearing anything good about Hannah Butler, either."

"Emma and Meredith were both fine," John pointed out. "I've seen Anna's report on Lauren, and she's fine, too."

"But she caused a lot of pain for others," Bessie said.

"I can't argue with that," John replied.

"The baby is smiling now," Hugh said.

Bessie gave him a grateful smile. "That's good to hear. I needed some good news tonight."

He patted her hand. "She slept for six solid hours last night, which was pretty wonderful, too," he said. "Grace is starting to feel better, physically and mentally. She told me that she might not go right back to work after all. She's starting to enjoy spending time with Aalish."

"It just keeps getting better," John said. "The more they learn to do, the more fun they are to be around. Then they get even older and you can spend time with them almost as friends. Thomas will be thinking about university in another year or two, and it seems wrong that he's just starting to be great company and he'll be leaving."

"I can't imagine letting Aalish go away to university. I know I have eighteen years to get used to the idea, but she's never going to seem like an adult in my eyes," Hugh said.

"You'll be surprised," John told him. "Enjoy the baby stage, though. It's much shorter than it feels when you're in the middle of it all."

Hugh nodded. "She's already looking less like a newborn and, I don't know, older, somehow."

A loud ringing noise made everyone jump. Hugh pulled out his mobile. "It's Grace," he said, looking worried. The conversation was short and Hugh was on his feet as he put the phone back in his pocket.

"The winds have caused a power cut at home," he told them. "Grace just wanted me to know so that I wouldn't worry if I came home to a totally dark house. I need to go and make sure everything is good."

"Of course," Bessie said. She walked him to the door and gave him a hug. "I'm sure the power will be back on soon."

"I hope so. The house will get quite cold without any central heating," Hugh replied.

The wind was howling as Bessie shut the door behind the man.

"I'd better get home as well. The children are both out, but if there are widespread power cuts, one or both of them might want collecting. Knowing my children, they'll want me to bring their friends to our house, too," John said.

"Assuming you have power," Doona suggested.

"There is that," John frowned. He got to his feet and then looked at Bessie. "Thank you for talking to Andrew Cheatham about Sue. He's definitely making things happen in Africa, although I'm not entirely certain what is going on. That's no different to before, though."

"I hope he can help," Bessie said.

"I've been told that Sue has been moved to the nearest hospital. A doctor there rang me to inform me as to her location. I haven't heard anything from Harvey in days."

"Let's hope she can get the care she needs," Bessie replied.

John nodded. "Thank you again," he said before he let himself out.

"And then there was one," Doona laughed. "I should go, too, but I'll help with the washing-up first."

It only took the pair a few minutes to take care of that job.

"Thank you," Bessie said.

"Not a problem," Doona replied. "I wanted to give John plenty of time to get away before I left, anyway."

"Why?"

She shrugged. "We're sort of avoiding one another at the moment. Things are, well, awkward and uncomfortable. Until the situation with Sue is sorted, I think it's probably best if we see as little of each other as possible."

Bessie nodded. "I'm sorry."

"If Sue does recover, I may just kill her," Doona added.

"I know you're kidding, but I understand the sentiment. She's caused a lot of problems for John and the children."

"Yes, she has," Doona sighed.

Bessie let Doona out and then finished tidying the kitchen. Tomorrow was another day. Maybe by the end of it they'd know what had happened to Hannah Butler. Anna seemed determined to pursue the case even after that, but Bessie wondered how far she would go to try to identify the castle skeleton. Maybe it would be better for everyone if Anna simply dropped the investigation.

The wind was slightly less ferocious when Bessie took her walk the next morning. She found herself wandering along the sand, feeling at loose ends. It was frustrating being on the fringes of the investigation. What she really wanted to do was to talk to Daisy, but that was Anna's job. It wasn't the first time that Bessie had felt annoyed with the constabulary's policy on age. She knew she was too old to apply for a job with them, no matter how much she helped John with cases. As a light rain began to fall, she turned for home.

The day felt long and dull. Intermittent power cuts kept her from getting much of anything done. She tried working on Onnee's letters, but with the lights going on and off, all she managed to accomplish was getting a headache. She read for a while, when she had power, and did a few household chores. Knowing that she was simply waiting to hear from Anna annoyed her, but there was nothing she could do about the situation. When the phone rang, she grabbed it quickly.

"It's Anna Lambert. How are you?"

"I'm fine," Bessie replied. "Just impatient to hear what Daisy had to say."

"She hasn't said anything to me, not yet," Anna sighed. "She never rang this morning, so I rang her after lunch. No one answered. I left a message on her machine, but she hasn't rung back."

"That's frustrating," Bessie said.

"Yes, it is. I don't know what else we can do at this point, except wait for her to ring me back. If I don't hear from her tomorrow, I may send someone from the local constabulary to speak with her. I don't think she's taking the situation seriously."

"You said she seemed distracted when you spoke with her. Maybe she didn't really comprehend what you told her."

"Maybe. Time will tell," Anna replied.

Determined not to waste another day worrying about Hannah, Bessie rang her taxi service and arranged for a car to collect her the next morning.

"Where will you be going?" the dispatcher asked.

"I'm not sure yet," Bessie replied.

"No problem," she laughed.

Another grey morning had Bessie cutting her walk short. As she got ready for her taxi, she still hadn't decided where she wanted it to take her.

"Aunt Bessie, how are you?" Dave asked when he arrived to collect her.

"Out of sorts and at loose ends," she replied. "I need to get away and do something, but I've no idea what to do."

"It's a lovely day on the other side of the island," he told her. "I took someone to Peel Castle this morning and it was beautiful and sunny there."

"Really? Maybe a walk on Peel Beach would be good for me," Bessie said.

"It's windy, but sunny," Dave promised.

The drive across the island didn't seem to take long as Dave told Bessie all about his family as they went.

"Are you sure you want me to leave you just here?" he asked as he pulled to a stop on the promenade.

"Yes, this will be perfect. I'll walk from one end to the other and then maybe stop in a café for some lunch. I'll find a taxi rank when I'm ready to come home."

"You can always ring me if you can't find a taxi," he told her.

"Thanks," Bessie replied. She climbed out of the car and shut the door behind her. The wind was strong, but the sun was shining, so Bessie began her brisk walk. An hour later she was tired of fighting the wind and feeling as if she had sand in her hair and stuck in her teeth. It was too early for lunch, but just the right time for a cup of tea and a toasted teacake, she decided.

Many of the seaside cafés were shut during the winter months, but Bessie found one that was open and went inside gratefully.

"Sit anywhere, love," a voice called from behind the counter at the back of the room. "I'll be over to get your order in a minute."

The room was nearly empty. An older couple were sitting together near the counter, each reading the local paper. At another table, a woman was sitting on her own, staring out the window with tears in her eyes. She looked to be in her sixties, and Bessie wondered if she should speak to her or pretend she hadn't noticed the tears.

"Are you okay?" she asked after a moment.

The woman looked up at her and gave her a shaky smile. "I'm fine, really, just feeling incredibly sad over the loss of a dear friend."

"I'm sorry," Bessie said.

"I lost her a long time ago, actually, I just didn't realise it, until a few days ago. Life gets in the way, and then one day you realise that it's been thirty-two years since you spoke to your friend. I didn't expect to find out that she was gone, but it's hardly surprising. We're all getting older, of course."

"Losing someone is never easy under any circumstances."

"I've lost people who were much more important to me, really. My husband, my parents, close friends and family members. They were all sad, but this feels sadder for some reason. Maybe because of the way she died. I feel as if I could have saved her if I'd been here."

"What can I get you?" Bessie hadn't heard the waitress coming up behind her.

"Oh, tea and a toasted teacake, please," she replied.

"Will you be joining your friend?" the waitress asked.

"We aren't friends," the other woman said. "But you're welcome to join me anyway."

Bessie sat down across from the stranger and smiled. "I'm Elizabeth Cubbon," she said.

The woman looked startled. "Your name was in the papers. I read all about the body at Peel Castle on the ferry yesterday. You found the body."

"I was at the castle when the body was found. I didn't actually find it myself," Bessie replied. The distinction was important to her, even if no one else seemed to think it mattered.

"Did she look unhappy?" was a question that surprised Bessie.

"I'm sorry, but I'm not sure what you mean."

"The woman that you found, did she look sad?"

"All that was left was a skeleton," Bessie said gently. "I only glanced at it. I couldn't see her head."

The other woman nodded and a single tear slid down her cheek. "I wish I knew what she was thinking. I should have known from her last letter what she was planning, but I was too busy with my own life to give it any thought at all."

"I'm not following you."

"I'm not surprised. I doubt I'm making any sense. It's all been such a shock. I've always been one for making plans and sticking to them. I planned my wedding for over two years, so long that my husband very nearly decided not to marry me. I planned all of our holidays and family outings, birthday parties, anniversary dinners, everything for the last thirty years or so. When the police rang and said they thought they'd found Hannah's body, I did something impulsive. It's odd and it's left me feeling off balance, but here I am, babbling to a stranger in a nearly empty café on an island that used to be home."

"You're Daisy Evans," Bessie said.

"I was, but I'm Daisy Eckles now. You sound as if you were expecting me."

"Not at all, but I've spoken to the police at length about who the body could be, and your name came up as the only person who might know what happened to Hannah Butler," Bessie tried to explain.

"Hannah was my closest friend on the island," Daisy replied. "That isn't saying much, as I didn't know very many people here. My father was offered a job over here and my parents thought the change of scenery would be good for all of us. I liked it well enough, but when my father was given a chance to move back to the UK, I decided to go with my parents rather than stay here on my own. It was the sensible thing to do."

"Tea and a teacake," the waitress said, putting them on the table in front of Bessie. "Anyone need anything else?"

"May I have more tea?" Daisy asked.

"Sure," the waitress replied. Bessie waited until Daisy's cup had been refilled before she spoke again.

"So you left and Hannah stayed behind?" she asked.

"I did invite her to come with me. She was so very sad, you see. I thought she needed a fresh start."

"Why was she sad?"

"Her parents both died in a house fire. She was out walking on the beach when they died, otherwise she probably would have been killed as well."

"Walking on the beach?"

"That was what she did when she couldn't sleep. She'd take long walks, sometimes going many miles. Her favourite place to go was Peel Castle. It was almost something of an obsession with her. She knew how to get in when the castle was closed. Once her parents were gone, she used to go there nearly every night."

"It's a very long walk from Kirk Michael to Peel Castle," Bessie pointed out.

"She said it used to take her about two hours each way. She'd started doing it when her parents were still alive. She suffered from insomnia, you see. I believe, in those days, she didn't walk all that far, just for an hour or so to clear her head before she went to bed. After the fire, though, she found sleeping almost impossible, especially after dark. She worried about getting caught in a fire herself. She sold the house and took a place as a lodger, thinking that might be safer, but it didn't seem to help her sleep. That was when her obsession with Peel Castle grew stronger."

While Daisy sipped her tea, Bessie tried to work out how to put her next question to her. "Was there anything else that made her sad?" she eventually asked.

"There was a man, too," Daisy sighed. "There's always a man, isn't there? He was kind to her when he was in the shop where she worked. I don't know that many men had ever been kind to her. She was odd, and her parents had been somewhat overprotective, as well. Anyway, one day he happened to mention that he was getting married. Prior to that, Hannah had always believed that some day he was going to ask her to have a meal with him or something. She was, well, heartbroken when she discovered that he was simply being kind to her."

"The poor girl."

"When I told her I was leaving, she told me that she thought she should go, too. At first I thought she meant that she was going to come to the UK with me, but then I realised that she was talking about killing herself. Of course, I did everything I could to talk her out of it. I thought I'd succeeded, too."

"Did you stay in touch after you left?"

"For a short while. I've brought some of her letters with me, the ones that I kept. I'm not sure why I kept them, really, but in light of what's happened, they may help the police."

"You think she killed herself at Peel Castle?"

"I'm almost certain of it," Daisy sighed. "By the time I left, the castle was the only place that felt safe to her. Stone can't catch fire, you see. She used to sneak in after closing and sleep inside the castle. I'm not sure where, but she said something once about moving around and trying out different locations every evening."

"I suppose there are a number of different places she might have tried. In those days, they might not have had locks on most of them, either."

"She never mentioned locks. What she did say, in her last letter, was that she'd decided it was time to leave. I thought, at the time, that she was moving. She'd been sounding happier in the last two or three letters I received, so I thought maybe she was feeling better. She told me that she wasn't certain where she was going, but that she'd write as soon as she was settled. I never heard from her again." Tears streamed down Daisy's face as she put her head in her hands.

Bessie swallowed the last of her tea. "Maybe she truly was planning to start over somewhere else. Maybe she just wanted to spend one last night at Peel Castle before she went. There's no evidence to suggest that she died of anything other than natural causes."

"I'd really like to believe that you're right. I hate the thought of my friend choosing to kill herself in a dark corner of Peel Castle."

"You should believe whatever you want to believe," Bessie told her.

Daisy sighed. "I'm going to have to think about all of this. When that policewoman rang me, I was so shocked that I nearly cancelled my appointment with my doctor. All while he was telling me about my blood pressure and my medications, I kept thinking about Hannah. As soon as I left the doctor's surgery, I went home, threw things into a bag, and took the train down to Liverpool. Except the next ferry wasn't until the next morning, yesterday, so I had to stay in a hotel in Liverpool overnight. That gave me time to do a bit of planning, anyway, so that by the time I arrived yesterday afternoon, I had a hotel for a few nights, at least. I was too tired to do anything yesterday, so I rang for a taxi this morning and had him bring me out to the castle. I thought I would visit Hannah's last resting place, but the castle is shut."

"I might be able to arrange a visit for you," Bessie said. "You really need to talk to the police, though. Inspector Lambert has been trying to reach you for days."

Daisy nodded. "I wasn't ready to talk about Hannah, not knowing that she'd died all alone in the dark. What you said, about her maybe dying of natural causes, that's helped a great deal, though. I feel somewhat better about the whole thing now. I just wish I'd written back after I received that last letter. She said she'd be gone before I'd have time to reply, but I should have tried."

"It wouldn't have made any difference," Bessie told her reassuringly. "You did your best to be a friend to her when you were on the island. I'm sure she appreciated that."

"I don't think she'd had many friends in her life," Daisy mused. "As I said, her parents were very protective. She should have been relieved when they passed away. It gave her a chance to start living her own life for the first time."

"Let me ring Anna Lambert," Bessie suggested. "I'm sure she'll send a car for you."

"And you'll see about arranging a visit to Peel Castle?" Daisy asked.

Bessie nodded and then pulled out her mobile. "Inspector Lambert? It's Bessie Cubbon. I'm at a café in Peel having a lovely chat with Daisy Eckles. I'm sure you'll be interested in what she has to tell you."

There was a long pause and then Bessie could hear the inspector counting to ten. When she kept going on to eleven and twelve, Bessie laughed. "It was just a chance meeting," she explained.

"Of course it was," Anna sighed. "I have a car on the way now. She'll be brought to my office, where she can explain her disappearing act before she tells me all about Hannah."

"Once you're finished speaking with her, she'd very much like to visit Peel Castle, to pay her respects to Hannah."

"She's that certain that we've found Hannah, then?"

"Indeed."

"I'm sure you can arrange that with your friends at Manx National Heritage. I can have her delivered to the castle at three, if that works for everyone."

"I'll make it work," Bessie promised.

"If I've not finished questioning her, she may need to return to the station with me after the castle tour."

"I'm sure that will be fine."

Bessie put her phone down on the table and smiled at Daisy. "Someone will be here in a few minutes to take you to see the inspector. I'm to try to arrange a tour of Peel Castle for three o'clock. The inspector has promised to bring you to the castle, even if she hasn't finished questioning you."

"Thank you so much," Daisy said, grasping Bessie's hand. "You've been wonderful."

The uniformed constable who arrived a short time later was a stranger to Bessie.

"Miss Cubbon?" he greeted her. "Inspector Lambert sent me."

"This is Mrs. Daisy Eckles," Bessie replied. "The inspector is waiting to talk to her."

"And how," the young man muttered under his breath.

Daisy let the constable escort her out of the café. As soon as they were gone, Bessie rang Mark. It only took her a moment to persuade him to arrange to have the castle open for their tour that afternoon.

"I may well be there myself," he said. "Having found the body, I'd like to know what happened to the woman."

"I'm not sure we'll ever know the answer to that, but at least we may know her identity now."

Bessie paid for her tea and for Daisy's. With nothing else to do, she set off towards Peel Castle. When she reached the House of Mannanan, she stopped for a rest. She had a hot and filling lunch at the café next door to the museum and then walked the rest of the way to the castle down the long causeway.

"You look as if you've been walking for miles," Mark greeted her at the gate.

"I walked up from the beach," Bessie explained. "I stopped for lunch and a quick tour of the House of Mannanan along the way, but it was still a very windy walk."

"You should have told me where you were when you rang. I would have been happy to collect you on my way here."

"I needed the walk. I've heard too many sad stories in the past few days. I needed to clear my head and let the wind blow through me."

"It appears to have done just that."

Bessie went into the small staff loo and ran a comb through her hair. It was pointless, really, as she was just going to be back out in the wind in a short while, but it made her feel better. She and Mark were talking quietly when Daisy and Anna arrived.

Daisy greeted her with a hug. "The inspector said the same as you," she said through tears. "That Hannah truly could have died of natural causes."

"I hope you'll believe her."

"I really hope she's right. Hannah did have heart trouble, you know. That was one of the reasons why her parents were so protective of her. It was also why she didn't work very many hours. She got tired very quickly. I think she thought that her long walks were building up her strength, but maybe they were simply wearing her out. I can almost picture her crawling into the tower wall, curling up to go to sleep, and simply never waking up again."

"Let's hope that was exactly what happened," Bessie said.

She introduced Mark to Daisy and listened as Daisy told him a shortened version of Hannah's life story. The foursome then walked slowly around the castle site, talking about the site and the island's rich history. When they reached the tower where the body had been found, Daisy stared at the police tape that covered the door.

"You can have a look," Anna said. She carefully removed the police tape and then unlocked the padlock on the door. Pushing the door open, she switched on a powerful torch.

Daisy approached slowly. "Where was she?" she asked in a whisper.

"Along the back wall," Mark told her. "She truly did look as if she'd simply fallen asleep there."

"Why wasn't the body found sooner?" was Daisy's next question.

"I wish I knew," Mark sighed. "I suspect it was simply a case of no one needing to be in the tower for any reason. There never used to be locks on any of the doors, but at some point, maybe twenty-five years ago, one of my predecessors added them. It's entirely possible that he or she simply locked everything without even glancing inside the various spaces. I did dig out old records from the site. This tower is listed as being empty, unused, and unsafe, in the records that date from fifty years ago. As such, I can see it simply being locked and left untouched."

"Does the castle have ghosts?" Daisy wanted to know.

"There's the Moddey Dhoo, of course," Mark replied. "I don't know that there are any other ghosts, though."

"That's the black dog, right? Hannah used to see him all the time when she visited the castle at night. She said he was really friendly and used to lie down next to her while she slept."

Bessie and Mark exchanged glances. "He isn't typically thought of as friendly," Mark said after a minute. "But maybe he doesn't deserve his reputation."

"If Hannah was right, he definitely doesn't," Daisy replied. "I hope he was with her when she died. I hate the idea of anyone dying alone."

Anna carefully replaced the police tape and then the foursome walked back to the castle entrance.

"Thank you for opening for me," Daisy told Mark. "I feel much more at peace now that I've seen where Hannah spent her last hours."

"I appreciated hearing more about her. I'm sorry that you lost your friend."

"It seems odd to feel so sad, after so many years, but I do feel as if I've lost a good friend. I suppose I always hoped that one day we'd find one another again."

Mark let them out, locking the castle behind them. He gave Bessie a hug before he headed back to his car.

"Was there anything else you need to ask me?" Daisy asked Anna.

"No, we're done. We'll check everything you said and see if we can't make a formal decision on the skeleton's identity. Thank you for your assistance," Anna said. She nodded at Bessie and then turned and walked briskly towards the car park.

"Do you have a car here?" Daisy asked Bessie as Anna disappeared from view.

"I don't drive," Bessie replied. "I came by taxi."

"What do we do now?" Daisy asked, looking up and down the deserted causeway.

Bessie pulled out her mobile and rang Dave. "Any chance of a ride from Peel Castle?" she asked.

"How did you end up at Peel Castle?" he replied. "Never mind, I just dropped someone off not far from there. I'll be there in five minutes or less."

Bessie had Dave take Daisy to her hotel in Douglas first.

"Thank you for everything," Daisy said as they went. "I'm going to see if I can get a ferry home tomorrow. Right now, the island has too many sad memories for me to want to see any more of it. I may come back one day, though, once I've worked through it all in my head."

When Daisy got out of the taxi, Bessie moved up to sit next to Dave.

"That was the passenger that I took to Peel Castle this morning. I did warn her that the castle was shut in the winter, but she didn't seem to be listening. How did you happen to find her and end up with her at the castle?" he asked curiously.

Bessie thought about telling him the whole story. She knew he'd never repeat anything she told him in confidence, but it seemed easier to give him a significantly simplified version of events. They were back at Treoghe Bwaane by the time she finished.

"Thank you," Bessie told Dave as she climbed out of the car.

Inside her cottage, she sank down in a chair and stared out the window at the sea. She was exhausted from all of the walking she'd done, but also emotionally spent from her conversation with Daisy.

CHAPTER 15

*B*essie was taking an afternoon stroll a few days later when she saw the car pull into the parking area next to her cottage. She quickened her pace towards home when she saw Anna climb out from behind the wheel.

"Good afternoon," she called as she approached.

"Good afternoon," Anna replied. "Do you have a minute?"

"Of course. Do you want to come in and have a cuppa?"

"Could we sit somewhere out here and talk?" Anna asked. "I could do with some fresh air."

"The rock behind my cottage is perfect for that, assuming the tide isn't in."

The tide was going out as they walked behind the cottage. The sand was still damp, but they were able to reach the rock without stepping into water.

Bessie sat down and, after a moment, Anna carefully climbed onto the rock next to her.

"I've spoken to Daisy again," Anna said after a minute. "She was able to confirm that Hannah had told her that she'd broken her left arm twice and her right arm once as a child. She also told Daisy that

211

she'd broken her right leg in her teen years. Those injuries match what we found on the skeleton."

"So you're certain it was Hannah?"

"We're certain. We'd like to compare the skeleton's DNA with a relative, but we haven't found any yet. What we have found are some medical records for her. They confirm what Daisy said about her having a heart condition and her childhood injuries."

"So she may have actually died of natural causes?"

"It's one possibility, the one I prefer, really, although that's the human being in me, not the police inspector. Without any evidence of foul play, the chief constable wants to close the case as undetermined."

"Are you happy with that?"

"I get credit for closing the case, so I won't complain. I've spoken to LouLar and John has spoken to Rosemary Quayle, but we're just going around in circles now. No one knows what actually happened to Hannah Butler."

Bessie sighed. "It still feels unfinished."

"I think she killed herself," Anna said quietly. "That's the police inspector in me talking now. The notes from her doctor also suggest that her father was abusive. Small children don't generally break their arms, not three times in as many years. The doctor had concerns, but such things weren't handled in the same way then as they are now."

"The poor girl."

"Yes, but here's where it gets even more interesting," Anna said. "I went back over the reports on the fire at Hannah's house, the one that killed her parents. It wasn't an accident."

"It wasn't? What do you mean?"

"Someone spilled a large amount of petrol in the sitting room and the bedroom where the parents were sleeping. Then that someone lit a match."

"You think Hannah caused the fire that killed her parents?"

"That's one possibility, certainly. I was going to ask Daisy for her views on the matter, but I didn't want to upset her. I don't know that it matters, not after all these years."

"Why wasn't there a police investigation at the time?"

"It was ongoing when Hannah disappeared. They didn't have enough evidence to charge her with anything, but I know the investigators thought she'd been behind the blaze."

"And they still didn't charge her?"

"As I said, there wasn't any evidence against her. She didn't drive, and they couldn't work out how she could have acquired the amount of petrol that was used. When the fire was discovered, she was miles away, walking on the beach. With the amount of accelerants used, she shouldn't have been able to get that far away before someone raised the alarm."

"If she didn't do it, who did?" Bessie demanded.

"The investigators were convinced that she'd done it. Their reports of the conversations they had with her after the fire were definitely odd, anyway. They could be read as the ramblings of a guilty woman or the confused thoughts of a woman who'd led a sheltered life up to that point."

"She was the latter, certainly."

"She was, which means we'll never know what actually happened."

"Did she have any idea who might have started the fire?"

"She suggested that her father may have done it to kill them all. He was having financial difficulties, so that's another possibility to add to the mix."

"It's very frustrating, not knowing and not having a way of finding out the truth," Bessie said.

"We've identified the skeleton from Peel Castle. That's a major accomplishment and one that no one thought we would manage. I'm happy enough with that for today."

"Let's hope your next case is an easier one," Bessie said.

"I'm leaving the island," Anna told her.

"I thought you wanted to stay here."

"I did want to stay here, more to prove that I don't run away when things go wrong than for any other reason, but I've been offered a position in private security, working for my brother, actually, and the offer is too good to pass up."

"Are you sure?"

"I'm tired of working all hours, day and night, being on call and never knowing what I'm going to have to deal with when I get wherever I'm going. This job comes with regular hours, proper holiday entitlement, and a salary that makes my eyes water when I think about it. I'd be crazy to turn it down, especially now."

"When do you go?"

"In about six weeks. I have things to wrap up here, and my brother will wait for me, however long that takes."

"That's nice."

Anna laughed. "We may end up killing one another once we actually have to work together, but for now it all sounds wonderful."

"Let's have lunch one day before you go," Bessie suggested.

"I'd like that," Anna replied. "I'll ring you."

"If you don't, I'll ring you."

"See that you do."

Bessie walked back up the beach with the inspector and then watched as she drove away before she let herself into Treoghe Bwaane. Her phone was ringing.

"Bessie, John wants us all to have dinner at his house tonight," Doona said. "I know it's short notice, but he said it's about time we had a nice social occasion. Hugh and Grace are bringing Aalish, and the kids will both be there."

"Is everything okay?"

"As far as I know, everything is just the same. Sue is still in hospital and Harvey won't answer when John rings. He won't talk to the children, either. They spoke to Sue yesterday and she told them that she's feeling much better."

"That's good news. Did she say anything about coming home?"

"No, which is probably a good thing. John isn't looking forward to fighting her for custody. Anyway, I'll collect you at six. John said that Amy and Thomas are doing all of the cooking, so don't come too hungry," she laughed.

Bessie spent the rest of her afternoon with a good book and then changed into a nice dress for dinner. Doona was right on time, and the drive to John's house only took a few minutes.

John lived in a modernised bungalow a few streets away from Doona's home. She found a parking spot on the street nearby and she and Bessie walked back to the house.

"Bessie, thank you for coming," John greeted her with a hug. He gave Doona a very quick embrace, too, before pulling away. "I have to get back to the kitchen to keep an eye on everything. Hugh and Grace are in the sitting room."

Grace was pacing back and forth with the baby as they walked into the sitting room.

"She's only happy when I'm moving," Grace said apologetically. She stopped to give Bessie an awkward hug around Aalish. As soon as Grace stopped moving, Aalish began to wail.

"Give her to me," Hugh said. "Then you can sit and chat with Bessie and Doona for a short while. You deserve a break."

"She'll fuss for you, too," Grace warned. "She's only happy with me right now."

"A bit of fussing won't hurt her," Hugh said. He took the baby and held her close. "Hush, now, you pest," he told her affectionately. "Mummy needs a break from all your shouting."

The baby seemed to study him for a second. As she opened her mouth to yell, he began to stomp back and forth across the room. The movement seemed to surprise Aalish enough to keep her quiet, at least for a short while.

John and the children joined them a few minutes later.

"Everything is ready," John announced. "We've arranged it all like a buffet in the kitchen."

The roast chicken and all of the trimmings smelled delicious. Bessie filled her plate and then followed the others into the small dining room. Everything tasted as good as it smelled, except for the roast potatoes. They'd come out rather harder than they should have been. Bessie tried to cut into one and found it was impossible.

"Sorry about that," Amy said, flushing. "I think I may have baked them for too long. Last time I did them, they went black, so I knew I'd overcooked them. This time they've simply gone rock hard."

"Never mind, everything else is delicious," Bessie assured her.

They were clearing away dishes, ready for pudding, when the phone rang. John grabbed it and everyone went quiet.

"Yes?"

"But that can't..." he glanced over at Thomas and Amy and then quickly left the room.

"Let's get these plates into the kitchen," Bessie said brightly. "You have a dishwasher, don't you? I've never used one."

John joined them in the kitchen a few minutes later. Bessie could tell from the look on his face that he'd had bad news. He glanced around and then sighed.

"At least we're among friends," he said softly. "Thomas, Amy, that was the hospital where your mother has been staying. She passed away this morning."

Thomas stared at him for a minute and then shook his head. "There's been a mistake. We talked to her yesterday. She was feeling better."

"I'm sorry," John said.

Amy burst into tears and threw herself into her father's arms. Thomas kept shaking his head until Doona pulled him into a hug then he too, began to cry. Aalish had been sleeping. Now she woke up and joined in.

"What can I do?" Bessie asked John over Amy's head.

"I don't know that there's anything anyone can do," he replied sadly.

GLOSSARY OF TERMS

Manx to English

- **moghrey mie** - good morning

House Names – Manx to English

- **Thie yn Traie** - Beach House
- **Treoghe Bwaane** - Widow's Cottage

English to American Terms

- **advocate** - Manx title for a lawyer (solicitor)
- **aye** - yes
- **bin** - garbage can
- **biscuits** - cookies
- **bonnet (car)** - hood
- **boot (car)** - trunk
- **car park** - parking lot
- **chemist** - pharmacist
- **chips** -french fries

- **chippy** - fish and chips shop
- **cuppa** - cup of tea (informally)
- **dear** - expensive
- **estate agent** - real estate agent (realtor)
- **fairy cakes** - cupcakes
- **fancy dress** - costume
- **fizzy drink** - soda (pop)
- **holiday** - vacation
- **jumper** - sweater
- **lie in** - sleep late
- **midday** - noon
- **pavement** - sidewalk
- **plait (hair)** - braid
- **primary school** - elementary school
- **pudding** - dessert
- **skeet** - gossip
- **skirting boards** - baseboards
- **starters** - appetizers
- **supply teacher** - substitute teacher
- **telly** - television
- **torch** - flashlight
- **trolley** - shopping cart
- **windscreen** - windshield

OTHER NOTES

The emergency number in the UK and the Isle of Man is 999, not 911.

CID is the Criminal Investigation Department of the Isle of Man Constabulary (Police Force).

When talking about time, the English say, for example, "half seven" to mean "seven-thirty."

With regard to Bessie's age: UK (and IOM) residents get a free bus pass at the age of 60. Bessie is somewhere between that age and the age at which she will get a birthday card from the Queen. British citizens used to receive telegrams from the ruling monarch on the occasion of their one-hundredth birthday. Cards replaced the telegrams in 1982, but the special greeting is still widely referred to as a telegram.

When island residents talk about someone being from "across," they mean that the person is from somewhere in the United Kingdom (across the water).

ACKNOWLEDGMENTS

My editor, Denise, is incredibly hard working, kind, and patient with me. I know I keep making the same mistakes over and over again, but she simply corrects them and keeps going. Thank you!

Thanks to Kevin for the wonderful pictures that grace my covers.

Thanks to my beta-reading team who polish out my rough edges.

And thanks to my readers, who keep me writing!

AUNT BESSIE WONDERS

RELEASE DATE: JANUARY 17, 2020

Aunt Bessie wonders if a holiday is a good idea.

Thomas and Amy Rockwell have had something of a shock. When Doona suggests a holiday to Lakeview Holiday Park, their father, John, isn't sure whether to agree or not. In the end, Bessie, Doona, John, and the children make the journey during the February half-term break.

Aunt Bessie wonders why Doona's solicitor, Stuart Stanley, happens to be at the park at the same time.

Stuart fills Doona in quickly enough. He's there because another solicitor is about to challenge Doona's right to the estate of her former husband, Charles Adams. Carl Dietrich is working for Lawrence Jenkins, the man who was a business partner to Charles, but who is currently in prison for fraud and other crimes.

Aunt Bessie wonders what it would be like to have a holiday where no one is murdered.

When Carl turns up dead, Doona, John, and even Bessie seem to top the list of suspects. Can Bessie help the local police inspector, Margaret Hopkins, work out what really happened to Carl? Was it murder, or is too much to hope that Carl simply had a heart attack? When a second man dies, Bessie can't help but wonder why she keeps finding herself tangled up in murder investigations.

ALSO BY DIANA XARISSA

Boats and Bad Guys

Cars and Cold Cases

Dogs and Danger

Encounters and Enemies

Friends and Frauds

Guests and Guilt

Hop-tu-Naa and Homicide

Invitations and Investigations

Joy and Jealousy

Kittens and Killers

Letters and Lawsuits

The Markham Sisters Cozy Mystery Novellas

The Appleton Case

The Bennett Case

The Chalmers Case

The Donaldson Case

The Ellsworth Case

The Fenton Case

The Green Case

The Hampton Case

The Irwin Case

The Jackson Case

The Kingston Case

The Lawley Case

The Moody Case

The Norman Case

The Osborne Case

The Patrone Case

The Quinton Case

The Rhodes Case

The Isle of Man Romance Series

Island Escape

Island Inheritance

Island Heritage

Island Christmas

ABOUT THE AUTHOR

Diana grew up in Northwestern Pennsylvania and moved to Washington, DC, after college. There she met a wonderful Englishman who was visiting the city. After a whirlwind romance, they got married and Diana moved to the Chesterfield area of Derbyshire to begin a new life with her husband. A short time later, they relocated to the Isle of Man.

After more than ten years on the island, it was time for a change. With their two children in tow, Diana and her husband moved to suburbs of Buffalo, New York. Diana now spends her days writing about the island she loves.

She also writes mystery/thrillers set in the not-too-distant future as Diana X. Dunn and middle grade and Young Adult books as D.X. Dunn.

Diana is always happy to hear from readers. You can write to her at:

Diana Xarissa Dunn
PO Box 72
Clarence, NY 14031.
Find Diana at: DianaXarissa.com
E-mail: Diana@dianaxarissa.com

Made in United States
North Haven, CT
06 November 2023

43689076R00134